I0535395

"I've been told I'm magical with my mouth, hands, and...uh um...other parts, but to show you would require a lot less clothing."

He didn't pause as he headed toward the stairs to the right of the receptionist's desk, but she stood staring dumbly after him, imagining the magic of those amazing lips on her mouth, neck, and lower. Much, much lower. Heat bloomed in her mid-section and she felt the rush of wetness at his provocative words.

"Coming?"

She snapped a wide-eyed gaze in his direction. "What?" *Not yet. But, she was hopeful.*

The Vampire Next Door

Also by Cherie Marks

The Fae Next Door

Lost in New Falls

Into the Fire

And writing as C. C. Marks

Edge of Mercy

Heart of Mercy

Mercy

Range of Mercy

The Vampire Next Door

by

Cherie Marks

This is a work of fiction. Names, characters, places, and incidents are either the product of the author's imagination or are used fictitiously, and any resemblance to actual persons living or dead, business establishments, events, or locales, is entirely coincidental.

The Vampire Next Door

COPYRIGHT© 2014 by Cherie Marks
All rights reserved. No part of this book may be used or reproduced in any manner whatsoever without written permission of the author or except in the case
of brief quotations embodied in critical articles or reviews.
Contact Information: authorcheriemarks@gmail.com
For more interesting reads, visit the author at
http://www.authorcheriemarks.com
Published in the United States of America by Cherie Marks

Thank you for purchasing this book. This book is the copyrighted property of the author, and may not be reproduced, copied and distributed for commercial or non-commercial purposes. If you enjoyed this book, please write a review at your favorite online book retailer and either share with or encourage your friends to purchase their own copy, where they can also discover other works by this author. Thank you for your support.

Dedication

This is dedicated to my wonderful sisters and brothers. Heather, Becky, Amber, Christy, Brandon, and Samuel. You've been my friends as well as my family. Though we didn't get a choice, I'd choose you all over again. So much love your way!

Acknowledgements

Thanks again to my editor and to my many favorite authors who inspire me to be better with every story I write. I love to write because I love to read. Thank you for opening my mind to the magic of fiction.

Chapter 1

Mia Alexander woke, hands around her neck. They were her own and there to protect against an attack, guarding her exposed skin from some unknown horror. Yet, she recognized there wasn't any real threat near her. A quick glance around reassured her she was still in her bedroom and seemed to be completely alone.

She dropped her hands to her sides, using them to brace herself on the mattress below her and sit up, slick droplets of sweat sliding down her torso. Another nightmare. She'd had another nightmare. One just like the others where she fought for her life against dark figures she could never quite bring into focus. And as before, she'd reacted in real life, trying to protect herself against the acts going on in her dream world. These vivid dreams were driving her crazy.

A quick look at the red glow of the clock showed 2:34 A.M., the same time she always woke when she had the nightmare. An odd coincidence, surely, but not one easily explained away. Something was off in her brain, and it was beginning to affect her everyday life.

She'd researched the heck out of repetitive dreams, specifically about ones in which the dreamer was attacked, but all she'd figured out was that she might have trust issues with the people around her or she might be beating herself up over recent experiences. *Well, duh!* Either way, with such vague answers, she was pretty sure dream interpretation was a throw-a-dart-at-the-wall kind of science, and she'd better look for answers elsewhere.

The t-shirt she'd worn to bed stuck uncomfortably to her skin. She threw the covers back, deciding to change before attempting to drift back to sleep. As she rose, a feeling she was being watched raised the hairs on the back of her neck. Using the scant light from the streetlamps and the moon shining through the closed French doors that when opened led to the tiny balcony outside, she scanned the bedroom. Nothing seemed out of the ordinary. She shook off the sensation, feeling a little silly. Must just be a remnant of the nightmare.

She turned to the oak wood dresser and pulled another shirt from the top drawer. With careful movements, she peeled the damp shirt she wore over her head. Thank goodness she'd gone braless tonight. One less piece of sweat-dampened laundry to worry about.

She jerked her head up at a low, strangled sound behind her and covered herself quickly as the cool night air cascaded through the now open door to the outside. She caught a glimpse of a shadow exiting and took two steps back toward her closet as the figure turned one last time before disappearing over the rail of the balcony. Her instincts had been on target, and she didn't have a weapon. *Why didn't she have a weapon?* There had been someone in her room. From the tall, broad frame, over six feet at least, it had to have been a man. And son of a beezy, she'd undressed in front of him. *Eeeewww!*

Mia swallowed a few times and waited, paralyzed. After a few moments, she realized the intruder was truly gone and crossed to the open door to search the grassy area below, but nothing stirred. Whoever it was seemed to disappear in the blink of an eye, but he'd left a trace of himself behind. A rich, spicy aroma, a sensual promise in its very essence, still floated in the air and tickled her nostrils. She paused, processing the enticing smell, committing it to memory. Her skin sizzled and electric fingers slipped down her spine, spreading through her mid-section. Surprised by the intensity of her reaction, she worked to slow her breathing and stepped back into her bedroom. She closed the door and turned the deadbolt, watching the metal slip into the casing to be sure it was locked.

Nervous energy fired through her as she stood in the dark trying to understand what had just happened. *Someone had been in her bedroom while she slept.* Tune her guitar to freaked-the-hell-out. That shit was scary.

The first call she made was to the police. Once they took down her information and assured her a squad car was on its way, she turned her attention to the necessary moral support she needed right now.

Even at three in the morning, Janna Thompson, Mia's best friend until the end, picked up on the second ring. "You need bail money?"

The tension eased the minute she heard Janna's voice, but she couldn't help but ask, "Now why would you automatically assume that's why I'm calling in the middle of the night?"

"You're right. Does Hope need bail money?"

"No. No one's in jail. Yet." Mia explained the situation, trying to downplay the seriousness of her internal panic, but Janna clearly wasn't fooled.

"I'm picking up Hope and Roxy, and we're coming over."

Mia sighed loudly. Nothing sounded better right now than being surrounded by her friends, but she felt guilty asking all of them to sacrifice sleep on her account. "There's no need for you guys to come over. We have class in the morning, and a policeman is on his way. I'm fine."

"Okay. How about just me then? I really need your advice about something anyway, so really you'd help me out."

A knock sounded at the door, and Mia crossed to peek through the peephole and check out the two officers on the other side. "Well, when you put it that way...I'd really appreciate having you here tonight."

"I'll be over as soon as I can."

Satisfied the policemen were the ones she'd expected, she began twisting the locks to open the door. "Thanks, Janna. You're an amazing friend."

"Hey, what are accountabilabuddies for?"

Mia paused in her motions. "Accounta...what?"

"You know, accountabilabuddies. A friend you get in trouble with who's probably the bad influence your parents warned you about."

"Well, that about sums it up. I'll have to remember that one."

They hung up the phone and Mia finally opened the door. The officers took down her information and scoured the apartment and the surrounding area, but nothing was out of place. None of her belongings had been touched and there weren't even any footprints in the soft dirt on the ground outside her balcony.

One of the officers, a tall, willowy fellow asked, "Has anyone shown unusual attention to you lately? Like making you uncomfortable at times?"

Mia thought through the people she interacted with regularly. "No. I can't say so."

The other officer, a wide-shouldered man with a tight buzz-cut spoke to her as they backed away from her door, "We can't find any evidence anyone meant you any harm. Still, not a bad idea to look into a home security system. Stalking is a real problem. "

"I'm not some celebrity. I'm a nobody."

"Often it's just a co-worker or ex-boyfriend who develops an obsession. Something to think about anyway."

"Thanks. I'll look into it." But the idea seemed absurd. Other than school at the community college, participating at the research lab, and the occasional lunch with her friends at a restaurant near the school's campus, she didn't go anywhere or do anything. No one came to mind as someone giving her extra attention, unless you counted the intern conducting the current study she was participating in. He'd shown a lot of concern for her lately, but that was part of his job. The study was for an experimental drug made to improve short-term memory. Part of his job was to ask her personal questions, draw blood occasionally, and give her weekly injections of an experimental drug that was in its final trials. It was a way for her to make a little extra money. And who didn't want to improve their memory? It was all pretty mundane.

When it came down to it, her life was actually boring, and the thought that someone would obsess over her was laughable.

Yet, as she checked the locks on her balcony door again, the faint odor of rich spice came to her once more, and she ran her hands along her arms, soothing the raised chillbumps there. One thing was certain, someone had been in her room, and she'd never forget the way he smelled or the sensual feelings his aroma evoked in her. It was...other-worldly.

* * *

Campbell Reid leaned against the wall in the shadows, arms crossed, gaze locked on Mia as she slept. She'd thought to keep him out tonight with an alarm system. It was high-end and probably would have stopped him if he'd been an ordinary man. In reality, it only took him a couple extra minutes to get past the top-notch security. It would take much more than an electronic alarm to keep him from completing his mission. It was humorous, really, if he could afford to laugh in this situation. He couldn't blame her for trying to protect herself after his amateurish slip-up last night, but an alarm was useless against him.

For one thing, the knowledge and skills about electronics and computer systems he'd gained over the years often came in handy to get him into, and sometimes out of, tight spots. This alarm system wasn't that complicated for someone such as he, who probably could've written the manual. Of course, if the system had stumped him, he could've shifted into a dark mist and slid through the cracks, something he'd had the ability to do since shortly after he was changed. It came as part of the vampire package, and though he'd not met another vampire who could, he'd been able to for almost five hundred years. The only thing that might block his entrance was a lack of an invitation from the human home-owner. It was an unusual curse placed long ago on his kind to protect humans at their most vulnerable, and it was unbreakable. However, he had a way around that. Though she didn't realize it yet, she was no longer human.

She shifted on the bed and mumbled in her sleep. Probably having another nightmare. Every night for the past week, he'd spent the night in the shadows of her bedroom, and every night she'd tossed and turned with nightmares. Perhaps if he were human, he might be drawn to give her some relief from whatever haunted her. He wasn't, and he clenched his fists to remind himself he was supposed to remain invisible. He wasn't supposed to want to comfort her with a light touch on the exposed skin of her arms or across her perfect cheek.

He'd almost blown it two nights ago, but he hadn't expected his reaction to her naked body to be so immediate and so intense. He'd lived for over five hundred years, had seen many beautiful women, and surprisingly only to others, he'd practiced a self-imposed celibacy for most of that time. After the tragedy that made him, it was the only thing he could do to keep his sanity. Yet, when the moonlight shone on this woman's curves, his body reacted as if she were the first he'd seen in centuries. It had caught him by surprise and the involuntary response had nearly exposed his mission.

The last thing she needed right now was more attention from Sup Co, otherwise known as the Supernatural Council, the group of supernatural beings who oversaw the paranormal world and worked to protect its secrecy from humans. They were already aware she was changing, and they'd sent him to watch over her during the transition.

Though they refused to intervene once the change was in motion, she would now be in constant danger and need to be guarded. Other vampires would fight to the death for a taste of her in her current state of being. Her transition phase held certain desirable side-effects for supernatural beings, and many would be willing to kill for them. It was his job to keep her safe for the next month, until the change was complete. He'd done this many times before, but somehow, something about her was different for him.

She grew restless again, turning onto her back and pulling her thin, cotton t-shirt tight across her chest. His gaze was drawn to the pebbled points showing off the feminine curves rising and falling as she breathed. He felt like the worst kind of voyeur and forced himself to shift his gaze elsewhere.

He traced his gaze to her face instead. Flawless skin, plump lips that slid into an effortless smile when she was awake. Everything about her facial features drew his gaze. Her auburn hair spread like a fan across her pillow. She was a sight for fantasies. He wished he hadn't noticed. He was having a hell of a time keeping his body in check as it was, and it was sabotaging his mission.

His job was to protect her without alerting her to his presence. Fledglings tended to run if they knew they were in danger, which almost always ended in them placing themselves even further into trouble. But it was becoming evident he wouldn't be able to continue with this particular job. He'd have to put in for a transfer in the morning and let someone else take over. How could he keep an eye out for intruders when he couldn't take them off her?

Out of the corner of his eye, he caught movement as a shadow passed the balcony doors, and he reluctantly looked away from the beauty on the bed. A tall, wide-shouldered silhouette filled the doorway. Someone or something was outside, and this was exactly what the council had hired him to take care of.

He inched toward the exit and waited at the side as the figure unlocked the door from the outside and slipped into the darkened room. *Interesting.* Campbell reached to his belt and pulled his gun. It looked like an ordinary 9 mm handgun, but the bullets were anything but ordinary. It would take much more than lead bullets to incapacitate a supernatural being. Hollowed and filled with a manufactured chemical created with a base that combined substances that weakened nearly every paranormal beast in the world, this weapon could take out an eight-foot troll, charging full-tilt. When aimed at a rogue werewolf, vampire, demon, or any other criminal para-being, this weapon could stop an in-progress attack with little effort. This creature would be no different.

Campbell needed to wait until whoever it was entered completely, then he'd give the creature a chance to surrender before unloading his weapon into its upper body, successfully ending its plan of attack before it even knew what happened.

The figure stood tall in front of the doors of the balcony, whole once again. Campbell tensed and lifted the weapon. The creature took a couple steps toward the bed but stopped cold at the sound of the gun safety being switched off.

"That's far enough. Turn back around slowly, keeping your hands up where I can see them." Campbell had spoken low, in a register some humans couldn't even hear, but his meaning was clear.

"Stand down soldier." Recognition clicked immediately. Campbell lowered his weapon, unsure why his superior officer was here, but together enough mentally to at least follow the order. He was still confused and didn't dare relax his guard yet. This was highly irregular.

"Forgive me, sir. I didn't expect you."

"We've received some intelligence about the fledgling. Information you need to know for the mission." He moved back toward the exit and Campbell hesitantly holstered his gun and followed. Something still felt off about the situation, but he knew better than to question his superior.

Once they were outside the apartment, on the balcony, he glimpsed the familiar features of Commander Riley Spencer and with a glance at the ground below, noticed a fellow freelancer, Kerenth Zeitler. He nodded and Campbell dipped his chin in return before shifting his focus back to his commander. Spencer's stern jaw tensed as he faced Campbell and crossed his hands over his broad chest. "I realize I took you off guard, but we've hit a complication."

Campbell hated complications. He did his best to avoid them at all costs, but this case seemed to be rife with complications from the get-go.

"With each case, it's important for us to know where the transformation began, whether it was natural or unnatural, whether the human sought the change or unwittingly stumbled into the paranormal."

"Of course. Standard protocol."

He ran a hand over his buzzed hair, too short to appear anything but brown and released a heavy breath before explaining, "This fledgling's transformation is nothing we've ever seen before."

"I don't understand."

He hesitated briefly, as if choosing his words carefully. "Conjecture is that she was injected in the research lab where she volunteered for a standard pharmacological study, but none of the experimental drug samples we tested had vampire serum in them. We also haven't linked any of the employees or personnel to our world. Something's off."

"Wait. How do you know she was injected in the lab if nothing contained the serum?"

Spencer gritted his teeth. "We received an encrypted message outlining who she was, that she'd been genetically altered, a hybrid of unknown origin and..." He paused, looking at the ground before continuing, "...that she will become a monster we've never seen before and have no means to control."

Hybrid? In the paranormal world, hybrids had been outlawed around five hundred years ago, around the time Campbell had become a vampire. Too many variables with the resulting mix of creatures caused more issues than could be controlled. Witches burned at the stake, plague, massive wars and invasions—all due to a few out-of-control hybrids. Campbell sighed loudly. If she was a hybrid, that changed everything.

"Well, that sounds like a big bag of what-the-hell."

"Understatement." Spencer braced his hands on his hips. "Kerenth and I are here to assess the immediate situation, but after that, the council's putting in a new protocol that involves you."

Campbell shook his head back and forth as he explained, "I'm putting in for a transfer in the morning. My head is no longer clear when it comes to this particular fledgling."

"Then do whatever you have to do to clear it. The council is counting on you to keep an eye on the situation here. You'll move into the apartment next door, get close to the target, ferret out the creator, and if necessary, protect others from whatever monster is developing in that bedroom." Campbell watched, slightly perplexed by the look of melancholy that slipped into Spencer's gaze as he looked toward the closed door.

With a muttered curse, Campbell turned away from Spencer and locked his fists on the balcony railing. Kerenth looked up a few long seconds before returning his focus to scanning the area. *Damn complications.* "The council will just have to get someone else. I..." Frustration made his chest tight, but long ago he vowed to live the remainder of his so-called life with honor, and that meant divulging anything that might compromise the mission. "...I find...that is...the target is an attractive woman. I'd be remiss to mention I might not be able to remain objective on this case."

Spencer growled and tensed at his confession, and Campbell got the feeling Spencer would like to throw a fist into Campbell's jaw. "Keep your dick out of this, soldier." He sighed loudly. "The council is counting on you. I'm counting on you because you're the best I've got, Reid. You're the only one I trust to do this right."

"What about Kerenth?"

Spencer spared a glance to the soldier below. "He'd do the job," he looked back at Campbell and continued, "but you'd do it right."

Spencer stepped to the side of Campbell, staring hard at his profile. "Now, are you going to do your job and take care of this situation, or am I going to have to do it myself and blow the whole thing the minute the creator makes me?"

Dammit! He was right. Campbell's job was to go unnoticed, to be a ghost, and he was good at what he did. As far as he knew, outside of his immediate superiors, no one could identify him as a Sup Co guard. On the other hand, Spencer was a well-known commander and council-member. His identity would be obvious to anyone familiar with the supernatural world. If this job was going to turn out right, Campbell would have to fight his body's reaction to Mia Alexander and do what he had to in order to save countless lives, both human and beyond-human.

"I'll do what I have to."

"Expected nothing less from a soldier of your caliber and experience." Spencer backed toward the balcony railing. "Just keep your damn hands off her." The threat in his voice held an unexpected heat, but Campbell nodded and Spencer seemed somewhat satisfied.

Campbell was hundreds of years old and had soaked up a lot of knowledge throughout the centuries. He'd experienced just about every possible historical event, repeatedly, as history tended to do. He'd battled in skirmishes, fights, small and major wars and come out the winner every time. Yet, something told him all that caliber and experience would mean nothing the minute he locked gazes with Mia Alexander. *Damn complications.*

Chapter 2

The minute she stepped out of her apartment door, Mia was nearly blinded. She fumbled for her sunglasses and quickly set them on her face. Was it just her, or was this whole global warming thing happening, like, now. Stinging prickles dotted her skin wherever the sun hit, and the thought occurred that maybe she should forget her classes, go back inside, pop open a bottle of wine, and wait for some clouds to roll in.

Wait! Was she really wishing for a rainy day? Something was seriously wrong with her brain.

She released a heavy sigh, adjusted the bag slung over her shoulder and locked her front door before walking toward her Chevy Traverse, parked in one of the covered slots in the row of spaces assigned to her particular section of the complex. She felt a little relief when she stepped into the shade of the structure covering the cars. As she approached her own though, the car next to hers drew her attention. It was a Jeep Wrangler, but more to the point, it was new. She'd never seen it here before. It was probably just a guest, visiting someone in an apartment close by, but guests were given specific spots to park. This space was reserved for residents only.

She was probably just being paranoid, so she shook off her concern and unlocked her car. It wasn't like she was going to the management to complain or anything. And it wasn't like whatever creeper was in her apartment the other night was going to move in next door and become her neighbor. That was too far-fetched to even consider.

As she was climbing in, a large rumbling sounded from around the side of the building. Too drawn out to be thunder, it didn't look like she was going to get a break from the sun today. She looked up just as a large moving truck rounded the corner and began to slow right behind her in the parking lot, blocking her exit.

Aaah, c'mon! Timing was everything. A few seconds earlier and she'd have been on her way, but such was the way things were going lately.

Two men climbed from the cab, one short and rotund, the other slant-shouldered and skinny and walked toward the apartments, passing her car in the process. Hello? Didn't they see her? Couldn't they hear the foul words flying through her mind right now? Couldn't they feel her desperation? Clearly her mental telepathy was broken. She'd just have to do this the old-fashioned way and threaten them within an inch of their life if they didn't crawl back into that metal behemoth and move it the hell out of her way.

She flung her door wide and stepped out, standing in the vee made by the door and the car. "Excuse me! Hey! You're blocking me in."

They didn't even pause in their strides, just continued to walk toward the apartment next door to hers. She growled in frustration and slammed her car door a little hard as she gritted her teeth and braved the sunshine again to stomp after them.

"Hey! Could you move your truck? I have to be somewhere, like, now."

They finally turned and stared wide-eyed as she made her way toward them, and at the same moment, the door to the apartment opened. Mia stopped in her tracks at the sight in the doorway. Arms crossed over his black t-shirt pulled tight across a muscled chest, his gaze met hers immediately, like he'd known she was there before he'd opened the door. His eyes were golden-green, so focused on her, she could almost feel his stare, and there was intelligence there, as if he already knew all her secrets. The thought he was nothing like other men jumped to the forefront of her mind. Like a lord of the underworld, he gave off the most dangerous vibe she'd ever felt, and in that moment, the urge to run was strong. It didn't help that the sun was burning her skin to a crisp, and she needed to be driving away at this very moment anyway.

"Something wrong?" His voice was rich and smooth, like cool water over her parched skin, and her feet moved toward him without thought until she stood between the two deliverymen. He gently gripped her upper arm, sending wild, electrical pulses chasing throughout her body, and pulled her through the door of his apartment. The relief from the sun was instant. "Maybe I can help you."

She nodded and for the first time, noticed features other than his eyes. He was tall, probably well over six-feet. His blond hair was a little long, falling soft and straight to his ears and to the back of his collar, and the thought of feeling the silk of his hair sliding through her hands sent a thrill through her mid-section. His sculpted cheekbones paired perfectly with his aristocratic nose and his prominent jaw, highlighting the symmetry of his tasty mouth. She wanted to lick his lips and see if they felt as soft to her tongue as they looked to her eyes. The thought brought a rush of heat across her chest and up her neck. This time she couldn't blame it on the sun.

He'd asked her something in a deep timbre and clearly expected a response from her, but for the life of her, she couldn't remember what she'd needed from him. He smelled so good. Her nose filled with a rich, delicious spice that was familiar, and she couldn't get enough of it as she pulled it into her nostrils again and again. Like the worst kind of chick flick, all she could do was stare, and a little laugh escaped at the picture of the surreal movie-moment she was currently living popped into her head. This was so unlike her. She didn't get rattled by anything. She rattled other people first.

"Did you need me to move our truck, sweetheart?"

The spell broke at the gruff sound of the stout mover's voice. She finally looked away from the gorgeousness before her and acknowledged the men on the other side of the threshold, "What? Oh, yeah." She looked at the watch on her wrist and then toward the truck. "You're blocking my car, and I have to be on campus in about thirty minutes."

"I'm sure they wouldn't mind letting you out before they start unloading my furniture. Would you, guys?"

"We're on it." The thinner mover was already heading back toward the truck as he answered. The stout one followed.

"Sorry about that. Moving in today, but didn't mean to hold you up in the process. "

She made the mistake of looking directly at the fine specimen of gorgeousness in front of her and had to shake herself free of his spell again before saying, "Thanks. Timing is everything, right?"

"Right. Campbell Reid." He extended his hand and she took it, feeling the same electric pulses she'd felt when he'd pulled her out of the sun earlier. *Interesting.* It had been awhile since she'd felt this level of attraction to a man. And he was moving in right next door to her. Maybe things were turning around after all.

"Nice to meet you. I'm Mia Alexander." She pulled back and slipped her hands into her pockets.

"Do you live around here?"

"Next door." She pointed to the apartment directly to the left of his, and his face rolled into a smile that made her heart skip a beat. He could be a model. For all she knew he was and had absolutely no problem finding available women to fall for him everywhere he went.

A knowing look glowed in his eyes again, and she got the feeling he was reeling in a big fish, and the taste of his bait was that of irresistibly rich, delicious chocolate dangling before her. It was irritating to say the least. He'd find out real quick that she wasn't that easy. As a matter of fact, she was downright distrustful of…well…everyone. Her grandmother had made sure of that. *"Trust no one, Mia. It's the only way to protect yourself from those who would hurt you."* A little paranoid, but so far, advice that had served her well and kept her safe.

Besides, the more she thought about it, the more getting it on with her next door neighbor seemed like a bad idea. What if he was bad in bed or annoyingly clingy? It wouldn't be just throwing away a phone number. She'd have to see him each and every day. She wasn't being pessimistic, just realistic. Despite what her friends would say.

"How about I take you to dinner tonight? You know, to make up for blocking your car in and all."

And there it was. Yep, he'd expected her to instantly fall for his usual game, but now that she had her wits about her again, he was in for a rude awakening.

"Look, I'm sure we can let bygones be bygones. It's not that big a deal, and I'm pretty particular about my food lately. I don't eat out a lot."

His face fell, and she almost grinned as his eyebrows pushed into a confused vee in the middle of his forehead. He hadn't expected that, had he? She stepped back outside and felt the heat immediately. The sun really, really was stronger today.

He didn't follow her out. He stopped just inside the door but leaned over the threshold just a little. "Are you sure? We could order in."

The delicious aroma of him filled her nostrils once again, and she had the strangest feeling she'd smelled it somewhere before. The thought tickled her brain, but she couldn't place it, and she shook the notion away, along with the rogue idea she should go back inside and wrap herself around his sexy body. But reality's sharp teeth bit hard sometimes, and she knew she didn't need the complication of dating her hot neighbor right now.

Mia couldn't keep the smirk off her lips. He really was good-looking, and power was heady, and by the sound of desperation in his voice, she had most of it right now. Of course, her grandmother, who'd raised her from a baby, taught her to treat people as people, so she didn't press her position, didn't turn it into a game. Instead, she called over her shoulder, "Tonight's a no, but maybe another time."

And, funny thing, she kind of meant it.

* * *

Campbell rubbed his eyes and yawned as he stood in the shadows of Mia's bedroom. He was tired. He hadn't gotten much rest this evening before starting his nightly vigil over the exceedingly attractive and possibly mutant fledgling in front of him. The deliverymen had taken longer than he'd liked to carry in the furniture the council purchased for him to use on this detail. To their credit, it was an apartment-full, but if he was being honest, the two men were a little free with the number of breaks they took between carries.

He could have handled that though and still gotten a good amount of rest, but after they left Spencer called on the secure phone for an update. Needless to say, he hadn't been impressed with Campbell's strike-out. He'd had quite an earful to say about it actually.

To be honest, Campbell still couldn't believe she'd turned him down. No woman could resist him. He wasn't conceited, just armed to the gills with attractive weapons. It was part of being a vampire. His eyes, his voice, even his smell were all meant to draw others in. They were another thing that came with the package when his evil-bitch creator turned him hundreds of years ago. If he turned on his charms, there wasn't a single person in the world who could resist him. Except her. It was damn freaky.

Maybe it was part of her mutation. Super-rejection powers. Not that he took it personally. Okay, maybe a little bit, but the point was she shouldn't have been able to walk away from him until he'd released her. But she'd shaken his weapons off like they were broken. He'd thought they might be, so once the sun was down, he'd woken early and gone out to a bar in the shopping center next to the apartment complex to test them out. Every woman, even the supernatural females he'd encountered, succumbed to the irresistibility. As soon as he was satisfied, he'd released them and walked away, still scratching his head as to what made Mia different. He had to admit though, despite the cut to his ego, he admired her strength. Whatever she was, he was impressed.

Now he was back on guard-duty, going crazy himself as he tried to resist her weapons-of-mass-attraction. It didn't help she'd worn a nearly see-through tank top and a pair of flouncy, barely-there shorts to bed tonight instead of her usual t-shirt, and the silky garments left nothing to the imagination in the moonlight. Her covers had been kicked off not long after she'd nodded off, and for his sanity, he needed to get the blanket back over her from head to toe and was willing to risk alerting her to his presence to do it. But he remained strong, stood in place, and pulled up the most mundane thoughts he could muster. He went back over the earlier conversation with his commander, trying anything to keep his mind off this attraction he was hard-pressed to fight.

One thing about the dialogue still bothered him. Spencer made it clear the council had given Campbell a week to find out the identity of the creator and what exactly Mia was changing into. The information that followed is what he found difficult to digest. If he failed, the council had given the order for her to be put down. Because they weren't exactly sure what she'd be capable of when she'd changed fully, they didn't know if they'd be able to kill her after her transformation. With that in mind, they didn't want to risk any dangerous outcomes. She'd have to die. To say the least, the thought didn't sit well with him.

Now he was determined to ferret out the information as quickly as possible. Though he had to continue his guard duty at night, tonight there were other agents he trusted checking out the research facility where she'd volunteered, and he was sure her creator would be coming for her soon. It was usually just a matter of time before he or she showed up and harvested what had been sown. Of course, normally the makers simply feasted on the fledglings, absorbing the immunities stirring in their half-human, half-otherworldly blood. Most creators never planned for the fledgling to make it through the entire transformation. However, Campbell didn't think Mia's originator wanted that. He was sure her maker had bigger plans, and it was up to Campbell to find out exactly what he or she was up to before it was too late for Mia.

Chapter 3

Why did a rare steak suddenly sound like it would hit the spot? Mia was in her kitchen, debating another peanut butter and jelly when the charcoal smell of a grill heating up drifted in. She followed her nose to the back patio and stepped out of her apartment. The wooden divider between the parallel patios was more ceremonial than an actual separator. It was only about five and a half feet tall, so a much taller Campbell swiveled his head in her direction the minute she stepped out, pinning her still for just a moment with those mesmerizing eyes. Wild energy danced in her mid-section at the sight of him. It was unnerving how beautiful he was, and as he stood there in the body-hugging, long-sleeve t-shirt he wore, images of the delineated muscles underneath invaded her mind. Would his skin feel as smooth as it looked?

She switched her thoughts back to the safer subject of the food. "Something smells delicious."

"Thanks. You caught me on a clean day. I do like a good shower now and again."

She laughed easily and approached the divider. Something deep inside pushed her to get closer. Thankfully, the sun had almost sunk below the horizon, and the evening breeze cooled her down. The scent of the raw steak waiting to go over the coals was delectable. Was she really salivating over the *uncooked* meat? She usually liked her food well-done and practically burned to a crisp. But right now, her mind screamed it would be a crime to even put the meat on the grill.

He gave his attention to his preparations again then swiveled his gaze back to her and said, "At the risk of another rejection, I have an extra steak in the refrigerator. Care to join me?"

On a logical level, she knew it would be a bad idea. Sure she'd held her own against his attractiveness once, but was she strong enough to keep up the resistance? Then again, she really, really wanted a steak. "I don't think I should."

"No pressure. Just two neighbors getting to know each other. I promise."

It was bordering on just-plain-hateful to reject him twice in one week. Plus, the thought of another sandwich made her nose wrinkle in disgust. "Alright. You talked me into it." She started around the divider but stopped and asked, "I could bring the drinks. Thirsty?"

She could have sworn his gaze intensified for a moment and dropped to her collar. She probably wouldn't have noticed, but the sight of him was almost impossible to look away from, she felt like she was cataloging every little detail about him in her brain. She really needed to slow her roll on this overwhelming attraction to him.

But he blinked and gave her a genuine smile, lifting his gaze to meet hers again. "You don't have to go to any trouble. I was just going to open a bottle of wine."

She began to back up and head toward her door. "I actually have a great bottle of red that pairs really well with steak. Will that work?"

"Sounds perfect."

* * *

"You're a student, right?" At her nod, he asked, "So, what're you studying?" Campbell leaned back in his chair, working hard to remain casual. He already knew the answers to the basic questions but jumping right into the information he needed to know would make her suspicious.

"Graphic and web design. I'm one of those computer geeks with artistic tendencies."

She finished off her glass of wine, and he poured her another. "I do quite a bit with computers myself."

"Really? Like what?"

"I design security software." Though he did security work for the council, it was more like an occasional freelance situation. His software design business was what paid the bills, and it was something he could do at night.

"No way. You're a geek too?" At his revelation about himself, he noticed her soulful blue eyes brighten up like the sky over a sparkling ocean. The sight made his chest tighten just a little bit in reaction, and he realized his attraction to her was deep. He could get addicted to that look. He could get addicted to her, but he needed to remember he was centuries-old and had a job to do, and it couldn't involve impressing her with the few modern-day skills he'd picked up.

If she knew how hard he'd had to push himself to embrace computer technology in the first place, she'd probably think his bones would creak with every movement. He was a timeworn vampire, and very set in his ways. But once he'd realized it wasn't going away any time soon, he'd taken it upon himself to learn as much as he could. The weird thing was he took to it like he was born with a keyboard in his hands. Maybe that did make him a geek of sorts and it gave them common ground. "I guess you could say that."

They talked in length about where he'd gotten his education and the companies he'd designed security systems for. A few had impressed her. He went into as little detail as possible, but still felt he'd revealed too much about himself. She was easy to talk to, and he had to remind himself this wasn't really a social visit. It should be more like an interrogation--an easy-going, unbeknownst-to-her interrogation--but one nonetheless. It certainly wasn't going the way he planned it.

Her blue eyes were alight with curiosity as she asked, "What about family? Where are you from?"

Her questions were innocent enough, but he really needed to steer the conversation back away from him. "Enough about me. I've got a question for you."

"Shoot. I'm an open book."

"Do you always like your steaks rare?"

She bit her lip and paused to think before answering, "No. It's weird. I usually like my food fully-cooked, but today, I could've eaten it raw and not batted an eye. Do you think I should be worried?"

"Probably not. You're allowed to change your mind about things. Have you noticed anything else out of the ordinary?"

She cocked her head and pulled her eyebrows tight together. "Now that you mention it, I've been more sensitive to sunlight lately. And this is going to sound really weird, but my senses have gone into some kind of superpower-mode."

Now it was his turn to be confused. He thought he had an idea of what she was saying, but he had to ask, "What do you mean by *superpower-mode*?"

She took a deep breath and released it heavily before explaining, "I could smell the raw meat from inside my kitchen. Weird, huh?"

No denying it, she was definitely changing. "Believe it or not, not the weirdest thing I've ever heard."

"Well, that's good to know. I probably should see a doctor or a psychiatrist. Could be a brain tumor."

He couldn't hold back the chuckle that escaped his mouth. "It's not a brain tumor." More than likely he'd thought something similar when he was changing. As he recalled, it was very much like that. At the time, he was pretty convinced he was going insane or dying.

"How can you be so sure?"

Because I know things you don't. "Trust me. It's not a tumor." But he decided it was time to get back to figuring out the identity of the source. "When did everything start?"

She thought about it a few seconds and answered, "Probably about a week ago."

"What'd you do in the past couple weeks that was different from what you usually do?"

"Nothing. Go to class, eat at the same places, come home." She stared into her glass of wine and shook her head back and forth, but stopped suddenly and looked up. "Wait. I've been participating in a medical study. Do you think I could be experiencing side effects from that?"

Now they were getting somewhere. "A medical study? You volunteered to be a guinea pig?"

She snorted and rolled her eyes. "The drug already passed several trials before now. I'm at the tail-end of the final trial."

"Well, you're braver than I am. How'd you find out about it?"

"One day in class, one of my professors announced it to everyone. I dismissed it at first, but he pulled me aside after the next class and offered to put in a good word for me. The researchers offered a substantial amount of money, so like a bajillion students applied to participate. And considering I'm only able to take on a few, low-paying web design jobs in my spare time, it was a good opportunity. I felt fortunate to be chosen." She shrugged one shoulder before giving a sheepish smile. "Hey, don't judge me."

He put up his hands in surrender. "No judgment here." He'd like to know who that professor was though. It sounded as promising a lead as he'd had so far. "Was the professor involved in the study or something?"

"Not really. He teaches one of my graphic design classes. But he'd stop by often. It was a little odd to see him there so much, but I guess he was hanging out with friends or something."

She still hadn't given a name. "Was he one of those professors that was like, 'Call me Jeff'?"

"No. We just called him Professor Tipton." *Ding! Ding!* He had a name. But his internal celebration was cut short as a pained look came over her face.

She leaned forward with concern in her shining eyes. "You don't think the side effects are permanent do you?"

More than you could possibly know. The urge to ease her anxieties came over him, but he'd save that conversation for another evening. And if he were being honest with himself, he wanted there to be another evening. Despite the secret agenda, he'd enjoyed spending time with her. He hoped this lead panned out. The alternative would put the council on the path to destroy her, and that was suddenly unthinkable to him.

He would at least give her a little reassurance, "Nothing on you looks broken. Don't worry about it too much." And he meant it. This transition looked good on her. Her hair shined with flashes of liquid red fire mixed with lustrous brown. Though he'd found her attractive just yesterday, today, he was having trouble keeping his hands to himself. As they'd headed from the kitchen to the living room, she leading the way, he'd reached out, almost involuntarily, to take a strand of her hair between his finger and thumb and feel the silky, irresistible beauty, but at the last minute, pulled his hand back as she turned and sat in a plush chair facing the couch. Reluctantly, he'd sat across from her on the couch. Everything inside him said to get right next to her. If he didn't know any better, he might think he was falling for her. Yet that was impossible. His own, long-ago change was so charged with trickery and loss by a deceptive female, he'd worked unfailingly to harden his heart.

He was probably too jaded to do more than give into his lust now. But, to be honest with himself, he'd never felt an attraction this strong, not even to the wicked woman who'd made him believe he loved her, until she turned him and then turned on him.

She took another sip of wine and stared at him thoughtfully. "I'll call for an appointment with the doctor tomorrow."

That's the last thing she needed to do. Though human doctors would see most paranormal beings as just a healthy human, normally that wouldn't be a bad thing. Yet, since he didn't really know what manner of creature she was becoming, he couldn't have a physician figuring out she was different. Like, dissect-and-study different. He had to do something to convince her she was fine for now.

He stood and walked toward her, holding out his hand for her to take. "Come here. Let me show you something."

At first, she just stared at his outstretched hand, but with apprehension in her eyes, she finally took it and let him pull her to a standing position in front of him. "Is this where we have a long look in the mirror and a talk about how beautiful I am? Because, if so, we can skip it. It doesn't work on me."

She had a sense of humor and could coax a smile from his bitter lips. Not many could. He liked that and he liked that she kept surprising him.

With gentle motions, he turned her to face him until she met his gaze full on. The minute he had her attention, he explained, "Watch my eyes closely."

Though he had the ability to hypnotize humans, that wasn't what he had in mind. After all, it was highly likely she would be able to resist him. Instead, he'd have to convince her with something he'd never shown anyone. At least anyone who'd lived to tell about it.

He recognized the moment she saw the iris of his eyes change from their usual light green to a deep midnight within a matter of seconds.

Her breath caught and she covered her mouth with her hand before briefly reaching out then dropping it by her side. "That was amazing. Do it again."

Perhaps the last sight an enemy saw before Campbell ripped his throat out, the color change of his eyes usually indicated he was nearly mindless with aggression, or possibly lust. Occasionally, he could flash them for a few seconds, if he was feeling charged up, and right now, being this close to Mia was pushing his adrenaline higher and higher. A pounding sounded in his ears, and he recognized it as his own heartbeat. His heartbeat pounded in his chest and reminded him with loud, staccato beats of another fallacy of vampire lore. Humans believed vampires didn't experience normal bodily functions, and they no longer had to worry about many human necessities like filling lungs with air, but without a doubt, they had beating hearts.

"Can you do it again?"

He stared at her with renewed awe. His overwhelming attraction had to have something to do with her--something to do with her mutation. Whatever was going on, something about her brought his soul to life when it'd been dead for far too long. "Uh. I don't think so."

"How did you do that in the first place?" She looked closer at him, as if the answer was written on his forehead. But rather than make him feel prickly and uncomfortable as in past instances, it made him wonder instead if her plump, red lips were as soft as they looked.

"You're not the only one with unusual talents." His voice sounded low and gravelly to his own ears.

Like him, she seemed suddenly aware of their close proximity as something like electric energy pulsed in the air between them. Time seemed to slow as he leaned toward her, focused only on touching her mouth to his own. *This.* This is what he craved. He felt as if he'd go mad if he didn't know her taste in the next few seconds. A mere whisper away, he paused, feeling as if he were standing on the edge of a cliff, about to dive into a shimmering pool below. He wasn't keen on flinging himself off a ledge, but somehow, he knew it was inevitable. He was lost to his lust and couldn't have stopped himself even if her touch was as damaging to him as the sun. He'd gladly burn to a crisp for a brief taste of her lips.

But just as she softened and her eyelids slid closed and he was sure he'd have his kiss, she pulled back suddenly, a look of wide-eyed terror marring her face. She stumbled slightly before regaining her balance and putting a healthy amount of space between them. Something had her in a panic. He wondered if his fangs had descended without him realizing, but he would have felt that change. *Yeah, like he'd felt his body strangely coming alive again?* He was thoroughly confused by the events of this evening, but she looked downright terrified.

"I...I should go. I just remembered something. Something I need to take care of tonight."

"Was it something I did? I can behave myself if I've crossed a line."

Her mouth dropped open as if to say something, but she quickly closed it and shook her head instead, backing toward the door. Once her hand was on the knob and she'd flung it wide, she glanced back at him with a puzzled look before saying, "Just leave me alone."

Reflexively, he stepped toward her, in an attempt to fix the mess he'd apparently stepped in. But the minute she held up her hand, he slammed into an invisible wall and couldn't move any further. Even as he pushed, the muscles in his arms straining in mid-air, whatever she was manifesting was impossible for him to get past.

He backed off and looked at her. Her face clearly said *What. The. Fuck!* And she stared at her hands for a few shocked moments before recovering enough to rush out his door and, with a quick unlocking motion, into hers.

Her change was escalating at an alarming pace for both of them. One thing was for sure. Campbell's timeline just took a screeching turn into *figure-this-the-hell-out-now* or the council would destroy her in a couple days. After tonight, the thought of the council laying a hand on her sent his emotions into rage-mode. The strange thing was he hadn't allowed himself to feel anything since he'd walked away from his small village in Scotland five-hundred years ago, right after the loss of his king, James IV, at the Battle of Flodden—and right after the loss of everything else he'd ever cared about. And though he hadn't done anything differently, somehow now he felt he'd rip out the throat of anyone who harmed this thoroughly modern woman. If he didn't know better, he'd think he'd been bewitched. But he knew firsthand what that was like, and this was stronger, more intense, and way scarier. At this moment, he'd die for her.

And if he didn't deliver her creator to the council before they tried to destroy her, he just might.

Chapter 4

Mia worked to slow her racing heart and quick breathing as she leaned her back against the back of her front door. *Impossible!* But the aroma was unmistakable. It was the same one that filled her nose on the night of the break-in and it had been his. He had been the one in her bedroom that night. He'd been in her *home*, and it freaked-her-the-hell-out.

She knew he'd had a familiar smell the day they'd met, but she'd dismissed it at the time when she couldn't place it. Now she knew. And things were getting a tad stalker-creepy. *Understatement of the year.*

For a brief moment, she wondered what might have happened to the little, old lady who'd lived next door before Mr. Dangerously Disturbed moved in. Should she check on her whereabouts? Maybe she should just go straight to the police.

And say what? She'd *smelled* the person who broke into her apartment the other night and now he lives next door. Yeah, that didn't sound crazy at all. There's no way they'd believe she'd identified someone by their scent. It sounded strange to even her brain, but there was no denying she'd recognized the same rich, spicy, other-worldly aroma when they'd nearly kissed tonight. And for just a crazy moment, everything in her wanted to dive right in and wallow in all his irresistible attractiveness. Until she'd come to her senses. Well, she came to one sense in particular--her sense of smell finally gelled with her memory.

She knew one thing for certain. She wasn't staying here. Camping out with one of her generous friends appealed suddenly. Hope, Janna, or Roxie would be more than willing to help a girl-in-danger out.

Without wasting another minute, she busted toward her bedroom, grabbed a duffle bag from her closet and began throwing a few key items inside. Mostly she tossed in various dark colored shorts and t-shirts, some underwear, and a couple pair of socks. She crossed the hall to grab her toothbrush and other necessities, but as she stepped back into her bedroom, she noticed it seemed darker. A quick glance at the balcony doors confirmed her suspicion. Someone was outside.

Mia backed into the hallway slowly, duffle in hand. She'd set the security alarm earlier, but she wasn't taking any chances. She went to her spare bedroom closet and pulled out her second wave of security--Bertha--a well-used aluminum bat. Thank you high school girls' softball. If Campbell dared step into her apartment, she'd go *homerun hitter* on his head.

Of course, if she could just get past him to her car, she'd be so gone in a matter of minutes. But she'd have to sneak by him somehow. Best to sprint to the nearby supermarket and wait there for one of the girls to come pick her up. *Damn!* This was getting complicated.

Just as she heard a loud noise, like her balcony doors being smashed open, the alarm started pulsing shrill beeps. He really was crazy, but she didn't wait around to see for herself. She flew down the stairs and headed through her kitchen to the patio door. She could hear what sounded like several bodies in hot pursuit, heading her way, but she was already sliding the heavy glass door open and stepping outside. Just as she thought to run toward a second set of apartments behind her building, Campbell slid around the divider, a gun in his hand.

Startled, she stopped so quickly, she was sure her sneakers had squeaked on the concrete, and she dropped Bertha with a ringing clang. How had he gotten here so quickly? Something wasn't clicking in this situation. If he was the danger, who was in her apartment right now? And what was he planning to do with the weapon in his hands? But he didn't aim the gun at her. He put his finger to his lips and motioned for her to get behind the wooden divider as he edged his way into her apartment. Did he really expect her to stick around?

The minute he was out of sight, she took off toward the other block of apartments. For all she knew, the other person was just someone he'd planted in the house to seem more heroic when he "defended" her against the intruder. She was nobody's fool and didn't even look back as she slung the duffle bag over her shoulder and ran full speed away from the chaos behind her.

She didn't stop until she was outside the supermarket, two blocks away. It really hadn't taken her that long--maybe a double-digit number of seconds. Matter of fact, she seemed to make it there in record time, almost like her feet barely touched the ground. And as she thought back, she had no recollection of cars or people on the busy street, like they'd just been a blur. It was all very strange, but she shook her head, not ready to really think through the possibilities. That would have to wait until later when she could actually take time to reason it all out and not feel like her life had taken a sudden TV-dramedy turn. Instead, she pulled her cell phone from her pocket, intending to dial Hope, the first contact of her little circle that showed on the screen. Yet, before she could punch her index finger to the bar on the touchscreen, a hand covered it.

"I wouldn't do that if I were you."

She looked up into his green eyes, practically glowing, and she nearly took off running down the gift wrap aisle, but held her ground, determined to end this here and now.

"Why are you following me? Just leave me alone."

"It's too dangerous to leave you alone now."

She couldn't help but roll her eyes at that statement. "Or you want me to think it's too dangerous. I bet if I went back to my apartment right now, I'd find a few things turned over and broken, but no dangerous intruders hanging out."

His brow tightened slightly before he explained, "You wouldn't find intruders hanging out. Unfortunately, you'd find two dead bodies."

That's when she noticed the speckled pattern covering his shirt. *Blood.* It was blood. He was a killer, had killed somebody. He'd certainly tangled with someone and had obviously come out on top. Had there really been an intruder in her home? Someone else? More dangerous than him? Maybe she needed to consider he might be telling the truth. No, she wasn't ready for that yet. It was all too unreal.

She looked at her phone screen again, preparing to dial someone to get her out of this crazy mess. At this point, she wasn't even particular who that was. Hope, the police, a freaking circus clown might cause enough of a distraction for her to get away. She just needed someone other than the entirely too attractive lunatic in front of her.

"I was serious about not involving anyone you care about. You'll just put them in danger."

She cocked her head to the side. "Then I'll call the police."

"That would be fine, but just so you know, by the time they walk into your apartment, the creatures there will be gone. Cleared by a task force assigned to keep humans from discovering our kind."

She had to get out of here right now. But she couldn't help her curiosity as she asked, "Oh, everything makes perfect sense now! You're an E. T.? What planet are you from?"

Now he rolled his eyes. "I'm not an alien. Look, we can't discuss this here. We need to keep moving." He gently grasped her upper arm and turned toward the exit. "Come on."

She dug in her heels. "I'm not going anywhere with you, you giant cuckoo." But she might as well be glued to him for all the good her attempts to get away did. He hadn't tightened his grip a bit, but it was unbreakable and she couldn't get free.

"I don't want to scare you, but Mia, those *side-effects* you described aren't going away. You're changing, and you're going to need answers."

They were back outside, and she was perturbed no one had stepped in as she'd expressed her need for help the whole way. "Why isn't anyone paying attention? This is ridiculous."

He took a deep breath before explaining, "Human minds are easy to manipulate. To anyone who happens to glance our way, we appear to be a couple deeply in love."

She stopped struggling as the sad truth set in. She was in the hands of an escapee from an asylum. "So, you've finally mastered the force, Luke?"

"What? I'm not trying to force you and who's Luke?"

Her confusion grew. "How do you not get a Star Wars reference? No way you're a geek."

He approached a little red hatchback and tried the handle, but it was locked. After a few more attempts, he found a blue four-door sedan, unlocked, and stuffed her inside, making her cross over the middle console to get into the passenger seat.

Self-preservation took over, and she reached for the door handle. But by the time she'd flung the passenger door open, somehow Campbell was standing right outside the door. She did a double take. *How'd he get around the car that fast?*

When he held up his hands as if he meant her no harm, she paused, totally staggered by the situation. "How did you…?"

"I know this all seems absurd, but give me a chance to explain. Your life *is* in danger. I was tasked with your protection. I know I scared you the other night in your bedroom. I promise, I'll explain everything."

"Do you know how crazy you sound?"

But he didn't get the chance to answer. Out of nowhere, a seven-foot-tall, hairy man with jagged teeth grabbed him from behind. Mia screamed once before shock took over. *What the hell is that?* It looked like a bigfoot crossed with a dog-man. She had to be seeing things. *Not real! Not real! Not real!* This couldn't be real. A costume? It had to be someone dressed up. But if it was someone in a costume, they were using Hollywood-grade materials because nothing suggested the shaggy, light brown fur covering the creature was zipped onto the wearer. The hair sprouting on every inch of exposed skin looked as natural as what normally grew on a head, and its mouth was elongated to accommodate the canine-like teeth sprouting from its gums, with no sign of make-up or prosthetics. It was jaw-droppingly unbelievable— downright horrifying even.

She scanned the parking lot to see if anyone else reacted to the struggle going on to her right. Every person went about his or her business like nothing out of the ordinary was going on, like there wasn't some storybook villain trying to remove Campbell's head from his body. Was it like he'd explained--a trick of the mind? Maybe she was freaking losing her mind.

And then something even stranger happened. Across the parking lot, Mia saw the familiar face of a woman she recognized but couldn't place. They'd interacted with each other at one time, but nothing jogged Mia's memory as to who she was. Even weirder, the woman watched the whole scene with intense, glittering eyes and an otherwise expressionless face. Rather than being horrified, she seemed involved in the outcome, like she had something to lose.

Out of nowhere, Mia had a sudden urge to leave the car, cross through the other cars around the lot, and go wherever this oddly familiar woman asked her to go. She looked down at her hand reaching seemingly on its own to push the door open and run from the brawl going on between the two beings right outside the car.

"The time is now, Mia. Come with me!" The words were in her head but as clear as if they'd been spoken right into her ear. Even more disturbing, the voice sounded similar to her grandmother's. It made her grief-stricken and attentive all at once. The urge to do as she said grew, but something about the woman felt off. She shouldn't listen. Mia's inner warning bells clanged like a wannabe trying to steal some cred. *Not friendly.*

With a shake of her head, Mia fought the impulse and looked down at her lap before swinging her gaze back to the fight.

Campbell struggled to break the hold of the unbelievable creature, but the angle made it difficult. With the monster still attached, he slammed his back into the side of the truck next to them, rocking it on two wheels for a moment before it thumped back into place with a crash. A huge dent covered most of the side of the truck now. The must-be-imaginary dog-creature finally released Campbell and he turned swiftly, raining blurred punches into its torso and face. He backed off long enough to ease his hand inside his jacket and pull his gun. Breathing heavily, the creature raised its hands the minute it saw the weapon and began to back away slowly.

With a growl, it turned and sprinted away, jumping over two cars as it went. Campbell looked like he wanted to give chase, but he turned his heated gaze to her, lowering his gun and urging her to settle back into the car with a wave of his hand. Adjusting her position, she closed the door, begrudgingly admitting to herself she'd rather be in the car with her stalker than out there with that...whatever it was.

Once the monster was out of sight, she searched the parking lot again for the mysterious woman she'd seen earlier, but she was nowhere to be found. Just another unexplainable puzzle in this very mixed-up horror flick she was currently experiencing.

She sat stunned as he walked around the front of the car and got in. He didn't say anything as he rubbed at his neck. Instead, he switched his focus quickly, fiddled under the steering column a few minutes, and started the car.

"This isn't even your car? You're a stalker *and* a thief." She strapped on her seatbelt as he put the car in gear and gave it gas. "What have I gotten myself into?"

They pulled out of the supermarket parking lot and headed away from the apartments. She wasn't sure where they were going and knew she ought to be thinking of a way out of this situation, but it was too weird to even assimilate what she'd just seen with reality, matter alone how she was going to escape. She must be experiencing some kind of psychological break. Yes, that was it. She needed to take the advice she'd given to Janna recently and see a professional as soon as possible.

He adjusted the mirrors and cleared his throat. "I know what you're thinking. You're not crazy."

A humorless laugh bubbled up from her chest. How had he known that's where her thoughts had gone? The funny thing was she felt perfectly sane. And one thing was for sure, she wasn't going to let him see any weakness in her. "Despite the events of tonight, I'm fairly confident I'm in my right mind. You, on the other hand, strike me as the type who wears aluminum foil hats on his head to protect himself from the little green men."

"That was a typical, American werewolf. Though they're naturally very strong, they're not always so aggressive, but that male was doing the bidding of a very powerful being."

"Of course. That doesn't sound far-fetched at all."

"And he's not finished yet. He'll be back."

She crossed her arms in front of her and stared straight ahead. "What'd you do to him? Move in next door, gain his trust, then scare the shit out of him?"

He paused, glancing at her briefly before focusing on the road once again. He seemed hesitant to say anything, but finally explained, "Fair enough, but he doesn't want me."

She turned her gaze to his face as the realization of just who he thought the werewolf was after sunk in. "What are you talking about? Don't be ridiculous. What would that thing want with me?"

As she noticed his nostrils flare and his face tense up, she realized the subject made him uncomfortable. How bad could it be? When he didn't answer right away, seemed to be deep in thought inside his mind for so many silent moments, she knew it had to be pretty bad.

"You're changing."

She felt another eye-roll coming on. "So you've said. How exactly am I changing?"

"That's the thing. I don't really know."

Another unsettling revelation. "How can you not know?"

"We think, someone who's dabbling in bio-engineering targeted you during the research study you participated in. Whoever it was, and I don't have a definite identity yet, injected you with a serum that bonded with your human form on a cellular level. The basis of the serum is clearly vampiric with some mutations. However, we don't know yet the differences that will manifest as you develop."

"One question. Who's 'we'?"

"I work for a group that governs the beings of the paranormal world. The Supernatural Council. They set the limits and decide how to deal with situations like yours.

"Oookay. This is all quite disturbing. Let me get this straight." She swallowed, cocked her head to the side, and said, "Assuming I'm buying any of this, I'm changing into some, as-to-date unknown creature. And a mad-scientist-type wants to get his hands on me because I'm his latest lab creation?"

"Sums it up."

This was all so unbelievable, but strange things were happening. She couldn't deny that. A stray thought confused her though as she clarified, "I thought a vampire had to bite someone to change them."

He laughed lightly, but squashed it quickly. "It's nothing like the movies, Mia. To change into a vampire, a human must ingest the blood of a vampire. Or in your case, be injected with it."

"And that will change me into a monster."

His forehead wrinkled with what looked like concern. She assumed he didn't appreciate her terminology as he responded, "Something like that."

"And exactly what kind of monster are you?"

His eyes widened again as he took a quick look in her direction. "You're laying the sarcasm on a little thick, aren't you?"

Now it was her turn to innocently widen her eyes. She pointed her index finger at herself briefly before relaxing with a smile. "No, seriously. Are you human?"

He sighed heavily. "I was at one time."

"And now?"

With a curl of his upper lip, she watched fangs descend from the top of his gums. His eyes blackened as he answered, "Now, I'm a vampire."

How did you fake teeth sliding through holes in your gums? And blackening eyes? The only logical explanation that came to mind was radioactivity. Maybe he'd played with plutonium toys as a kid. All joking aside, though she didn't want to, Mia had to admit, *this shit was getting real.*

Chapter 5

"So, you're a vampire. Like, suck-blood kind of vampire?"

"Yes." He didn't add more. It was usually best to leave out the details and let a new vampire ask specific questions. The impending freak-out was less explosive that way. This would be the moment she'd break down, Campbell was sure of it. Most fledglings dwelled on the eating habits more than anything, and it was usually a deal-breaker.

"Do you hunt and kill people? Like drain all their blood?"

"Nowadays, I don't consume blood straight from the source. Haven't since the invention of modern medicine. Much more sanitary to purchase from a reputable dealer." He paused. He hadn't always been so benevolent though. And there were still many vampires who killed for sustenance...and for pleasure. Truth was he hadn't been a saint himself. There was a time, in the beginning, when his urges were nearly uncontrollable. "In the past, I drank from others, but I didn't make a habit of killing. Unless they deserved it, of course."

"Oh, of course."

Her sarcastic tone made him smile. She'd genuinely surprised him with how calm she appeared, at least outwardly. It was likely because she still didn't believe him completely. Denial was a strong and protective force when applied correctly. Possibly, it would keep her from reacting rashly to her situation and keep her safe from those that would do her harm.

She seemed a little more reserved as she clarified, "And I'm turning into something like a vampire?" It came out as a question, but it was more like she was working through the reality of the situation aloud.

He answered her anyway, "There's no doubt you're becoming a vampire, but because of the biological tampering, no one is sure what else will manifest."

She sounded breathless as she asked, "Oh, holy fat cakes on a platter. That's comforting. And how long will it take?"

"Normally, the transition lasts a few weeks, but it can take up to three months. However, it's clear you are changing at a much faster rate than is usual."

"Well, isn't that just sparkly rainbows and unicorns." She covered her face with her hands. The reality was starting to sink in, and she was reacting like he'd expected. "There's a thought." Surprising him yet again, she pulled her hands away, as if an idea occurred to her suddenly. "Are unicorns real? No. Nevermind. I don't want to know. I've had too much of fantasyland for one day."

"I understand."

"Do you? Were you changed against your will?"

He sighed heavily. Now was not the time to get into his own sordid transition, but it had certainly shaped his inability to trust others. The truth would probably ease her frazzled nerves slightly though. "Yes. I was misled until it was too late to turn back."

"Wait. Is there a way to turn back? Is there a cure?"

He paused, trying to word the truth carefully. How did he get stuck with the job of disappointing her constantly? But once again, the truth was the way to go. Though there were some who'd gladly take your money and promise to fix you, it was nothing more than a scam. No sense in giving her false hope. "No. There's no cure."

She nodded but didn't say a word. Her hands tented over her forehead, elbows on the armrests, she seemed to shut down for a little while, and he drove on in silence in the direction of a hotel next to the interstate. He'd contact his commander tonight and update him on the situation. Tomorrow he'd drive to a house he had near the coast. He'd drive a few hours in that direction tonight, but they wouldn't make it by sun-up. It was the most secure place he knew, and he'd decided he didn't want to head to the Sup Co headquarters just yet. It concerned him they were so anxious to dispose of her and the black-eye she represented on their control of the world's supernatural beings. He wasn't entirely sure why he gave a damn really. But handing her over right now felt wrong. The thought of anyone hurting her, not to mention killing her like she was just an annoying insect, made the muscles in his shoulders and arms tighten, and he didn't want her anywhere near them, just in case their trigger fingers got a premature itch.

She finally pulled her hands away from her face and inhaled deeply, staring straight ahead, and again it struck him. She wasn't taking this the way new fledglings usually did. There were usually tears and hysterics. He was beginning to worry her mindset might not quite be as calm as it appeared. He wondered what circumstance caused her to perfect her outward mask so well.

They drove a few quiet hours until sunlight began to peek over the horizon. She stirred as he exited the interstate.

"Where are we?"

He pulled into the lot of a major-chain hotel, parking in front for now. After they checked in, he'd pull the car around back. "We'll stay here tonight. Tomorrow, I'll take you somewhere safe until things settle down."

"Two rooms."

His gaze swung to her as he stopped the car. For the first time, he noticed the puffiness around her pinkened eyes, and realized she'd been crying. He hadn't even heard so much as a sucked-in breath. Even his jaded heart softened at the thought of her sobbing so quietly, he couldn't hear. Again, it made him curious to understand just who this fledgling really was.

"As it turns out, I'm not letting you out of my sight. We'll share a room."

"Well, if you get thirsty in the night, you'll have to get a bite to eat elsewhere."

He gave a short laugh before explaining, "I'm not bragging, though it will sound like it, but there are many women who would beg for my bite. Apparently, it brings orgasmic pleasure."

A scoffing sound rose from her throat. "Oversized ego much?" She shook her head and crossed her arms. "Let's get one thing straight. I'm not one of these, many women and I don't need you to bring me any kind of pleasure."

"What is it they say? Don't knock it 'til you try it." An impulse to touch her came over him and he reached out to trace her shoulder and upper arm with the backs of his fingers. At the last minute, he stopped himself and his hand hung in mid-air. He couldn't allow himself even a slight touch of her cool, smooth skin. It would never be enough to satisfy the need building inside him. Already, her vanilla and lavender scent filled his nostrils, and his gaze drifted down her body where, even through her layers of clothing, he watched her nipples tighten under his perusal. His body reacted. His cock hardened and he pulled his hand back to adjust the damn thing. He couldn't remember when he'd last lost control of his body, if he ever had. He wanted to sink his hands into her reddish-brown hair and pull her in for a long, drawn-out kiss. He wanted a kiss that would turn her knees to jelly, and he wouldn't stop until they were both on their backs, side-by-side, exhausted but well-satisfied.

The reality of their situation, though, cooled his sudden need. Preservation had to come first. And he couldn't forget this was a job and he was a professional. A good soldier didn't get mixed-up with the target he was protecting. It was pretty obvious he was already too close to her. The whole thing was a tangled mess inside a hurricane, but if they fucked, he knew he'd be lost forever. And the way he was feeling right now, afterward, he'd probably never let her go.

"Oh, whoever *they* are, they don't know me. I'm not trying it. Consider it knocked. Got it?"

"Of course. I wasn't serious. Same room, separate beds, and I'll keep my teeth to myself."

She glanced at him hesitantly. "Are you sure you can?"

"I've been in your bedroom for a little over a week and not a mark on you yet from me. You can trust my word." He hoped he hadn't just made a promise he couldn't keep.

Seemingly satisfied, she nodded once and said, "Okay. I'm exhausted. I need a shower, some clean sheets, and some shut-eye. Let's go."

As they climbed out of the stolen vehicle, Campbell couldn't help himself from one more jab. "However, if you change your mind, there's a spot on the neck, just below your ear, that I've been told just a light scrape from a vampire's fang will bring waves of sexual release in seconds." He stepped toward the building but turned back when he noticed she hadn't kept up with him. She stood beside the car, her gaze locked onto his mouth, most likely lost in the image he'd painted for her. "I'd be willing to test it out if you're game."

She shook her head and looked as if she were emerging from a daze. Her feet moved quickly as she made her way to Campbell's position. "Don't hold your breath waiting, okay?"

He laughed low, leaning closer to her as he whispered in her ear, "For you, I'd hold it for all eternity."

He only gave her a brief look, noticing her blue eyes widening and her pulse racing faster. What a beautiful thing--that pulse. He felt the tips of his fangs emerge slightly before he got himself in check and retracted them. He turned and headed for the door, satisfied she'd be thinking about his bite just as long as he'd told her he'd hold his breath.

* * *

The warm water of the shower hit Mia's spine, and she tipped her head back, releasing a moan of appreciation for the liquid cascading over her. For at least a few seconds, she could forget she might be irrevocably changing into some sort of fairytale monster. Except, the problem with finally being alone was the dam of thoughts she'd been holding back gushed into her mind.

She was a freak! Some might think throwing up force-fields and super speed would be convenient problems to have, but she just wanted her crappy, un-super-powered, life back. Whining about her situation so wasn't her. She'd grieved her parents' deaths. She'd grieved for her grandmother, but this...this was so beyond her realm of dealing with it, she didn't even know where to begin.

So many questions to which she needed answers, and though she had Campbell here, much too close for her mental comfort, part of her just wanted to stay in denial that anything would be different for her now that she'd been introduced to a world she'd never known existed and of which she was apparently about to become a card-carrying member.

Reality hit suddenly, and she sunk to the floor of the shower, tears spilling unchecked down her face and sobs racking her body. How could she be losing her humanity? She didn't want to believe any of this was real, but she'd seen too much to think Campbell was making it up. She couldn't deny the werewolf in the parking lot had been real. And her sensory side effects, her sudden speed, and the ache in her gums right where her canines were clearly made the truth undeniable. Her change was very real and inevitable. She raised her knees to her chest, resting her forehead on top and let the water fall over her head and down her back.

She didn't want to be a monster. Who had time to live out Halloween all day every day? Too many things in her life were finally falling into place to change everything now. How was she supposed to go to class? Vampires didn't go out in the day, did they? Of course, her sun sensitivity made sense now. And she'd been ready to go on an Anti-Global Warming, Go-Green campaign. Well, she'd planned to recycle more at least. Now, she couldn't even go outside at all anymore. How was she going to get her recommended daily Vitamin D dose? She apparently wasn't drinking milk anymore. Supposedly, she'd crave blood. Just the thought of consuming blood made her want to retch. Did it even contain vitamins?

A frustrated groan rumbled in her throat. And what was she supposed to do about Campbell? He was currently her only source of information, supposedly protecting her from all sorts of evil, and about the sexiest man…er…vampire she'd ever met. When she'd thought he was a stalker, she could dismiss her growing desire for him. She'd been freaked out, with good reason. Now that she was beginning to believe he was actually watching out for her, it kind of changed things. She'd have to be careful not to develop strong feelings for him given her present predicament. Something told her in the middle of a transition from human to vampire was not the time to get between the sheets with someone. More pressing matters took precedence, but she had to admit, no matter how much she tried to repress it and focus on the realities of the situation, her body reacted to him anyway. She had ninety-nine problems but sexual attraction wasn't one of them.

Briefly, the image of his teeth grazing her neck below her ear eased into her head. She couldn't seem to shake the idea. Would it really bring waves of instant orgasms? Her sex throbbed and her nipples ached at the thought, but it confused her more than anything. How could she be thinking of sex at a time like this? She wasn't sure what was going on, but it was like her skin was on fire and she needed the release of a mind-blowing climax right this minute. And the thought of seducing Campbell into giving it to her seemed like the best idea she'd had all day. How was that even a remote possibility?

What if this was part of the transition? What if she went into some kind of sexual frenzy and attacked any male unfortunate enough to be close to her? Maybe she'd be better off being locked up for the rest of her horrific life. A hideous, horny vampire like her shouldn't be running around, randomly sucking necks and male body parts with no control over her urges. Life was completely impossible to live suddenly.

Stop it! She had to stop this pity party immediately. Now she had to wonder if raging self-pity was a side effect.

Her grandmother, who'd raised her after her parents' car accident, certainly hadn't taught her to sit around kicking herself when she was down. She'd tell her if there wasn't a way then you just had to make one. But how could she make a cure where there wasn't one?

She looked up and stared straight ahead at the shower wall. There had to be a way to fix herself. Surely, she wasn't completely doomed and there was some way to put everything right again. Of course, she hadn't missed Campbell's pause before he told her there wasn't a cure. He knew of some way, she was sure of it. She just had to convince him to tell her what he knew.

Chapter 6

Campbell paced the tiny hotel room, growling in frustration.
Confused as to how, but able to all the same, he could feel Mia's
unsatisfied sexual desire, and it was driving him crazy. He adjusted his
hardening cock and tried to remember a time when a woman affected
him this much. *Never!* All he could think about was her naked, wet body
just feet away from him. He'd seen a glimpse of her curves and knew
exactly where he'd run his hands to feel his way over her skin and pull
her against his body until her head fell to the side and her neck was
exposed to his aching fangs.

Shit! He really needed some way to push his mind off that
dangerous path. With a groan, he ran his hands roughly through his
hair. He was close to losing control, which he hadn't done for hundreds
of years, since he was a fledgling himself. If he didn't get a grip on his
urges, he'd have no other choice than to hand Mia off to someone else
from the Sup Co secret force. The problem with that though, he couldn't
guarantee they wouldn't just dispose of her immediately. He wasn't
entirely sure what he was going to do if they insisted she be destroyed.
Just the mere thought of someone laying a hand on her made his brain
buzz with thoughts of severing the head of anyone who dared go near
her with the slightest violent intention.

Aaarrgh! This was getting out of hand. He needed to contact his
supervisor and let him know he had a name of their likely evil bio-
engineer. Maybe when they found the one who'd started this whole

mess, they'd figure out a way to help Mia and he could turn her over to the experts before he did something they would both regret later.

He dialed his phone and quickly relayed all the pertinent details to Commander Spencer, including the special skills she was manifesting and the werewolf attack in the store parking lot. He left out the possibility that driving males desperate with lust might be part of her skill set. He wasn't ready to divulge how far his own struggle had come, and figured they'd find it out eventually. But it felt good to show progress, even a small amount.

"Good work, soldier. You've done an admirable job maintaining the safety of the target. Perhaps tonight would be a good time to bring her to the Supernatural Council Compound. Her safety could be assured and we could begin her training."

He'd been waiting for this exact opportunity. Finally, he'd be able to put her somewhere safe and go on with his own existence, without the distraction of his body's constant reaction to her. He could get back to his usual routine, writing code for security software at night and sleeping through the day. His gaze drifted toward the bathroom door just as the water shut off. Why did his life suddenly sound so depressing to him?

And if he were being perfectly honest with himself, something about this situation still didn't seem right. Deep inside him, it felt wrong to hand her over to anyone else, like she was his responsibility. No, it was more than that even. It went beyond his obligation. It was like she belonged with him. *Mine!*

"I think it best we stay put tonight. Too much movement might draw attention. I'm ready for anything that comes our way."

"Perhaps you should just tell us where you are currently. We could extract you both before dawn."

A niggling worm of suspicion burrowed itself under Campbell's skin. Why was Spencer so adamant about getting Mia into their custody? He felt it was imperative he keep their location secret. Something about this didn't set well with him. As a hybrid, there was no telling what they'd do to her. "I don't know if this line is secure, sir. I'd rather not reveal our current position." It was complete bullshit, and Spencer probably knew it. Of course Campbell's line was secure. He was a freaking security specialist when it came to computers and electronics. Nothing he owned would be unsecured. But he hoped his commander didn't insist or make it an order.

He heard only silence on the other end and wondered if the connection had been broken.

Finally, he heard a deep sigh. "Okay, son. I'm going to trust your judgment. Keep her there today, but at the first sign of dusk, get her to our facility pronto.

"Yes, sir."

"I'll look into this Dr. Tipton. Hopefully, he's our guy, and this whole mess will be over by nightfall."

"It sounds promising." At the sound of the click of the bathroom door, he ended the call and settled on the bed closest to the most likely exit. She walked out fully dressed in shorts and a t-shirt, but rather than making him less interested, it only emphasized her shapely legs and how the fabric of her shorts stretched nicely across her ass. The t-shirt molded to her torso and left so little to the imagination, considering he'd already glimpsed the delectable body beneath it.

"Stop looking at me like I'm dinner."

He snapped his gaze to the phone in his hand. *Dammit!* He was making her feel uncomfortable. "Sorry. I'm just not used to having others around."

"Haven't you ever had...I don't know...like a pack or nest or some kind of vampire family?"

The media had really fucked with human's minds when it came to vampires. So much in books and movies was made-up crap that had nothing to do with the real existence. Most vampires were anti-social loners. He'd heard of some forming pair-bonds, but for the most part, as alpha-predators, they were rather territorial. He tended to avoid other vampires unless it was council related.

"No family. Few friends."

"Hmmm...that's a little...sad."

"For humans, it would be. It's the way I like it. Less ties and less for my enemies to use against me."

She crossed the room, sat on the bed across from his and pulled her legs up, cross-legged, back straight. It was such a feminine thing to do, and he was impressed she was still standing, so to speak, after all they'd been through, though he did notice the puffiness of her eyes. She'd been crying recently. "So, why exactly does anyone want to become a vampire?"

"Mostly immortality. Often, it is like what happened in your case.

They aren't made with the intention of allowing them to develop fully. They are a means to an end."

Her eyebrows dipped to the middle of her forehead, and he noted how her eyes practically glowed with curiosity.

"And what end would that be?"

He took a deep breath before giving her an answer he knew she wouldn't understand or like. "Vampires evolved centuries ago and have remained top of the food chain for all this time. Then about fifty years ago, a researcher noticed a pattern of disease beginning to wipe-out populations of vampires in Asia. The pathogen was unlike any discovered before, almost like it was engineered."

"Chemical weapons?"

"Exactly." One thing he could say about her, she was sharp. "Nothing developed could combat the infection, and vampire numbers dropped drastically. Then, it became clear, newly made vampires were immune because their lingering human immunities protected them. It didn't take long for older vampires to put the evidence together and begin making vampires just to drink them before they transitioned completely, absorbing their immunities."

"How horrible. It worked though?"

"Only for those not yet infected. But they had to drain the fledgling vampire in order to benefit completely."

She sucked in a deep breath. "They killed them?"

"Since they weren't fully immortal, yes, the process resulted in their deaths."

A look of intense concentration entered her eyes. He knew what he'd be concerned with, and as much of a thinker as she was, she was bound to come to the same conclusion. "If I was created just for the purpose of my immunities, why go to the trouble of bio-engineering the injection before giving it to me?"

A few different reasons came to mind. For one thing, her creator could have been making a never-before-seen paranormal being to be used for some immoral purpose. Another idea came to mind--one that concerned him more than anything else. What if she was a walking chemical weapon? Maybe her creator was engineering a super-bug inside her, one resistant to even human immunities. He didn't like to think about the choice he'd have to make in that case. He was intelligent enough to realize, as tragic as it was, her one life wasn't worth the few thousand or so remaining vampires it would kill. Yet, as he stared at her, sitting relaxed across from him, her wet hair falling in reddish curls around her shoulders, her eyes so innocently wide, he couldn't consider harming her, matter alone killing her. But he'd have to keep those thoughts to himself anyway.

"We're probably overthinking the situation." He needed to distract her with something else, and though his gaze strayed to her mouth once again, he didn't think that distraction was one she'd be willing to delve into. He decided on a neutral subject as he focused on her eyes again. "What about you? Any family?"

"Not since last year. My grandmother passed away last winter. She raised me after my parents died in a plane crash fifteen years ago."

An ache for her set up deep in his chest. He'd lost his own parents and sisters during his transition long ago, and had still yet to recover. "I'm sorry. Were you still close to your grandmother?"

"She was the only one I can say was always there when I needed her. One of the kindest people I've ever known. There wasn't a person in need she ever passed by. I just wish I'd been there for her when she needed me."

"Could you have really done anything to save her?"

"She died peacefully in her sleep, and the doctors said there was nothing anyone could have done, but part of me will always wonder, you know?" She shrugged one shoulder pitifully, and for just a moment, he caught a quiver in her chin, but she drew in a calming breath, seeming to push away the emotion. "I have to admit, it's been harder than I expected. Before she passed, Gran insisted I take classes. You know, get my degree. Kind of a last dying wish. I don't know what I'd be doing now otherwise. Probably drunk, dancing on a bar in some run-down, college dive."

He smiled at the image of her sexy body moving in time to music. That was a sight he'd be willing to do almost anything to see. "I'm sure we could find a liquor store still open somewhere if you wanted to see what it's like to be drunk as a vampire."

"Is it different?"

He laughed hard, remembering the last time he got so shit-faced, the one friend he trusted whole-heartedly, Mac, had to come pick him up on the side of the street after he got kicked out of a bar. It catered to paranormal beings, but he'd tried to defend a female vampire from the overly aggressive flirtations of a werewolf. She hadn't appreciated his interference and told him so with a few snide remarks. The owner, who tolerated him as long as he was spending money, asked him to leave, afraid the wolf would try to pick a fight. He was probably right. Campbell loved a good brawl, but he didn't like the idea of taking on a werewolf as messed up as he was, especially not over a woman who obviously didn't want his help, so he did what any self-respecting drunk would do, he threw the first punch, knocked the wolf flat on his ass, and literally, got thrown out the door. Not one of his finer moments.

She waited expectantly for him to answer, so he finally said, "Not a bit. Still gives a false sense of invincibility and a splitting headache in the morning."

She shrugged, calling his attention to the fantasy-inspiring places on her t-shirt where her hair dripped as it dried. They were strategically placed over one of his favorite areas on a woman's body, and her nipples were hard and visible through her shirt. He knew he shouldn't be looking, but his brain didn't seem able to think logically when she was near. His mind clouded with thoughts of her that night in her room, but instead of him rushing out, she beckoned him to her, a look of desire in her sexy eyes. He shook his head to push the image away. The last thing he wanted to explain was why his pants were suddenly so tight.

"I could use a little liquid courage about now, but keeping my wits about me might be a better way to go."

"I think you're one of the most courageous people I've ever met. I mean, anyone who keeps pushing herself the way you have, even without the family support others take for granted..." *Damn!* It suddenly occurred to him why she'd been targeted. Without a family, no one would be around to miss her if she disappeared. He was almost completely certain whoever had created her had planned to drain her for some biologic advantage. More than likely, she was still just a means to an end.

"You barely know me."

"More than you realize."

The skepticism was written in the twist of her mouth and the raising of one of her dark eyebrows. "Okay, I'm going to call you on that. What do you know about me?"

Time had given him the ability to read people, and though he knew there was much he still didn't know about her, identifying what made her tick was not difficult. "You spend most of your time alone, either working or studying. You have a close circle of trusted friends and that's the only socialization you allow yourself." Her eyes enlarged as he lifted slowly from his bed and slid onto hers, feeling the bed depress with his weight. "Your sarcastic responses and your humor hide your insecurities. But most interestingly to me, it's apparent no one's ever kissed you passionately enough to make your toes curl and your protective shell crack."

She watched him intently as he reached out a hand and gently pushed a ruby piece of wet hair behind her ear. Instead of pulling his hand back though, he rested it on the back of her shoulder and upper arm. Time slowed down as they stared into each other's eyes. She swallowed hard and he grinned crookedly because he knew he was on the right track. "How'd I do?"

For a few extra seconds, she sat still, breathing quickly, and the temptation to lean forward until their lips met and he demonstrated exactly what she'd missed all these years was strong. Like all his blood suddenly rushed to the front of his body, his body felt heavy as he moved toward her ever so slightly. But, she shrugged his hand free and it fell back in his lap.

"I'm feeling a little tired. We'll have to save this enlightening conversation for another time."

Oddly, her rejection stung a little, but he nodded and stood slowly, crossing to his own bed and grabbing the remote. He turned the TV on with the volume low. Taking it personally was not normally something he did. Of course, no one could resist his charm if he turned it on. No one before her anyway. How was it possible she wasn't affected by his vampire weaponry, and more to the point, why had she rushed to push him away? He must have hit a nerve. His description must have been a little close for comfort. He'd been spot-on about how she hid her anxieties and how she didn't trust easily. But he'd have to gain her trust somehow because it was obvious she was metamorphosing into a very powerful being. One who would be a force with which to be reckoned.

He'd just have to find another way to deal with her. And for fuck's sake, he'd have to find the strength within himself to stop trying to kiss her every time they were together.

Chapter 7

Mia lay awake in the quiet room, unable to sleep despite her exhaustion. The sun shone brightly outside, but the heavy curtains covering the hotel window didn't allow even a drop to leak through. Thank goodness for that, considering it would apparently be painful on her skin the more she transitioned. As if she weren't pale enough, now a tan was completely out of the question. Less wrinkles that way, she figured. Though thinking on the bright side wasn't her usual M. O. But what choice did she have?

In the other bed, Campbell lay sleeping, the back of his broad shoulders facing her. She'd always thought vampires slept in coffins, on their backs, rising board-stiff to their feet at the end of their death-like slumber, but Campbell slept so...human. He'd tossed and turned with every noise outside the room, lifting his head slightly from the pillow until the possible danger passed them by. His breaths fell evenly, and she was almost certain she heard his heart beating steadily in his chest. She didn't realize vampires even had hearts, but that had to be her Hollywood-influenced imagination. She obviously had a lot to learn about vampires.

And to make matters worse, her mind was playing cruel tricks on her. It was impossible to know when humans were passing nearby, wasn't it? Surely that wasn't the aroma of those humans' blood filling her nostrils so sweetly? Her stomach rumbled and cramped tightly, and she moaned low in reaction, wrapping her arms around her mid-section.

Her ears picked up the rhythmic beat of multiple pulses close by, perhaps in the room next door. She felt a slight ache in her upper gums and gently prodded there with her fingers. Two bumps that weren't there yesterday, rested above her canines, one on each side. The changes taking place in her were undeniable. *I'm a freaking vampire!*

She was baffled by the reality taking hold of her life, but as it turned out, Campbell was sane after all. Her doubts were melting away with each new development, and the facts were becoming irrefutable. She was a real-life, and as-of-now, still-breathing paranormal being. She shook her head. *A freaking vampire!*

As two people passed the room, the delectable smell of their blood filled her lungs, and she felt the bumps elongate and break through her gums. She touched the newly-sprung fangs and winced at the sharp sting as they sliced into her finger. Hesitantly, almost afraid of what she might see, she lifted her cut finger in front of her eyes and stared at the drop of red welling up there. Her stomach muscles contracted tightly, and rational thought emptied from her head.

She had to drink right now. Those humans were prey, and she was a hunter. But above everything else, she was starving and needed to feed immediately.

Quicker than she'd ever moved before, she leapt from the bed, toward the door, and the food on the other side. But before she could grasp the doorknob in her hand, Campbell grabbed her from behind and spun her around, blocking her exit with his body.

"Get out of my way."

"I can't. I won't let you do something you'll regret later. And believe me, you will regret it."

She doubled over as her abdomen seemed to cave in on itself, and all her strength left her. "But I'm so hungry. I need to eat."

He lifted her in his arms and carried her to his bed, sitting there with her still cradled on his lap. "You don't look good. Very pale."

She looked up at him and her gaze locked onto the pulse beating a rhythm in his neck. Her fangs throbbed with each beat. "I feel like I haven't eaten in a week…maybe even a year."

He pulled back, staring at her thoughtfully, a look of utter distaste in his eyes, like he was picturing something horrible. Did she really look that bad?

"You're gaunt, like you've been starving as long as that, if not longer."

In desperation, she reached her arms around his neck, pulling him against her. The scintillating contact of his skin against hers felt like a hot, summer storm breaking over a mountain range. She rubbed against him in desperation and had him groaning as well. She hugged him to her chest, desiring to have him close, not caring about the intimacy of having him crushed against her breasts. In that moment, only hunger mattered. "Please, please, I need to eat. Help me, Campbell."

With acceptance, he nodded and situated himself against the headboard without letting her go. As she writhed on his lap, he stroked her hair and back gently. Unrelenting and punitive, her stomach rolled like ocean waves smashing against the rocks of a cliffside, and she twisted in agony. The necessity of food wouldn't be denied.

"I can't leave you, and I can't take you with me. Either way, you'd probably attack someone in your current condition." His brow wrinkled in concentration, and she could see him coming to a conclusion right in front of her. "It is rare that I've ever shared my blood with another, mostly it was involuntary, but desperate times call for desperate measures."

He gently pried her arms free and bent his wrist back to give her access to the veins there, but just the idea of biting him repulsed her. Not because it was him, but because she'd never done anything like that before. How could she possibly sink her teeth into another being?

She shook her head back and forth. Despite her incredible hunger, she couldn't bring herself to break his skin with her fangs. There had to be another way.

"You need to eat. In your transition stage, you can still die without sustenance."

"Another way. Another rare steak."

He shook his head and sighed deeply as he lifted his hand to his throat and sliced open a wound with his fingernail. He pulled her toward him again until his neck was in front of her nose and with one whiff, she felt the irresistible pull. "I don't think you have time for a plan B."

She held out as long as she could, but with a groan of resignation, she grabbed his shoulders and tentatively touched the red liquid flowing at the juncture at his collarbone with her tongue. At just that small taste of heaven, she was lost and didn't hesitate any longer as she sank her fangs deep into his skin and began to draw his blood into her. Like warm rain, it flowed throughout her body and she began warming up in some strangely surprising places. Her breasts felt swollen and heavy. She shuddered with intense pleasure as she drew in the delicious taste. Her pussy tingled, becoming wet instantly, and she rocked her hips involuntarily and moved to straddle Campbell's lap, the need to close the distance between them growing stronger than she could resist.

He growled low in his throat, drawing her attention to the fact he was feeling the effects of their connection too. Desire burned out of control as he rubbed his hands up and down her back and subtly thrust his hips upward. Everything inside her wanted him naked beneath her, and she could feel his very male reaction pressing at her core. The size nearly made her release his neck, just to determine whether it could possibly be so long and thick. But, she held tight, as if he might pull away any minute. Truth be told, neither seemed too eager to end this anytime soon.

"Don't stop, little vampire. I've never felt anything better." His voice sounded rough, like sand crunching under heavy boots, and she felt it in her abdomen like a tingle of hot sauce on her tongue. Her need burned strongly, and she recognized stirrings of a massive release in the making, pushing her inhibitions away.

She was openly grinding against him, and he was lifting his hips to intensify the friction between them. Unwilling or unable to stop, they moved against each other, desperate to get to their imminent climax.

But just as the end was in sight, Campbell's phone began to ring on the bedside table. He gave a frustrated groan and thrust himself against her a couple more times before halting his motions even while his hands remained pressed to her back.

She pulled free of his neck slowly, and he shuddered as if she'd touched him intimately. The reality of her position began to sink in. With careful motions, she slipped off his lap to the bed beside him, feeling boneless but satisfied for possibly the first time ever. She felt her fangs retract as she wiped her mouth with the back of her hand and let it drop to her side on the bed. A feeling of euphoria washed over her as she lay prone against the pillows, trying to catch her rapid breath. With a quick glance up, she met his heated gaze, and she recognized the promise shining from beneath his lowered eyelids. Whatever this was between them, wasn't over.

He leaned down and brushed his lips lightly over hers once before straightening. The fire in his eyes made her want to reach out and pull him back for a deeper kiss, but she just stopped herself as the ringing continued.

He grabbed his phone from the bedside table. "What?" His tone was rife with frustration, and she could totally relate. Wasn't that always the way? Just when things were getting good, something had to interrupt.

"How is that possible?"

Mia sat up straighter, her passion cooling quickly at Campbell's incredulous tone.

"I see." His gaze strayed to hers, but he shifted his focus swiftly away, and she realized she was the topic of conversation. The thinning of his lips told her the news wasn't good.

"There has to be another option."

He turned his back on her and walked from between the beds, toward the window. Just the slightest part in the curtain with his hand, and he glanced outside like he was searching for something...or someone.

"Okay. I'll relay the target by morning." He touched the screen to end the call and placed the phone against his forehead, eyes closed, like he'd received terrible news. "Dammit."

As he slowly shifted his head and rolled his gaze in her direction, his eyes glowed intensely amber. "How about a little road trip?"

"Now? I thought we needed to lay low for a while?"

He shrugged and walked toward her duffle bag, scooping it up and approaching her on the bed. He reached out a hand, and when she laid hers in his, pulled her to standing. Instead of letting her go, his hand gripped hers tighter for a moment. In his eyes, a struggle played out as he stared at her, the confusion written in every wrinkle between his brows.

His forehead smoothed as he seemed to come to a decision, and he laced his fingers in hers briefly before turning toward the door. "I've got a better place than this. Safer. We need to get you there now."

As strange as it was, as many bizarre things as she'd experienced in the last twenty-four hours, until that moment, she hadn't truly feared for her life. His words held an ominous undertone. He was completely serious that her life was in immediate danger. Now, she wasn't just scared. She was flat-out terrified.

* * *

His order was to kill her.

Or, at least, he was to bring her to the council headquarters where the facility staff would put her down like an animal. Either way was the same in his mind, and just the thought of it turned his stomach.

Apparently, Dr. Tipton was dead, murdered yesterday in his campus office, and since he was the only lead into what she was becoming, the administration wanted it taken care of now. They wanted all the loose ends tied up, and to them, she was nothing more than a dangling string that needed to be dealt with.

He'd made his decision before he'd hung up the phone. She would live. And he'd do everything in his power to guarantee it.

She sat in the passenger seat, staring out the side window without saying a word. He'd stolen another car, one with tinted windows, but the sun had been descending when they'd left anyway. An hour later, it was below the horizon.

He slid his gaze to her for the thousandth time, the memory of her bite and his very sexual reaction still prominent in his mind. Never in his long life had he experienced anything so dizzying and pleasurable. He'd nearly come in his jeans and couldn't seem to muster a bit of shame at that admission. Just the thought of her grinding on him gave him a sudden jolt of fiery desire and his cock shot hard as rock again. This was going to be one long-ass ride at this rate.

Was it just him or did she look different?

Her hair seemed longer, her cheeks pinker. Even her lips seemed to be a deeper shade of red and her blue eyes were brighter than they'd been before. Again, the idea that this overwhelming attraction could be a result of her mutation occurred to him. Maybe his desire for her was enhanced by whatever biology had been mixed with the vampire serum. Perhaps she had some characteristics of the mysterious succubae. It was rumored, they were nearly irresistible to all males, human or supernatural. She certainly seemed to be displaying the features of an alluring sexual being he was finding near to impossible to resist.

He rubbed his hand down the center of his pants, trying to adjust himself without her noticing and wondered how he was going to survive hours in an enclosed space without yanking the car to the side of the road and picking up where they left off earlier. And, more importantly, when would she feed again and how did he convince her sooner was better than later?

"Are you hungry?"

She shook her head, but he felt her gaze on his neck like a beam of heat. Her eyelids lowered, desire expressed in every flutter of her lashes. She clearly wasn't unaffected by their earlier connection, and the need he saw in her eyes went beyond basic hunger. He could feel her sexual need almost as strongly as he felt his own. Lust, either for blood or sex, was ruling both of them at the moment. One thing he knew for certain, he'd gladly offer up his neck to her any time. For that matter, he'd be the only one to feel the pleasure of her bite if he had anything to say about it.

"Do you think I could call my friends? They'll be worried about me."

He rubbed his hand over the stubble on his chin. "Probably best not to. I'm serious about the danger they'd be in if you contacted them. Whoever created you wants you back, and he'll stop at nothing, it would seem."

"What do you mean? Like sending the werewolf and the woman?"

"Wait." He understood her reference to the werewolf, but what woman was she asking about? *Had she been attacked some other time?* Other than the wolf, he hadn't known about any other attacks. "What woman?"

"In the store parking lot. She was a couple rows over from the fight and watching the whole scene. She was familiar and spoke to me *inside my head*, but I don't know who she was. I figured if she were human, she would have ignored the fight like every other person and couldn't have put herself into my mind. Instead, she seemed to watch everything eagerly, like she had something riding on the outcome."

No doubt about it, this was a curious twist. No one mentioned anything about the involvement of a woman. "What did she look like?"

"Though she looked as young as me, she had long, white hair, pulled back in a braid that reached below her waist. Her eyes glowed like stars and looked yellow from a distance. I remember thinking she had to be something supernatural. I'd never seen a human with yellow eyes."

It couldn't be. He'd only ever seen one person with the characteristics she described, and though he hadn't seen her in centuries, he'd recognize her anywhere. *Lisada!* The witch who'd double-crossed him and left him as a bloodsucking vampire. He'd thought she was dead, but Mia's description brought to mind the hated image he'd been sure he'd never see again. Clearly the death blow he'd dealt all those years ago hadn't taken.

"Did she have any distinguishing marks? Tattoos or scars?"

She sucked in a sudden breath. "Yes. Now that you mention it, she had something like a birthmark on the side of her face. Her skin was darker there and it seemed to be shaped like a star."

It was her. He knew it now. *Shit!* This situation just grew more complicated by the minute. "When she spoke her thoughts to you, what did she want?"

Mia thought back. "She wanted me to join her. Something about the time being right. The urge to go to her had been strong, but I shook it off. Didn't trust her intentions."

Campbell ran a quick hand through his hair. "Smart girl."

"I noticed something else too. Maybe it was a trick of the low light, but her neck had a raw, red scar stretching across it. I know this sounds morbid, but it looked like someone had attempted to cut her throat."

It hadn't been an attempt. He'd thought it a success. Clearly he'd been wrong.

Well, this threw them into a whole, different kind of shit-storm. If Lisada was alive--*God, he hoped she wasn't*--they were in for a world of hurt.

"Do you know who I'm talking about? You look like you're about to throw up."

"I know of only one woman who looks as you describe. She was a force to be reckoned with. A witch of great power. I thought her long dead, but now I'm not so sure."

She sat up straighter in her seat and untucked her shapely legs. He wished he didn't notice how long they were and how smooth her skin was. It threw him off balance and made his hand itch to slide over her exposed thigh. He had to remember he was trying to keep his hands to himself and off her. Near to impossible when she looked more and more like an irresistible fantasy and smelled like the most delectable vanilla cream he'd like to dip his finger in for a swirl and a taste.

"Sounds dangerous. What should we do?"

He sucked in a steadying breath and blew it out hard, forcing himself to focus on the road in front of them instead of the temptation in the seat beside him. "Nothing yet. Once we get to my house, we'll decide on a strategy from there. It's like a fortress, and I have a small army in the caretakers and other residents, so anyone would be a fool to attack.

"Other residents? You have roommates? Is the rent so high in a fortress?"

He glanced at her, noting the upturn of one corner of her mouth, before swiveling his attention back to the front again. Her dry sense of humor appealed to his jaded heart. He loved how she used her humor. It spoke to the cynic in him, and that she could laugh at all under her current circumstances impressed him completely. He tended to take everything too seriously and couldn't help but be a little awed by her levity.

"Not exactly roommates. I just have a few trusted friends who tend to crash at my house on occasion. I called a few of them at our last gas stop and asked them to come lend a hand in case we needed reinforcements."

"Vampires?" Her voice came out low and unsure. No doubt she was nervous about her reception with other paranormals. She might be right to worry. Thanks to years of persecution by humans and fighting between factions, most supernatural creatures were distrustful from the get-go. He wouldn't let anyone hurt her though.

"A couple, along with some of the Noble Faeries, a werewolf, and a few other creatures."

"Yeah, that sounds perfectly normal."

"You have nothing to fear. I'd trust them with my life, and they'd do anything for me."

Her teeth worried her bottom lip with persistent concern. "Even protect a mutant like me?"

He hated hearing the way she spit the word *mutant* like it was distasteful in her mouth. "Don't say it like that. Mutant describes every single one of us, and it's not a bad thing. I felt like you in the beginning, but the passage of time gave me room to think it through."

"And now you like being a blood-sucking vampire?"

She'd made her point with her word choice, but it wouldn't dissuade him from the argument he was trying to make. "Yes. There are perks."

"Not buying it. To me, it's clear the cons outweigh the pros. I mean, we suck blood, for heaven's sake. Why can't we just eat a decent, non-creepy meal?"

He sighed deeply. "Fledglings always get hung up on the feeding method. Trust me, in the beginning, I tried to go back to eating human food. But legend says, vampires were created from the blood of humans who'd been damned. Supposedly, to exist, we can only subsist on the blood of those same kind of humans. As you demonstrated, we can survive on the blood of other vampires and for a time, on the blood of animals. Take it from me, you can eat prepared human food as you did before, but you won't like the taste of it and it won't sustain you for long."

She crossed her arms and sharply asked, "Change of subject?"

Probably a good idea. "Actually, I have a question for you. You mentioned you were raised by your grandmother because something happened to your parents. When did you lose them?"

"Young. When I was six, they went on a sudden trip to Europe. I've often wondered why they left me with my grandmother. Money was never an issue for them. My father was a silent partner in an early technology start-up that took off. He'd had to travel for business at times, and I'd always been allowed on their trips before. For some reason, they were adamant I stay behind on this particular one." She paused and stared at her hands in her lap. "Their plane crashed on the flight over."

"I'm sorry. That must have been horrible."

"It was a long time ago."

"Time doesn't heal all wounds. At least not in my experience." And he understood this truth all too well. He blamed no one but himself for his family's deaths. If he hadn't fallen for Lisada's lies, they all would have finished out a normal, human existence. He'd have married and had children. Though his life expectancy would have been pitiful compared to modern day humans, compared to eternity, he would have taken normalcy over this existence. The perks were many, but not worth the loss of his mother, father, and three sisters.

She watched him in silence, waiting for him to elaborate, he was sure, but she'd have to wait a little longer. He still couldn't bring himself to speak aloud the sins of his past. Not to her, not to anyone. It was hard enough having the ripping guilt constantly rolling around in his head. To share his pain with another would be too...too...well, too weak. His weakness had been used against him before. He vowed he'd never open himself up to that kind of vulnerability again.

"Thank God I had my grandmother."

It was the change of subject he needed. "Made a difference in how you turned out, huh?"

"She was amazing. Warm and generous, but fiercely protective of me. She tended to wait on me hand and foot, even as I got older. Some said she spoiled me, but I think she just did what came naturally. I guess she felt she had to compensate for all the things I missed out on not having parents. Toward the end, I tried to care for her as much as I could, but I wasn't there when she passed, and I have to live with that."

Something about her words nagged at him. The way she described her grandmother was in line with how grandparents tended to treat their grandchildren, but he wondered at the apparent servant role she took on so well. "Which one of your parents was she the mother to?"

"Truth is, neither. My parents sort of adopted her somewhere along the way, and she never really looked like a grandmother, but she and my parents insisted I see her as such."

Definitely something about the situation wasn't completely normal. He stared at her out of the corner of his eye. Who was she really? He was sure finding the answer to that was the key. It was the key to figuring out who was after her, what she was becoming, and how to save her from the threats that seemed to be multiplying by the minute.

This was unquestionably not another routine job.

Chapter 8

Mia woke a little disoriented, unsure where she was for a moment. Nightmares plagued her sleep as usual, but the sudden shifting around woke her and made her straighten up from where her cheek rested against a wadded sweatshirt she'd used to buffer her head from the glass of the car window. A loud pounding filled her head, and her throat felt like it was lined with sandpaper. She worked the kinks out of her neck with a few twists and ducked her head to stare out the windshield at the looming castle-like estate coming into view in front of her.

They were traveling over a long, gravel driveway, lined with trees and heavy, wooden fences toward a Georgian style manor, with a red, brick front. Dark shutters sided each of the windows lined up in a straight line, five on top and four on bottom. Two slightly smaller, attached wings flanked the main house and were set back a little. The house was dark with the exception of the foyer light, streaming through the window over the gable and front door.

What was that pounding sound? Rhythmic and regular, she was having the strangest reaction to it. It made her feel restless, like it was telling her something important that she needed to take care of. The feeling intensified and was quickly elevated to emergency level. All she could focus on was that constant beat.

"What is that noise?" Her words came out broken and scratchy, like she'd screamed for hours on end. The beating grew louder still. She put her hands over her ears, but it didn't help. The sound was barely muffled.

He pulled the car to a stop in front of the enormous house and turned to her, concentration making deep furrows between his eyebrows.

"Do you hear it? It's so loud!"

Gently, he pried her hands from her ears and opened his mouth to reveal his lengthening fangs. Call her insane, but it was the sexiest sight she'd ever witnessed in her life. Nothing sounded better than his bite in that moment, and she tilted her neck involuntarily, as if to give him access. Then, an even bigger surprise made her draw in a deep breath of the most mouthwatering smell that had ever filled her nostrils. As it wafted in her direction, her own fangs descended, and she hyper-focused on the pulse at his neck. Its rhythmic undulation matched the noise perfectly, and understanding began to dawn on her.

"Don't go so long without feeding. The need to survive is impossible to ignore. At least every twelve hours from now on. The noise is my heartbeat, and if we were around humans, the urge to attack would be uncontrollable."

"Are you saying I wouldn't be able to stop myself from hurting someone?" She rubbed a hand through her hair, pausing at the nape of her neck as she thought the reality over. "I'm a real-life monster."

"Eventually you'll learn to control it, but fledglings have a long way to go before they can fight the urge."

The back of her head hit the headrest as her options became clear. This wasn't going away. "I can't bite you every time my stomach growls." A flash of memory reminded her just how things would go if she sank her fangs into him. Sparkling sensations traveled down her spine to her core at the image of grinding herself on top of his stone-hard erection as she sucked at his neck. She shook her head to evict the provocative picture, but her breathing grew shallow and her skin heated up all over. The thought occurred to her that, at the moment, as hungry as she was, she probably couldn't spare the blood it took to get turned on. She needed to stay focused on the problem at hand and not create more for herself. "Isn't there like a vampire carry-out service or something? You know, to you in thirty minutes or it's free."

He gave a half-hearted laugh and shook his head. "Don't worry. I keep a supply ready here. My freezer is well-stocked."

"What are we waiting for then? I'm starving."

They climbed out of the car and headed toward the front door. It opened as they reached the top step, and Mia stumbled at the behemoth standing in the doorway. *What the hell was he?*

"What tasty treat did you bring me, Campbell?"

"Don't get any ideas. This one's not for you, Donovan."

"Not a maiden?"

What the hell was that supposed to mean?

Campbell put his hand on the small of her back and moved her toward the entrance and the large, brick-wall of a man/beast, who had a decidedly feral look about him and seemed ready to devour her like a tasty snack. She moved a little closer to Campbell as they approached.

"I can't say that I know that information first hand. Regardless-- hands off." The hard edge of Campbell's voice surprised Mia. The threat of violence lacing each word was unmistakable.

"Whoah! Sorry, didn't realize you'd staked a claim already. Very unlike you, dude."

As they climbed the spreading, brick staircase, Donovan stepped inside and gave them a pathway to pass into the house.

"No claim staked."

"Then, she's up for grabs?"

Finally fed up with the whole talk-about-her-as-if-she-wasn't-there routine, Mia grated, "*She's* right here, in case you hadn't noticed, and nobody's staking claims or grabbing anything. Understand?"

"Her eyes glow when she's mad, dude. What is she?"

Mia gave an exasperated growl, stomped past the beast/mountain spouting idiocy and stepped passed him, wrinkling her nose as an unpleasant odor hit and two pounding beats picked up in her head. It was a mix of sulfur and a strong musk.

"Pungent, ain't it?"

Campbell pushed in behind her, wrapping his arm possessively around her waist. "It's a defense mechanism. Though it's rumored dragon's blood is the most delicious in all existence, no vampire can get past the smell to see whether it's true or not."

"Dragon?"

"In the flesh, love. And from the way you're eyeing my pulse, I'd say I'm one lucky bastard to be a dragon right now. "

She shook her head, unable to process completely what he'd said. He looked nothing like a dragon to her. He was kind of handsome, in a rugged, mountain-man way. Maybe it was the dark beard, covering his lower jaw or the midnight-colored, shaggy hair, curling around his ears and nape. If he was a dragon, why didn't he have scales, wings, or a tail? Did dragons have tails? "How is that possible? You look like a man. A *huge* man, but a man all the same."

"And I will remain in this form if all goes according to plan."

Her confusion only grew, but Campbell steered her away from the door and away from Donovan, the supposed dragon. "A story for another time. We have a hungry vampire to sate."

For the first time, she turned her attention to the decadence of the foyer. She was immediately impressed, and her anger and confusion dissipated as she took in the richness of the sight in front of her eyes. Dark, hardwood floors looked freshly polished and gleamed under the glow of an elaborate chandelier. The walls were decorated in champagne-colored and taupe striped wallpaper from floor to the middle of the wall, where it met ornate wainscoting. From the middle upward, another wallpaper with ornate designs, repeated around the room. A small semi-circle mahogany table sat against one wall with a decorative lamp atop, and across from the table was an elaborate staircase trimmed in white and fanning out at the bottom, the balustrade ending in a swirl at the bottom. "This is lovely."

He shrugged. "I had a human decorator come in a couple years ago. Unfortunately, she figured out things weren't quite what they seemed, and I had to get rid of her."

"You killed her?"

He met her gaze, a look of utter horror on his face. "Good God, no!

I'm not that far removed from my humanity. I wiped her memory and sent her on her way." He returned his focus back down the hallway and shook his head. "The point is, unfortunately, several rooms remain undecorated, but she certainly did well on the places she got to, I suppose."

She followed him down a hallway formed by the stairs and the opposite wall, relieved to hear he wasn't a complete monster, even if he was a vampire. What was she saying? She was apparently a vampire too. It was a good thing he still held some respect for life. It gave her hope that she would remain herself and could still exist among humans, especially her human friends.

A quick glance through a wide archway, showed a comfortable sitting room with a fireplace as a focal point. They didn't stop there though, instead continuing toward the back of the house and into a magazine-spread-worthy kitchen. Pristine, white cabinets surrounded the area. They were oversized and perfectly accentuated by the light-brown granite with veins of white and gold throughout. The appliances were stainless steel and industrial size. A deep, double sink sunk into a huge, center island where three barstools were pushed under a shelf on the back.

"This is gorgeous."

"I guess so. Other than the freezer, I no longer have need for most of the other amenities in here." As he spoke, he made his way around the island to the freezer and opened it, pulling two, red, plastic bags from inside. They were clearly frozen, but she felt her fangs lengthen and her salivary glands kick into overdrive at just the sight of the potential food.

Stinky followed them into the kitchen and moved up behind her. Before, she would have edged away from a behemoth such as him, who exuded certain danger like he did, but now she had a strong urge to draw him close to her, to gain his trust, and then sink her fangs deep into his skin. The only thing holding her back was the smell. It turned her stomach each time it hit her nose, and she could even taste it on the back of her tongue. It was a damn good defense against vampires; that was for sure.

"I know I may not smell like much, but you're kicking off some pretty intense pheromones, little miss trouble." He continued to stare at her, but he directed his next words across the kitchen, "You better see to your woman soon, Campbell. Otherwise, when the crew gets here, there's going to be bloodshed over her."

Something hot and dangerous zinged through her nervous system. "I'm nobody's woman, and I certainly don't need *seeing to*, thank you very much. I am visible, aren't I? I mean I didn't just develop some odd side-effect where I can't be seen or heard, right? In case you don't understand sarcasm, I really don't like being talked about as if I'm not in the room. Got it, stinky?"

He just stared at her with a big, stupid grin on his face, like she amused him in some way.

"You'll have to excuse Donovan. He doesn't get out much and has shitty social skills." Campbell slid a glass full of red slush across the massive island, and it stopped right in front of her. She slid onto the stool directly in front of where she stood, gaze locked onto the glass of nourishment as if it were the center of all the universe. Nothing had ever smelled sweeter, and though the idea of drinking blood still seemed very wrong to her, she just told herself it was a cherry slushy, and she'd down it so quickly, she wouldn't even taste it.

But at one sip, her eyes rolled back into her head, and an involuntary moan escaped her lips. It was just want she'd always craved even though she'd never known she craved it. It felt like heaven on her tongue, and she slowed down the pulls on her straw, wanting to savor every last drop of the delectable liquid.

Stinky's gruff voice came from behind her, "Okay. That's just bat-shit crazy, dude. How am I turned on by watching a bloodsucker drink from a glass? What's the world coming to?"

She barely acknowledged the big lug's comment with a quick glance behind her followed by a sour look and a nod before again returning her focus to her liquid dinner. *Screw him and the cave he crawled out of.* But one look in Campbell's direction and all thoughts of food slipped from her mind. His eyes shined with sensual promise, and she wondered if he were thinking about earlier when she'd fed directly from him. His heated gaze dropped to her neck, and fiery shocks swam through her body, accumulating at her core. Her pussy grew wet, and her heart revved up like the engine of a formula one car, pounding wildly in her chest. He wanted her.

The straw dropped from her lips as she worked to steady her breathing. How could one look affect her that strongly? Her body was on fire for him, and from the looks of things, he was feeling the lust between them just as strongly. Suddenly Mia couldn't remember why it would be a bad idea to feed directly from the source. Her mouth watered and she felt her small fangs grow longer, ready to pierce skin…his skin. It would give just a little before his skin would open and like being sexually penetrated, a shock of sensuality would assail her body before she even took the first pull. And there was no doubt the intense sexual desire generated by feeding from Campbell's neck was the strongest she'd ever experienced. The memory sent lingering tingles rushing over her skin. The anticipation was almost as thrilling as the feel of the warm liquid sliding down her throat, satisfying her carnal hunger.

She shook her head to pull herself out of her fantasy and noted the knowing smirk that planted itself on his face. Though she had to admit arrogance looked good on him, she hated that he knew of her hunger, both for blood and for sex. The one saving grace was the fact he'd more than likely experienced it himself. He knew what she was going through, and she was surprised he wasn't taking full advantage. Most men would likely see her ramped-up sexual needs as a way to satisfy their own. Why didn't Campbell? Maybe he didn't find her desirable? The thought cooled any lingering desire.

"Come on, Mia. Bring your meal, and I'll show you where you can rest for the night and through tomorrow."

* * *

Campbell couldn't remember a time it literally pained him to be in proximity to a female. He physically ached to be inside her. Everything about her spoke to him on a sensual level and made him want to grab her close and pick up where they left off in the motel room.

As he pointed her down a set of stairs and watched her as she went, he rubbed a weary hand over his mouth. If he were a different man, he might take full advantage of the side effects of her change. Her senses were on overload right about now. The slightest smells and sounds were amplified to a maximum level. And of course, her ability to perceive pheromones was on high alert as well. Whether she realized it or not, the longer they were in close proximity, the higher her sexual attraction would climb, which in turn would attract him and causing him to release more pheromones, thus creating a full-on passionate cycle that wasn't going to stop any time soon.

She paused at the bottom of the steps, and he slid by, feeling scalded by each whisper touch as he moved past her into the narrow hallway. Something had to give soon or he'd be buried to the hilt inside her, reveling in the feeling that she was *his* completely. *Damn!* She was like a dangerous addiction, and he was fiending for a taste.

He shook his head hard and turned to the right, leading the way down the hall. When they got to the end, he punched a string of numbers into a keypad at the side of his underground sanctuary.

"That's one big-ass, metal door. You keeping the baddies out or planning to keep one in?"

The door was large. Taking up the width of the hallway and just falling short of the ceiling. The polished metal looked dull in the low light, but it was solid steel and practically impenetrable. Necessary with his current lifestyle.

He couldn't blame her for believing he might lock her away. Unable to trust easily anyway, she couldn't possibly think he had her best interest in mind, but surprising even himself, he did.

"You are a valuable asset right now, and there are some who will stop at nothing to possess you. This is the safest place you can be."

"So, you're locking me inside?"

"No." The multiple locks released with a metal click, and the door opened slowly, allowing Campbell to grip the handle and help the thick heavy door swing free of the facing. "I'm locking *us* inside."

He placed his hand on her lower back and shifted her duffle over his shoulder as he directed her through the door. The minute they stepped through, sensors raised the lights gradually until they were at the dim level he personally liked. It reminded him of the soft glow of a room full of candles and a crackling fire in the fireplace. Though he appreciated modern conveniences, he'd lived long before the flip of a switch produced light, and part of him would always long for the ways before he lost his humanity. Besides, a vampire could see perfectly in low light anyway as evidenced by her dropped jaw as she spun in place, taking in the great room of his hidden world.

Campbell had never actually invited anyone into his private rooms—ever. She was the first, and by her reaction, she was impressed. He tried to see the large area from her perspective, but he was so acclimated to it, that the leather sectional and the 60" TV were all he noticed anymore.

"Is that bar fully stocked?" He glanced at the kitchenette that was framed by a large L-shaped bar, replete with barstools that never got used.

"Depends." He grinned, surprised at his own playfulness as he asked, "Are you going to dance on top of the bar if I share?"

Her easy laughter reached through his shields and pulled his insides tight. As a distraction, he turned his focus from her relaxed features and pulled the foot-thick door closed. He punched in the security code once again to keep any intruders out and felt the reality that they were once again alone.

"Sorry to say, that would probably cost you more in drinks than you're probably willing to pay."

She was more right than she knew. The cost to him wouldn't be monetary. When it came to getting involved with Mia, it would cost his body and his soul—what was left of it. Of that he was certain.

With curiosity in every touch, she walked around the room, skimming her fingers over the stone walls and wooden mantle over the wood-burning fireplace. It was swept clean, seeing as he didn't really spend leisurely evenings here beside a fire, sipping an after-dinner drink. The thought was actually laughable.

Yet, as he glanced around, he took in the pool table to the left of the room and the gaming table to its right. When had he ever actually spent a good amount of time in this ultimate man-cave? Considering most of the time he was out doing the bidding of the Sup Co, the answer was never.

As she came back around and stood beside him, apparently

satisfied she'd seen everything worth seeing, she covered her mouth with a yawn, and he remembered that she wasn't fully a supernatural being. Her needs were still human at times, and especially as she changed, she'd need to rest.

"Let me show you where you'll sleep."

"Separate rooms."

He nodded. "If that's what you want. Shouldn't be a problem while we're here. My security system is unbreakable."

"What about smelly up there?"

"Who? Donovan?" She gave an affirmative dip of her chin. "I'd trust him with my life, and he'll be joined by a couple other men I trust completely, but even he doesn't have access to this area of the compound. You're safe from intruders."

She looked thoughtful for a moment, chewing on that plump bottom lip and driving him crazy with desire. "Yeah, about that. We need to talk."

Never a good thing to hear a woman use those words, but he'd been waiting for this moment since she first realized she was living a real-life horror movie. "Have a seat at the bar. I'll fix you a drink, and we can discuss anything you want."

A few minutes later, she was perched on a barstool, watching him mix a drink on the other side of the bar. She rested her chin in her hand, and he figured the first question would be a tough one.

She didn't disappoint as she asked, "So, who's the witchy woman and why did my mention of her freak you out so much?"

He paused briefly and released a heavy breath before continuing to make her drink. He needed to be honest, but he also had a strong need for self-preservation. Once he set the glass in front of her, he kept his gaze lowered to the dark wood and rested both hands on either side of the bar beside him, answering, "She was my maker."

Her reaction was silence, and he finally looked up to see how she was taking this news. Her face said everything. No doubt about it, she hadn't expected that. "She's the one who turned you from a human to a vampire?"

"From what you described of her, she's the one."

Stunned into silence again, she lifted the glass to her lips and took a sip. She set it back down and asked, "What does that mean?"

"Not quite sure. I thought she was dead."

"You thought she was dead? Why would you think that?"

"Because I was the one who sliced her throat."

She choked a little on another swallow of her drink. For the third time in so many minutes, he'd managed to reduce her to speechlessness. She finally regained her composure enough to say, "Okay. Did not see that coming."

The story of Lisada's role in the deaths of his family wasn't one he wanted to reveal right now, but he knew he had to say something. He'd opened a box of jagged memories, but he wasn't ready to test each sharpened point just yet. He needed to divulge enough to make her understand. "Take my word for it, the death blow wasn't undeserved. She's the reason every member of my family died too soon."

"Not being judgy of you at all. I wasn't there to say one way or the other." He couldn't tell if she was just placating him or if she spoke true, but he accepted her explanation with a dip of his chin.

Her forehead creased in thought for a moment before she said, "One thing that's still a mystery to me. She looked familiar. How would I know her?"

Seeing as he hadn't a clue they'd ever even met, he'd like to know the answer to that too. "Up until you saw her last night, I hadn't thought she'd survived the sixteenth century."

Her face fell in utter shock. "You're that old?"

He nodded. He did feel ancient more often than not, but he had to admit her reaction bothered him a little. Not that he needed her approval or anything, but he didn't like the feeling he'd hung out at the party too long. It didn't help that she looked a little horrified by his admission.

"Sorry if I stepped on your antique toes, but I suppose you look good for your age."

Not the reaction he'd been expecting. Nevertheless, he needed to get to the bottom of where she'd met up with Lisada before that parking lot. Could she be Mia's maker too? Wouldn't he sense that in some way? "Did you cross paths with her at the research center?"

"Not that I remembered everyone I met, but I don't think so. It's almost like it was from further back, like from when I was a child."

That was even more confusing. He certainly felt more out-of-touch than ever with this situation. Who was she really? Could her parents' plane crash have been more than an accident? He'd suspected as much when she'd first told him, but had dismissed it as paranoia. Yet, the grandmother who'd cared for her, even though she wasn't a relation at all, sounded more a part of a gothic romance...well...than a brooding vampire-type like him, and the fact her parents never left her before that particular trip couldn't just be another coincidence, could it?

She covered her mouth again with a yawn, and he thought it was probably time to put her to bed, and not in the way his raging attraction suggested either.

He pulled her almost-empty glass toward him and dumped the rest of the contents.

"Hey, I wasn't done with that. I'm not even close to swaying, matter alone dancing on this bar."

"Well, that delectable thought and your interesting questions will have to wait until tomorrow. You need rest, and I need to meet with the men upstairs to see what information they've gathered about your situation."

He swung around the end of the bar and waved her toward the hallway which led to his bedroom and a guest room. With only the slightest hesitation, he directed her away from his room and toward the other room. Separate rooms, she'd said, and he agreed it was for the best. Yet, just the thought of touching her creamy skin made his fingers itch and made blood rush to some vital areas. One particular area, actually, which shot hard at just the mind-sight of the suggestion of her dancing. He could picture perfectly her gyrating body in front of him. He'd glimpsed her naked form once, and it had been his undoing. No taking that back, and he wouldn't want to. That sight would haunt him for the rest of his life—in a very good way.

"I should probably be there with you."

He shook his head as he opened the door and walked inside, waiting for her to do the same. "You will stay underground for the time being. At least until we figure out who is after you and how we can eliminate the threat...permanently."

She yawned again and didn't even bother to try to hide it this time. "I am rather exhausted. Maybe a short nap, but you have to promise me you'll share everything you find out. Promise."

Funny how easily he could've lied, how easily he could've said he would. He'd done it to countless other targets, but something about her made him want to be a better man all around. God that sounded sappy. But he still couldn't lie. "I'll tell you everything you need to know to keep you safe."

"I don't like the sound of that. That sounds like you'll keep stuff from me."

He ran a weary hand down his face. "I don't know what's going on, and I don't want to make a promise I can't keep." His resolve was melting under her wounded gaze. "Look, I'll make you a deal. I'll tell you everything I find out that won't jeopardize keeping you safe. Everything."

For a long moment, she just stared at him, but seemingly satisfied, she nodded and trudged past him toward the bed in a very childlike way, barely picking up each foot as she crossed the carpet.

She pulled back the bedding, and he was thankful he'd changed the sheets recently because he wouldn't have had time as she only paused a moment before she completely collapsed, face-first onto the pillow. He chuckled low and said, "There's a bathroom at the end of the hall. You're welcome to take a shower or bath, and you can borrow something to sleep in if you'd like."

Her muffled reply came to him clearly, "Nah. M'good."

With long, measured movements, she pulled herself under the blankets and turned to her side, facing him, her low-lidded eyes drawing him in until he had to mentally restrain himself from crossing the room and crawling into the bed with her. At the moment, he was having trouble remembering why that would be a bad idea.

With effort, he stepped toward the hallway and looked at her one last time before saying, "Get some rest. I'll be back in a little while. We can talk some more then."

And part of him hoped he had information he could share. He damn sure hoped he knew who had made her and for what purpose. But above all, he wanted to be able to tell her she was no longer in danger. Unfortunately, he knew all too well just how treacherous the supernatural world really was. He'd experienced betrayal first-hand, and now it had come back to haunt him all over again.

He punched in the security code and opened the large door enough to squeeze through, securing it behind him. One thing for certain, if the chance to kill Lisada came again, she wouldn't survive a second time. He'd make sure of it.

Chapter 9

Mia ran through a forest, faster than she'd ever moved before. She smelled blood all around her, but she didn't dare stop. She was the prey, and someone was closing in on her.

Unbelievably, she ran with agility, swerving in and out of the trees, barely skimming by them, but sure of her next move without a doubt of where to turn. The darkness around her suffocated, but she saw everything with precision. She heard everything clearly, including the footfalls quickly gaining ground behind her. With a heavy dread she'd never experienced before, she swiveled her head to look behind her, to try to catch a glimpse of who or what was chasing her. Yet, she only saw shadows and a looming, dark figure, so close, emanating danger. If she could just bring whoever it was into focus...she would know who or what threatened her.

Suddenly, she burst out of the treeline into an open meadow, the moon illuminating the expanse of land. She ran to the center of the field before she stopped and turned to see who came after her. At the sight of him, she dropped to her knees. Campbell emerged, covered in blood, feral eyes searching, searching...for her. The minute he saw her, he ran headlong in her direction, eating up the distance in seconds.

She threw her hands up in front of her face as he neared. This was it. She would die at the hands of the one person she thought would save her. Her heart raced and a broken sob escaped her lips as he descended on her, his fangs long and dripping.

Just as she felt the vise-grip of his arms clamp around her, she pulled a hard, cool breath into her lungs, pulled her hands down to cover her neck, and opened her eyes.

Mia woke, sucking air deep into her chest, her hands covering her neck, and looked around the unfamiliar room. A quick glance at the clock and she saw the numbers 2:34 glowing bright red. She lowered her hands to her side and sat up, feeling her sweat-slicked skin sucking her shirt in tight. Another nightmare. But different this time. Never before had she seen who was chasing her. Yet, clear as anything, she had seen Campbell. Covered in blood and thirsty for more—for her blood, it had been him.

Heaven help her, what an idiot she'd been. No matter how many times she tried to tell herself it was just a dream, she still felt like her life was in danger. With a sudden urgency, she swung her legs over the side of the bed. She didn't usually overreact, but panic filled her body at the thought that Campbell wasn't all he seemed.

With a few steps toward the door, she grabbed her duffel from the floor and gripped the doorknob tightly. A deep breath later, she turned it in her hand and was slightly surprised it was unlocked. Wouldn't someone who planned to jack-her-up make it impossible for her to get out.

What was she saying? It was impossible to get out. His words came back to her. *My security system is unbreakable.*

She wasn't safe here, and whatever it took, she had to get out now.

* * *

"You should've let them put it down. Kerenth could still be here within the hour. He'd handle the situation quickly and painlessly."

The fury welling inside Campbell at those words made him clench his fists on the countertop. To his credit, Ewen Mackenzie, known as Mac to the few friends he had, couldn't possibly understand the level of attachment Campbell currently felt when it came to Mia, but it didn't make the hot rage brewing in the pit of his abdomen go away any faster.

Through clenched teeth, he addressed Mac, his associate in many a mission and a werewolf to boot, "Don't refer to Mia as an *it*, and nothing about that whole 'bring her in and we'll take it from here' felt right." He drew in a deep breath through his nose and unclenched his jaw. "Besides the men in this room, I'm not sure who I can trust at this point."

He looked around at the small group. It certainly was a motley crew with creatures from many factions of supernatural beings, but without a doubt, every single one of them had his back, even the surly wolf Mac. To the were's right was the toughest being Campbell had ever met. He never would have guessed the guy was a Faerie, but Cade Lanter could throw down with the best of them. To the Fae's right was a creature few knew the existence of—a Kachina. Thought to be just an ancestral spirit worshipped by the Hopi Indians, Achak kept track of what was going on in multiple spiritual planes at any given moment. He had the uncanny ability to completely mask his face and shape-shift into different visages.

Then, there was Donovan. He was currently in the look-out tower at the front edge of the property, and no one was missing him all that much. The only person missing from their little circle was their own master magic-crafter, Linnetha, a sorceress of the highest order and one hell of a fighter. Right now she was off on another job for Sup Co. Otherwise, she'd be in it up to her long lashes and throwing elbows right alongside her male colleagues.

Cade ran a weary hand down his face like Campbell had so many times before, crossed his arms over his chest and summed up the situation. "You don't have any idea who the maker is. You don't know what she's changing into. And, to top it all off, you don't know who you can trust. Just for kicks, tell me something you do know."

"Lisada is involved."

Mac's face hardened at the mention of the witch's name. He'd been with Campbell those many years ago and knew what he'd gone through. But Cade and Achak both looked confused.

Achak voiced the question in his raspy, deep tone, "And just who the hell is Lisada?"

Where to begin?

Yet, Mac beat him to it and spat out, "Just about the most evil bitch you've ever met. She fuckin' messed with our boy Cam's mind and it resulted in the death of his family. Needless to say, we thought she was dead and gone because Cam killed her himself." He turned his attention back to Campbell. "Are you certain? How is that possible?"

"I wouldn't put necromancy above her, but more likely one of her many admirers came to her rescue those many centuries ago."

Mac scratched at his chin. "But I saw her bleed out myself. The life faded from her eyes."

"Then, it had to have been a vampire."

"And probably someone you knew." Cade's statement hung in the air, and once Campbell absorbed it, another reality sunk in.

"It's possible I still know the bastard."

Achak looked confused. "Now wait a minute. Why are we jumping to conclusions here? How do we know it was a vampire?"

Campbell met Mac's gaze, a look of understanding passed between them. How did they know?

"Because she started the whole, damn human-to-vampire line with a chalice with some kind of name of doom like the Ultimate or Supreme Cup or something Raiders of the...whatever like that. Before that, all vampires were natural-born, not made. I was one of many she spawned with it, and in a sick way, the original offspring bonded with her with unfailing loyalty. Whoever is helping her, had to have turned her after she died."

"What happened to the cup?"

"We stole the cup from her, and when they approached us, gave it to the members of Sup Co at that time. Some queen of the Faeries with serious power took it to another dimension to protect it."

Suddenly, something like a look of pain came over Cade's face. "You said it had a dooming name. It wasn't the Absolute Glass, was it?"

Campbell snapped his fingers and pointed in Cade's direction.

"Yeah, that was it. The Absolute Glass. Do you know it?"

"My mother was tasked with guarding it. She's done so for centuries, but recently, Aelfric the Touched, an Unseelie Faerie once imprisoned by my mother, used a kind of unknown dark magic to break into the palace at Eiru and take it. The baffling part was he was a weakling and never strong enough magically to accomplish anything like that."

"Could Lisada be backing him? Feeding him dark magic?" Mac's question was on everyone's mind and the most likely lead they had.

Cade answered, "If she's strong enough to magically overpower Orla, a high queen of the Fae, then I'd say it's likely." He sucked in a breath as if something occurred to him suddenly. "Here's a question for you, Campbell. Can Lisada change into a black mist like you?"

"Not that I know of?"

Cade looked thoughtful. "Besides you, do you know of any other creature that can mist?"

"I've never met another, but we all have abilities. Why do you ask?"

With pursed lips, Cade shook his head. "Probably nothing, but a 'not-entirely-credible' source mentioned Aelfric is working for a being who can change to black mist. No way it's you, so that leaves another creature out there who fits that description. The only person who knows for sure is Aelfric."

Campbell released a heavy breath. "This just gets stranger and stranger. We need to get our hands on this Aelfric character. Where is he and where is the cup?"

Cade sighed heavily. "Wouldn't I like to know? I've been searching for both for a while now. I think I'm close to catching him. He'll come for me soon, and I'll be ready."

Campbell nodded. "And when he does emerge, find out what he knows about the glass and one heinous witch with a scarred neck."

"It won't be a problem." Cade shifted and uncrossed his arms. "I've got to go now, but I'll report back to you in a couple days."

"Alright. Call as soon as you find something out."

Cade left through a portal he created called a Faerie gate, and not for the first time, Campbell thought it would be a convenient way to travel. Vampires could sometimes change forms, like Campbell and his ability to mist, but regardless of this ability, they still had to cross distances the old fashioned way, even in a different shape. Nevertheless, once Cade was gone, Campbell turned his distracted thoughts back to the small group because the conversation wasn't over.

Achak spoke up, "One thing I'm still unclear on. If Lisada enthralled the vampires she created, how were you able to turn on her?"

Even though it had been hundreds of years, it was impossible not to remember and feel like it'd just happened, but with as close to an indifferent shrug as he could manage, Campbell explained, "It wasn't easy." He swallowed heavily several times before continuing, "I think it was my mother's voice that woke me up finally. The rest of the family was gone by then, but she was still barely alive, and in her sternest motherly voice, demanded I stop and listen to her. And I did. I came to my senses. With my brain burning like an explosion had gone off inside,

I fought Lisada's pull, fought free of her hold like I was digging myself out of a grave. In a way, I was."

Silence fell heavy over the three men. There was much Campbell chose not to tell because the horrors of what he'd done still haunted him and always would.

Mac finally spoke up, "She could never enchant him again after that, and together we destroyed her. Turns out our version of destruction doesn't stick as well as we thought it did."

The part Mac glossed over was just how broken Campbell had been when he'd found him. At first, all he'd wanted was to die, and he tried too many times and too many ways without success. He always regenerated. His last resort was to find someone else to cleave his head from his body. It had to be done completely and quickly for it to work. He'd gone to Mac, who at the time had been Laird Ewen Mackenzie and one of Campbell's most trusted friends. When he'd confessed the entire sin-ridden affair, Mac had talked him down from the ledge and promised to help him avenge his parents' and sisters' lives.

He'd also attempted to convince Campbell it hadn't been his fault, but that was an impossible task. Campbell would always carry the burden of that guilt.

The strength of his determination rang in Campbell's words as he said, "Then, we'll just have to do better this time."

"Better is good."

As one, the men turned at the light, feminine voice behind them and pulled their weapons, aiming at the speaker. Campbell ducked his head curiously and stared at the petite, brown-skinned, pink-haired woman in front of him. The hair was cut close to her head but definitely bright pink, which brought out the intensity of her violet eyes. Her upturned nose twitched and an intelligent grin stretched across her mouth. He held his defensive stance as she stood with her hands on her hips, feet braced apart, and looked like no one else Campbell had ever met. "What the…? Not possible. Magic shields around this place keep beings from just popping in. Who are you, lady and how did you get in here?"

"Would you believe I'm your dream-come-true, and one of your best friends invited me?"

"Sounds like a lie. Did Lisada send you?"

She looked horrified. "Goodness, no! She and I aren't exactly on speaking terms." She shrugged. "Could be the saran wrap I put on her toilet seat when we were college roomies. Oh, wait! No, that was someone else."

In that moment, it occurred to Campbell whoever this was might just be completely insane, and he wasn't exactly sure how to handle her. "Look, you better start making sense and tell us who the hell you are or we'll be escorting you to the nearest exit with force."

"Wow. Caveman much?" She hopped up onto the kitchen counter in one graceful movement. "Name's Lily Bloom, but for obvious reasons, I just prefer to be called the Pixie. I was sent with a message—for you, Campbell."

Mac asked through clenched jaw, "You better be clear as to who sent you right now or I warn you, you willna like what I can do."

She sighed and crossed her legs. "So much testosterone. Don't go all wolfie just yet, Scot." She pointed her gaze directly at Campbell and said, "The message is for you alone, and only you will totally understand. I was told to inform you not to be such a blood-sucking vampire when it comes to Mia. It will most def, fo sho lead to the destruction of the world and other horrible things."

Achak grated a question. "What's more horrible than destroying the world?"

"Duck-facing selfies all over Pootter. That's the paranormal version of Twitter, and the duck-face alone has destroyed my love for sending several, hilarious Poots a day. Devastating, really."

Campbell stared at her incredulously. "Are you completely daft?" He couldn't very well kill her if she wasn't right in the head. That would be inhuman, wouldn't it?

"Don't know. Never been analyzed." She popped down from her perch. "Anyway…good luck storming the castle…er…oops…was thinking of someone else. Just remember to keep your teeth to yourself, Campbell. Now, time for me to make like a tree and…get out of here."

She crossed her hands and snapped, disappearing with a loud pop that sounded like weapons firing. The men ducked their heads, but there was no danger, only the lingering smell of cotton candy floating in the air.

Mac was the first to speak. "Well, that was…odd."

Achak straightened and scratched a hand over his chest. "Think I'm in love."

"You're as crazy as she was." Campbell shook his head and met

Achak's wide-eyed gaze.

The sudden sound of a piercing alarm snapped all three to attention and brought them back to reality. Damn, he hoped that alarm was Mia attempting an escape. That would be the best case scenario for why the warning had sounded. Anything else would be an all-out disaster.

Of course, it didn't escape his notice the timing of the alarm—right after the Pixie, as she wished to be called, had left. *Who exactly was she delivering a message for?*

The in-house intercom system crackled, and Donovan's shout came through the speaker, "We've got company! And she looks pissed!"

Dammit! So much for hiding out somewhere secure being an easy fix. "I'm going down to Mia."

Mac turned toward the door. "You need to get her and go. We'll handle things here."

Achak followed right behind him. "Meet us at the safe house in Alaska. We'll regroup and plan our next move."

Campbell hated to cut and run, especially when it was his battle to fight. Yet, Mia's safety was his first priority, at least until she'd changed completely and could use her own new powers to defend herself with control. "Okay. We'll be there."

Chapter 10

With long strides, he made his way downstairs and punched in the code, stepping through the door before it opened completely. The room remained dark, and he was confused as to why his sensors didn't immediately turn the lights up when he'd entered. Before he could turn to slam the door closed, something hard hit him on the back of his head. Stars swam before his eyes. He went down to his knees but managed to stay conscious. *What the hell?*

He rolled to the side, narrowly missing a second blow, but he jumped up as he spotted a flash of dark hair flying around the metal door. He gave chase immediately and wrapped his arms around her just before she reached the stairs. She was as fast as a vampire hundreds of years-old. Unusual, to say the least.

"Mia! Dammit, it's me!"

"Get away from me!"

She was so frenzied it took all of his strength to hold onto her. What had her so out of her mind to get away? Did she somehow know how much danger she was in? And didn't she realize he'd do everything in his power to keep her safe?

"Listen! We're under attack. We need to go back into the secure area before they breach the building."

With a look up the stairs, her struggles slowed. "They're already inside."

"What?" Campbell whipped around just in time to hear the howl of a fully-changed werewolf charging down the stairs. Immediately he knew it wasn't Mac, and even as fast as she could run, they'd never make it back to safety together. "Go! Run and close the door behind you."

He watched her follow his order without hesitation, and he kicked himself for not showing her the code. Too late for regrets, he braced for the impact of the gigantic wolf as it leaped from the last landing onto him, knocking him into the wall, which crumbled behind him like bread. He used what was left of the wall to push the wolf backwards to the other side of the hallway, slamming its head into the concrete. Campbell began throwing his fists into its snout a few times before it recovered fully, trying to daze it enough to get to the security panel and make sure Mia was protected.

But the wolf snapped its jaws, thrusting large incisors at Campbell's face and pushing him down the hallway toward the dull shine of the door. He couldn't let this beast anywhere near Mia, but it was clear she was the objective as his beady, ice-blue eyes flashed in the direction of where she hid. When Campbell's back hit the steel hard enough to dent it, the reality of how close this monster was to the woman he'd been charged to protect, a rage he'd never experienced before fell over him like a blanket and he felt the pop and swell as deep, unreal strength pervaded every muscle. A haze covered his vision, and he went crazy as he sliced and tore at chunks of flesh until they were both covered in a layer of blood that filled his nostrils with a sour odor. He wasn't entirely sure whose injuries were mostly to blame for the liquid covering them, but he refused to stop until one of them was on the ground, unable to rise again.

The wolf went down to his knees, head lolling as Campbell continued to strike at him over and over. Just as he felt certain he'd won this battle, the wolf suddenly lunged and sunk its teeth into Campbell's torso. He staggered backward, but the werewolf growled and clamped his jaws tighter. He lifted Campbell in his mouth and shook him like a ragdoll once before flinging him into the metal door.

For the first time ever, Campbell felt a niggling of panic spark to life in the back of his brain. He'd been knocked down before. Had been bloodied and bruised beyond recognition. But never before had he felt like he had so much to lose. Like never before, this mission mattered. Not because he felt obligated to complete the job, but because he didn't like the idea that he might let Mia down or, if he was being honest with himself, lose her. Already she meant more to him than he was ready to admit.

As he lay there on the cold, hallway floor, blood pooling around him, he ached at the thought of watching this creature take her away from him. How could he allow that to happen?

* * *

Mia found his gun, and with shaking hands, stood with legs braced apart, feet back from the door, pointing the weapon and ready to fire at whoever or whatever came through that door. She flinched every time the crashing thumps hit into the steel of the portal. Surely one of them was winning the fight.

She wanted to say she didn't care one way or the other. After all, her dream seemed all too realistic to dismiss the idea Campbell might eventually hunt her down and drink every last drop of her blood, just like he told her the older vampires did with fledglings in order to absorb their immunities. Yet, she had such a hard time believing he meant her harm. It was just a dream. Wasn't it? Yes, it was a freak-her-out repeating nightmare, but that didn't mean it would come true.

Honestly, she had to think it through. Would he have protected her so many times and in so many ways, risking his own life, if he just planned to kill her himself? If he'd wanted to drink from her, he'd had numerous opportunities. Hadn't he?

And she was real enough with herself to understand how the subconscious worked. Wasn't it possible that all this running around and being chased by unknown enemies could cause her to dream about the danger, plugging in the one vampire she'd been with all this time because he was on her brain in more ways than one.

Yes! She would admit it. She wanted Campbell to come through that door, and no matter what else happened, she had to trust that he didn't mean her harm. He was doing everything he could to protect her, including battling a seven-foot werewolf that she could smell through the thick metal of the door. The dirty, rotten odor wrinkled her nose, and she felt tears sting the back of her eyes with the idea that the wolf might actually kill Campbell to get to her.

With a sucking sound, the door shushed open again, and bracing her spine, Mia shifted her weight between her feet a few times, gripping the gun tighter and hating that she still sweated like a human. Shouldn't that be one of the perks of changing into something supernatural?

Someone pushed through the small opening of the door and collapsed to the floor. She couldn't tell for sure who it was. She smelled both the horrible smell of the werewolf and the familiar scent of Campbell but couldn't be certain which one of them had survived the fight. What if the wolf had transformed back into its original form. The figure was large and coated in a slick layer of shine, further obscuring his identity. It was like oil, but from the smell, she recognized it as blood.

Her breathing sawed in and out heavily as her heart raced, and she debated whether to fire the gun or not. The figure lifted its head and raised a hand toward her, and Mia yelped in protest.

"Stay back! I'll shoot."

A worn voice rasped, "Mia…" He collapsed and certainly lost consciousness. *He'd called her name.* She rushed to his side as recognition sunk in and relief flooded her. It was Campbell.

Through the opening to the hallway, she spied what remained of the wolf. Completely eviscerated, he lay in a pile of gore and bloody tissue. She shivered. Campbell had gone wild on his ass, but he was a supernatural being, so he wasn't necessarily dead.

With a sudden definitiveness, she felt the presence of others headed their way, and from the energy she felt emanating from them, they weren't friendly. She stood and dragged Campbell the rest of the way into the safety of the room. With little effort, she shoved the heavy door closed. *But how was she supposed to lock it?*

"Put in the code." She flashed her gaze toward Campbell and was thankful to see his eyes open. He motioned for her to come closer, and as soon as she did, he whispered a string of numbers and letters to her.

Without any more delay, she rose and input the code. Even as she heard the sound of the system locking into place, she wasn't entirely at ease. This didn't feel safe. If felt like they were trapped like mice, and no doubt, the creatures coming for her would find a way through.

"Tunnel. You...go..."

"Without you?"

"Need time...to recover."

She shook her head hard. "There has to be a different way. What do you need? I'll get whatever it is."

He groaned and raised a shaky hand to his forehead to smooth the gunk away from his eyes. "I need blood."

With a mission in mind, she jumped up and headed toward the mini-fridge behind the bar. Inside she found a few chilled bags and brought them to him with a glass.

"Not enough." He pulled several drinks into his mouth but pushed the glass away weakly. "My bedroom, behind the bookcase...hidden tunnel. Go!"

"What do you mean, this isn't enough? You need more than this?" She shook her head. "Wouldn't this be enough to get you up and moving? At least until we can get away and get more."

"Need sleep. You...must...go."

Several fists hit the metal of the door to make sure their presence couldn't be denied, and it wouldn't be long until they found a way inside. They'd kill Campbell in his weakened state, but an idea from something he'd told her earlier surfaced in her mind. "Drink me."

She had immunities and other healing properties in her blood. According to Campbell, all fledglings did. Of course, she wasn't an ordinary newborn vamp. Honestly, who knew what she had in her blood? It was the reason she'd been created, and even Campbell couldn't know what would happen if he drank from her, but in her estimation, it was worth trying if the alternative was certain death.

"Couldn't stop myself."

"No offense, but right now, I think I could take you."

He shook his head and grimaced in pain.

Another loud crash came from the other side of the door, and it dented inward. "We don't have time to debate." She let her incisors slide lower and used them to slice open a place on her arm. "Just do it already."

As the scent of her blood hit him, he doubled over at his mid-section and his eyes shot wide—glowing with the light green she remembered well enough to feel her own abdomen twist at the sight. She held her arm over his mouth and let a few drops slip inside. His resistance evaporated as he pulled the limb to him and latched on with unexpected speed.

With the first pulls, euphoria like she'd never known, like a drug, filled her and her pleasure centers fired rapidly in her brain. A moan escaped her mouth as calm and something much hungrier overcame her. She crawled closer to him on her knees and only the lingering smell of the wolf kept her from straddling him and riding out the incredible desire building like a churning river deep inside her.

His strength increased, his flesh plumping before her eyes, and a sensation of floating in mid-air began to creep over her. She was slipping away, but she couldn't be upset by it at all. It was right, and she'd gladly fly away forever if he could just live on. Nothing but serenity occupied her mind, even as she realized he was taking too much blood from her. No panic, no anger, no protest came to mind.

Like she was made of fire itself, he suddenly pulled free and rolled away as she collapsed to the floor. His breathing was erratic, and as she met his gaze, it still held a feral danger, like he wanted nothing more than to cover her and drain every last drop.

He looked away, kneeling on hands and knees and concentrating on the floor. She guessed he was trying to get himself under control, but her eyes slid closed. Just a little sleep was all she needed. Then, she'd be ready to go.

When she awoke, she tightened her eyelids and squeezed her forehead with both hands. Her head pounded so intensely, she could hear it pumping in rhythm like it were outside of her. It felt like the hangover to end all hangovers.

With hesitancy, she finally opened her eyes and looked around the dim room. She realized she was in Campbell's bed. Earlier, before her pitiful attempt at escape, she'd explored this bedroom and thought she'd discovered so much about him from the lack of knick-knacks and pictures. It was very utilitarian and detached. Campbell didn't bond with others. He distanced himself, and at the time, it had confirmed her suspicions he wasn't helping her for benevolent reasons, but a more recent memory came to her, canceling out her previous beliefs. She glanced at her arm, but the cut and the bite marks were gone—healed completely. Yet, she clearly recalled the look in his eyes that said he was using all his willpower to resist killing her. It was enough proof for her that she could trust him—at least a little bit.

For a few quiet moments, the pounding stopped, and Mia realized it *had* been outside of her the whole time. The monsters were still trying to get through the metal door, and from the sounds of things, they wouldn't give up until they'd made it through.

The bookcase swung open, and she sat up slowly, still weakened. Campbell stepped out clean of the remnants of his battle with the wolf and swung a worried gaze toward her. "Good. You're awake." He approached cautiously, as if he wasn't sure if she might strike out at him for nearly ending her life. "Can you stand?"

She put weight on wobbly legs and nodded.

"Excellent. I've got the supplies inside the tunnel. We need to move now."

"I'm good to go."

He stepped beside her, put an arm around her waist to assure himself she was as strong as she claimed, and moved her toward the bookcase.

As he propped her up inside, he pulled the bookcase closed behind them and punched in his security code on the panel that hung on the wall beside the secret portal. "It will sound an alarm if they breach the tunnel before we've made it out."

"Sounds like a hellagood idea."

A tiny smile lifted a corner of his mouth, and he surprised her with a sudden hug, wrapping his arms around her body and pulling her into his warmth. She melted into his embrace, feeling like it was where she belonged. Scary, but her heart lifted with each stroke of his hand over her back.

His breath moved her hair as he explained, "Thank you, Mia...for allowing me to feed from you. I couldn't have survived if you hadn't. I won't ever forget that."

Heat bloomed in her chest, rose up her neck, and spread throughout her limbs. It was an unexpected promise, and her heart pinched tight at the commitment of his vow. "I still can't believe you pulled away when you did. I thought you said you wouldn't be able to stop?"

He pulled back enough to tip her chin up and cup her cheeks between his hands. For several frozen moments, he gazed at her and lowered his mouth inch by agonizing inch. Taking slow pulls, he kissed like they had all the time in the world. With the slightest swipe of his tongue, she opened her lips to him, allowing him to delve inside, making her feel cherished and special. The kiss deepened as he embraced her tighter to his hard body, and she felt his arousal pressing insistently at her lower abdomen. His hands roamed her back and sides, kneading her sensitive flesh. When she tentatively touched his chest with her fingers, digging them into the folds of his shirt, he groaned in reaction.

She heard and felt the pounding of someone's rapid heartbeat, but she couldn't distinguish which one of them it belonged to. Maybe they were beating in rhythm together. All she knew was that her fangs began to descend, and she was suddenly very thirsty.

A moan fell from her own lips as he picked her up and positioned her so that she wrapped her legs around his waist, putting her aching core flush against his hardness. She was mindless to anything but the sensations freely running through her body. All she wanted was to get their clothes off and let him sink inside her, bringing them both to the height of pleasure and beyond.

Beyond the hidden doorway behind them, a loud crash brought them back to reality, and they pulled apart, still breathing heavily in the darkened tunnel. From the continued sounds of constant pounding, she realized they weren't through yet, but clearly they'd brought out the big guns, and it wouldn't be long now.

Once she got her breathing under control enough to speak, she asked, "So how did you stop?"

For just a moment he looked confused, like he had to think back to what they were discussing before he went all making her feel like the center of all that was necessary and desirous in the world. Then, he nodded, understanding she was asking about when he'd fed earlier, not the melt-you kiss they'd just shared.

His eyebrows pinched together tightly before he spoke, "The thought of the light fading from your eyes, the warmth leaving your skin, the pink evaporating from your lips was…undesirable to me. It was enough to bring me back from the brink of insanity."

Her chest caved in just a little at his poetic words. "And how do you feel now?"

He released her and inched back as he rubbed a hand over his neck nervously. Seemingly a little unsure, his eyebrows dipped in the middle. "Like I could take over the world. Like lightning is flowing through my veins. Like an ocean-deep supply of adrenalin is pumping throughout my body." He looked at her like he'd just discovered the answer to the universe. "You're blood is magical."

"So, do you think my creator planned to drain me after all?"

He turned and busied himself with organizing the last of the supplies, zipping it up, and situating the backpack onto his back. For a moment, she thought he was avoiding answering her question.

"No. I think your creator plans to keep you prisoner as a regular supply of his or her own special performance-enhancing drug."

She straightened from the wall, feeling a driving need to escape such a horrible fate. "Well, that doesn't work for me. I refuse to be anyone's blood whore."

"One reason I won't be drinking from you ever again."

She wasn't sure why she should feel disappointed by his words. The act of feeding was too intimate for her, and she would do well to keep distance between them, especially until she understood his role in her dream. But she had to admit, she couldn't stop touching her wrist where he'd penetrated her skin, and her mind kept returning to how close she'd been to a mind-blowing orgasm just from his bite.

She looked up and met his heated gaze. Was he thinking about the same thing? His stare intensified as he tossed a bag of blood to her, and she caught it despite her sluggishness. "Power-up and get ready to run."

Chapter 11

After thirty minutes of non-stop jogging, they stopped below a round, metal hatch with a ladder leading up to it. Mia doubled over and braced her hands onto her knees. She'd gained some of her strength back, but she wasn't at full throttle, and she knew Campbell had gone slower for her sake. As a vampire, speed was natural, except when your body was recovering from nearly being drained.

He tossed another bag of the red liquid her way, and she downed it quickly, feeling the energy begin to sluice through her muscles and give her the life force she'd need to get out of this mess. The only problem as she saw it was that it was their last one, and she wasn't fully recovered yet. From the looks of Campbell's heaving chest, he wasn't full-strength yet either.

"Let me go through first and make sure it's safe." He started up the ladder. "Wait for my signal before you start up."

The hatch screeched loudly as he unlocked it and dropped it with a clang onto some kind of hard surface behind it. Mia looked around in the dark tunnel, but even when her night-vision confirmed she was alone down here, the panic making her heart flutter around all bird-in-a-cage-like didn't ease up at all. She watched Campbell disappear through the opening and nearly called for him to come back. This felt wrong somehow, like maybe they hadn't been running away from danger but straight toward it.

She grabbed the shoulder-level rungs of the ladder and twisted her hands around them nervously, sure Campbell had been gone too long. What if Lisada had been waiting for them to emerge? What if even now, she was cleaving Campbell's head from his shoulders.

Unable to wait any longer, she began to climb just as Campbell's face appeared in the round opening in the ground. "I told you to wait for my signal."

She continued to climb, shrugging unfazed by his censure. "I wasn't going to stay down there with the worms forever."

"Worms is good eatin', love. Don't knock 'em."

She pulled herself through and sat with her legs dangling over the edge for a few minutes as she enunciated each word, "Eeeww. Not even if they were dipped in chocolate and every last drop of blood in the world was contaminated."

He sucked air through his teeth like he was in pain. "Didn't I tell you? Chocolate is poison to vampires."

Her heart dropped to her toes. "What? No! What's the point of immortality without chocolate?"

A grin stretched across his sensuous lips which she could still feel the impression of on her own mouth. Teasing her, he laughed low and stifled, but shrugged finally and said, "Of course you can still have chocolate. But I'll warn you now, certain senses go into overdrive once you've turned completely and never ease up. Taste is almost always one of them. It's one of the reasons vampires don't eat more ordinary human food. The taste is often so changed, it's unpalatable."

"Well, that doesn't sound like a fair exchange." She looked around the random parking lot onto which the hatch opened. With the exception of a darkened, three-story building sitting at the opposite side of the stretch of asphalt, they seemed to be in the middle of nowhere. The building appeared completely abandoned, like a failed business, which if the location were any indication, probably was. "Where are we?"

He picked up the pack and moved toward the building, and she followed, throwing a few glances over her shoulders, hoping that whole feeling of being watched was just a remnant of the most recent threats on her safety.

"We're home. At least for the daytime."

"Will we be safe here?"

He shrugged but kept moving toward the imposing structure. As she got closer, she realized what it lacked in height, it seemed to make up for in width and depth. This really was a very large building. *What was it?*

"This is the former headquarters for the Supernatural Council of Paranormal Regulation. It has since been relocated, but it still has many of the bells and whistles it used to." They reached the door, and he went straight for the security panel to the side of it, dropping the pack to the ground. "I don't doubt they'll find us here, but with the armory that takes up residence far below ground here, we'll be better prepared for whatever they dish out."

Like he knew exactly what he was doing, he pulled the outside of the panel off the wall and pulled a small, metal box out of his pocket. He connected it to the wires that were now hanging free and pressed a button on the device, which now glowed as a series of numbers began blinking rapidly until the digital screen froze on seven numbers and the door buzzed and opened for them.

"Well, isn't that a nifty thing you can do. What other kind of magic tricks do you have in your repertoire?"

He swiped the pack up again and guided her toward the entrance with his hand in the small of her back. They walked through the glass doors into a massive entrance hall with an abandoned receptionist's desk she was certain was the hub of this place at one time.

With deft fingers, he found a way to reset the alarm and gave her a wicked grin as he said, "I've been told I'm magical with my mouth, hands, and...uh um...other parts, but to show you would require a lot less clothing."

He didn't pause as he headed toward the stairs to the right of the receptionist's desk, but she stood staring dumbly after him, imagining the magic of those amazing lips on her mouth, neck, and lower. Much, much lower. Heat bloomed in her mid-section and she felt the rush of wetness at his provocative words.

"Coming?"

She snapped a wide-eyed gaze in his direction. "What?" *Not yet. But, she was hopeful.*

"Are you coming with me downstairs?"

On every level, she knew he hadn't been asking about the state of her arousal, but her traitorous body didn't seem to care as she picked up her pace and inhaled the arousing, wild scent of him. So many reasons not to fall into bed with this man, but somehow, someway, she couldn't seem to think about anything else all of a sudden.

She wanted him. And with the end of her human life closing in rapidly, possibly the end of her freedom forever, in his arms sounded like the way she'd like to spend her final moments. Now, what would it take to convince him?

Chapter 12

They stepped out of the stairwell, far below the surface. They'd walked down at least ten flights of stairs, and Campbell strode quickly, determined to get his hands on some big guns as soon as possible.

Occasionally, he looked back to make sure Mia followed, and he fought the strong attraction that made him want to stop, get her undressed, and run his hands over every inch of her body. To take hours to explore each place that makes her breath catch in her throat was foremost in his mind. But her safety was what mattered most, so he pushed himself forward down the long, white-walled hallway to the last barrier between him and heavy protection in his hands.

"Almost there."

Fortunately, they'd both fully recovered and had no lingering effects from his reprehensible feeding on her earlier, unless you counted the fact he still felt like liquid electricity flowed through his body. He marveled at his willpower to pull away, but he hadn't been lying earlier. Her continued existence mattered to him. He didn't want to dig deeply into the reason why, but he admitted willingly that maybe he wasn't as jaded as he once thought. Maybe he still had the ability to care for others. Doubtful, but at this point he couldn't rule out the possibility.

He slowed and dropped the bag at his feet again, and pulled the security panel apart. He made quick work of the code. Easier than it should have been, but then again, he'd designed the system ten years ago, and though he wasn't given the updated codes, they weren't that difficult to break. He'd improved his system ten-fold since then, but he still kicked himself because he was sure he wouldn't be the only one to find a way inside. He just hoped anyone following them struggled longer than he had.

They stepped in and recessed, blue lights flashed on one at a time for the length of the room. The numerous weapons glowed in the pale light.

"Uh...holy shit. This is straight up stocked for the apocalypse." Her mouth dropped open and her eyes widened as more heavy artillery revealed itself.

"You ever shoot a weapon?"

"No, but I'm a fast learner. I'm so Will Smith to your Tommy Lee Jones, old man. Where's the Noisy Cricket?"

He grinned at her enthusiasm, and this time, he actually got her cultural reference. The weapons in this room appeared somewhat alien to most humans, but they'd been developed out of necessity because paranormal creatures were notoriously hard to kill, usually requiring much more than the standard gunpowder-filled bullets.

"Come on. I've got one that's just point and shoot. It sprays out such widespread fire, you won't need to be accurate for it to be affective."

Like a kid on Christmas Day, she edged closer to him, an excited gleam in her eyes. "That almost sounded insulting, but if you're giving me something cool, I don't even care."

He shook his head and moved toward the end of the long corridor.

In a drawer on the right, he pulled out a hand-held laser-blaster with a large body that she could wrap a firm grip around. "This one will do for a beginner."

"Well, don't sugarcoat it. Say what you really think."

He began loading a second duffel bag with as many weapons as he could fit inside. He worked quickly, but took a moment to reassure Mia. "I always say what I think, and I think you are a force to be reckoned with whether you have a weapon in your hand or not. So, what does that tell you?"

Her sly grin did things to his insides, made them feel all hot and scrambled. "I think it means you got a thing for me, vampire."

With sure fingers, he zipped up the bag and ambled over until he stood in front of her, looking down into her eyes. "What makes you think so?" He dropped his gaze to her mouth.

She ran her tongue along her lips, making them slick, shiny, and oh, so tempting. He knew he shouldn't, but the irresistible force pulling them together like magnet and steel felt heavy and inevitable.

"'Cause when you look at me, I see hunger, but it has nothing to do with feeding."

They weren't safe here, needed to keep running. He knew it as well as he knew every freckle on her face, but in that moment, if he didn't kiss her, life wouldn't even be worth living anyway.

He leaned down and placed a gentle kiss on her neck, moving upward, lightly running his mouth along her jaw line, before pulling back and whispering, "You might be right. Maybe I'm ten-times a fool, but the only thing I want to do right now is see if your luscious mouth tastes as good as it looks."

Campbell licked her lips with the lightest touch of his tongue and his fangs descended through his gums slightly. Her scent filled his nostrils, and he found himself committing it to memory. He'd never forget the vanilla and lavender smell as long as his immortal existence continued. With no more hesitation, he dropped everything in his hands, pulled the blaster from her grip and placed it on the counter. He wrapped her in his arms and covered her lips with a deep, meaningful kiss, giving her everything he'd worked to keep contained, to bottle up in order to keep his head on straight enough to keep her safe. Right now though, he didn't want to think about Lisada and the other creatures no doubt closing in on them. The only thing that mattered in that moment was Mia, him, and this need to make love to her, and in a way, make her *his.* He knew she wasn't an object to be owned, but something deep inside him said he'd want her for the rest of his life, whether she felt the same or not. He'd realized early on, she had the potential to become an obsession for him. It was why he'd attempted to get assigned somewhere else, far away from her. Thanks to Riley, he was way in over his head now, and now it was clear to him, he'd headed right down that road of utter fixation.

As the kiss deepened, he lifted her and sat her on the countertop, lining up his throbbing cock with her core, still frustratingly covered by her shorts. He ground himself against her and loved the moan she fed him as she wrapped her legs around his waist and rubbed herself back on him. She clutched his shoulders and he dared to bring his hands around to spread them over her breasts, lightly squeezing them in his palms, feeling the small kernel of her nipple harden to a point.

Reluctantly, he broke the kiss and pulled back to rip her t-shirt over her head. Her lacy, white bra barely covered the dusky circles that made his mouth water at the sight of them. He didn't even bother to lift her bra at first, just bent and licked and sucked a nipple into his mouth, loving the feel of the tightened bud rolling around his tongue. For the other side though, he lifted the fabric away and pulled the nipple into his mouth to feel tongue-on-skin in all its irresistible sensation.

Her breaths were rapid and heavy, small, keening sounds rising from her throat, ramping his own arousal to impossible heights. His nimble fingers slid down her torso and found the button at the top of her shorts. He made quick work of the closures between him and her. Without removing his mouth from her nipple, he slipped his hand inside, past her lacy panties, into her soft curls until he found her wet and hot, just like he knew he would. His cock felt ready to explode at the evidence of her extreme arousal, but he stilled a few moments, letting her delicious, rosy point go from his lips. Like a fucking kid, he needed a second or two to get a grip on his raging excitement before he embarrassed himself.

He almost laughed at the situation. A centuries-old vampire who'd seen and done most everything was nearly brought to his knees by a modern woman who considered herself nothing more than a computer-geek. Yet, to him, she was so much more. She was a reason his turning wasn't the worst thing that ever happened to him. Without it, he'd have been long dead before she was even born. It certainly brought things into a new perspective.

"Everything okay?" She sounded breathless, and he was ready to give her more, so much more. *Okay?* Right now, things had far surpassed okay, until he knew in this moment, they'd blown past everything good, great, or giga-fine on every level. They were no longer on the same scale as okay and never would be again.

"Everything's perfect." He worked a finger into her, rubbing the outer wall, in and out a few times, until she was writhing and mewling for more. With adeptness he knew she'd appreciate, he used his thumb to circle her clit, even as he continued to rub and pushed in another finger, running them in opposite circles and working her flesh expertly. She began thrashing her head back and forth and he knew he was pushing her to the edge. It was almost enough to push him over the same ledge, but he held on tight to his wits, wanting to see her tumble into her orgasm.

She suddenly stopped, met his gaze, and pulled her hair away from her neck. "Bite me, Campbell."

Everything inside him wanted to. He licked his own lips and felt his fangs descend completely through his gums. He wanted to feel her flesh give as he penetrated and took in that delectable essence flowing through her veins. But he shook his head and looked away, going back to making her crazy with his finger movements on her intimate flesh.

"Please, Campbell. I can't get there without your bite."

He'd been able to pull away before, but he seriously doubted he could do it a second time. The Pixie's warning came back to him. He truly understood how bad it would be for him to sink his teeth into her. Yet, she begged him so prettily, and it would feel so good.

Like the worst kind of junkie, he graze his fangs along her neck and felt the delicate taste of a touch of her blood on his tongue, sending electricity throughout his body. He felt her sex clench in orgasm and continued to rock his hand against her as he used the other to release his dick from his jeans. When she'd finished, her muscle spasms beginning to slow, he let go to grip her hips tightly in both his hands. The desire to thrust himself deep inside her was near overwhelming, but he knew he couldn't take her here, now, or ever. It would be far too difficult to let her go when the time came. He didn't dare create that connection, but his need for her was too great to deny completely.

Instead, he ground himself hard against her, feeling his own release building higher until he aimed his rock-hard cock toward the floor and exploded harder than he ever had, ropes and ropes of come. He couldn't believe how high she could take him with just a touch. It didn't escape him that he'd almost come inside his fucking jeans again. Like the teenager he could no longer claim to even remotely understand. But the minute he calmed down, he licked the scratch at her neck, one swipe of his tongue to seal the wound.

He stepped back from her and stared, trying to reassure himself he hadn't stepped over the line too far. His own body felt like he could take on the world and win without being the least bit out of breath, but he worried he wouldn't be able to resist next time—if there was a next time.

"Freak me! That was amazing, Campbell." She stood in front of him, seemingly unfazed. "Okay. It completely hurts to say these words, but you were right. Your fangs are addictive. Do mine feel like that too?"

He nodded as he ran his hands over her to reassure himself she was okay, and he'd admit it to himself, to continue to stay in contact with her soft skin. He couldn't seem to stop touching her, even after he knew for certain he hadn't hurt her at all. "Your bite sends me into a mindless race to the top of a mind-blowing orgasm on contact."

"Exactly! Can we do it again? This time with...full penetration."

Fire filled his veins at her loaded words. Despite his reluctance to acknowledge there would be another time, and despite the uncomfortable state of his pants right now, he had to admit to himself he wanted there to be many next times. He stepped back toward her, ready to take it even further this time when all hell broke loose. A high-pitched, screaming alarm sounded, and he knew their time here had come to an end.

"Looks like we'll have to pick this up later." He swiped a quick kiss over her lips. *And he was* damn *sure* t*here would be a later.* "Let's go!"

Chapter 13

Mia was hooked. Orgasms with a vampire were better than chocolate, better than finding a front parking space open right when you needed it, better than anything she'd experienced in her entire life. Clearly, there had to be some sort of pleasure-amping substance injected at the time of the bite, one of the weapons vampires had in the bag. If used for defense or even sustenance, a victim would lie there willingly and let the vampire drain every last drop, reveling in the enjoyable feelings flowing throughout his or her body until they were dead. Of course, from what she'd seen, there was one minor consideration—the vampire found the bite just as enjoyable.

Of course, all she knew was she'd gladly be the biter or the bitee, no complaints, especially if it were with Campbell.

She looked across the front seat of the car, studying the intense look on his face as he drove. They were speeding down the highway in some sort of armored car straight out of a Bond movie. It looked like a sporty Jeep Cherokee, but he'd explained that it had a few extra bells and whistles, such as weapons that fired at cars behind or in front of them with the push of a button and bulletproof glass in all the windows. Despite her normally aloof demeanor, she'd had to admit the truth. She was impressed.

They'd busted out the back of the building from an underground garage and bounced across the field with the headlights off. She freely disclosed she'd screamed the whole way, certain they were going to drive off a cliff at any moment. Eventually though, they'd made it to a deserted, country road. He'd flipped on the headlights, and they'd driven on like they were just passing through.

After they were about half a mile down the road, an explosion rocked the earth and a fireball lit up the night sky behind them. She hadn't had to ask. She'd watched him set the explosives. Her hope was they wouldn't be pursued, but again, she was smart enough to realize whoever created her wasn't going to give up until they found her, and considering they were likely immortal, the chase could go on indefinitely.

For now though, they progressed down the road, and so far, no one followed.

"Where're we going now?"

He inhaled deeply and blew out a heavy breath. "Can't get a hold of anyone. Not a single person I trust is picking up the damn phone. Mac, Donovan, Achak, and Cade all seem to be AWOL, or at least uncommunicative right now."

"What's that mean? Do you think they're okay?"

"Don't know, but if we followed protocol, our goal would be to head to the closest safehouse. However, if I can't get a hold of them, I have to assume they've been captured or in some other way compromised."

"So, no safehouse. Is anywhere safe?" She hated the pitiful sound of her voice, but already tired of running, she feared they'd never be secure.

He met her gaze briefly before turning his focus back toward the road, but she didn't miss the concern in his eyes. Yep, they were clearly screwed.

"I've got a place in upstate New York that's completely off the grid. We'll go there." He ran a hand over the back of his neck nervously. "We might have to stay there a while."

"How long's a while?"

"A few hundred years."

The air left her lungs. "What? A few hundred years? What about my friends, my classes? What about my life?" But the truth cut deep. Other than her friends, she had nothing she couldn't walk away from. No family, no significant other, not even a cat or a dog would be left behind to miss her. Honestly, it wouldn't be such a bad thing for her to disappear for some time. What if she struggled to control herself around humans, like that night in the hotel? She would rather die than hurt any of her friends or anyone else, for that matter. What were a couple hundred years in the scheme of forever? It was a small blip. She could do that, and having Campbell for company might make it somewhat pleasurable.

"It's best if you don't contact your friends ever again. I know it's hard to swallow, but any contact will only make them targets. They'll be killed to try to get to you." His voice broke and he cleared it loudly. It was clear, he spoke from experience, and Mia's heart clenched at the thought of him suffering that kind of loss. "Sacrifices must be made if you're going to make it. In a couple hundred years, your strength will be greater, perhaps unmatched. I'll help you hone your powers and get ready to take on anyone trying to hurt you."

"Okay. That's our plan then."

"Okay? You're on board? Just like that?"

She nodded slowly. "I don't want anyone to get hurt because of me. And I don't want to be anyone's blood slave. I'll do what I have to do."

"Well, don't sound so excited to hang with me. *Do what you have to do.* You'll make me blush with lovely words like that."

A smile settled on her lips, but anxiety erased it quickly. She hoped her friends were okay. The idea of putting them in danger continued to haunt her. How could she live with herself immortally, knowing it had killed the people she most cared about?

She stared at Campbell out of the corner of her eye. She was sure he knew all about that. "How did you lose your family, Campbell?"

His jaw clenched over and over as he drew air in and out of his nose a few times. They drove on in silence, and she mentally kicked herself. She'd crossed a line and brought up bad memories.

"So young and stupid, I believed I was in love with Lisada. My father tried to warn me away from her. Somehow he knew she was a witch, and a devil witch at that." His voice trembled with every word, and she laid a reassuring hand on his arm. "I drank her poison willingly, but I didn't know she planned to turn me into a killing machine."

An uneasy foreboding tingled at the back of her neck, pushing her to stop him, but too much of her wanted to know, wanted him to show the skeletons from his past, to lay it all out on the table.

"It actually took a whole month of ingesting her potion until I succumbed and died in her bed. Another week for my rotting corpse to reanimate. All that time, my father searched for me. Finally, he found her home, deep in the Scottish woods. When he saw what I'd become, he cried. The strongest man I'd ever known, and he broke down right in front of me.

"She ordered me to kill him, and in my blood lust, I nearly did. Choked as I pulled down long drinks of his blood, but at the last moment, I pulled away and threw myself across the room, hunkering in the corner like the monster I'd become. I couldna kill my da though. He was still alive, but barely."

The tremble faded from his words, but his breathing became rapid, like he was reliving the scene moment-by-moment. He was right back in Scotland, right back in the witch's clutches. "Didn't matter. With a wave of her hand, she snapped his neck right there in front of me. In a sickly sweet voice, she said, 'I forget how strong those human bonds can be. Well, we'll just remove all that ties you to your human life, so you can set aside that pitiful conscience you hang onto.'"

His eyes glassed over, and she almost suggested he pull the car over to the side of the road. She cringed, knowing what surely came next, but not sure she wanted to hear it.

"Should've stopped her then. Should've at least tried, but I let her go. Let them all die. My mother." He swallowed hard, like he couldn't quite get past a lump in his throat. "My…my sisters…all of them. She wiped them from the face of the earth forever, and I cowered in the corner, not even trying to stop her."

Mia wanted to wrap her arms around him tightly and reassure him it wasn't his fault, but he'd carried the guilt for centuries. She was certain too much time had passed for him to let go of such deep pain, but she had to try. Her hand closed over his and squeezed as she said, "Not your fault, Campbell."

He slammed his other hand on the steering wheel, denting the perfect circle. "Dammit! My da tol' me. He warned me to let the witch be, but I dinna listen. All dead, cause I dinna listen."

His accent became more pronounced, and she knew it would take so much more than she had to give to erase his pain. "Not your fault. No way could you have known what she planned, and you certainly weren't the first kid who didn't listen to his parents' warnings. Put the blame where it belongs. She schemed and manipulated you. Your family was targeted the minute she settled her plans on you. Nothing you could've done, except die beside them, and she wouldn't have allowed that anyway, probably would have brought you back to life again and again."

No tears fell down his face, but the effort it took to hold them back showed clear in his tightened features. He worked his throat a few times, trying to speak. Finally, he uttered, "Maybe you're right."

"Not your fault, and this time, you have me to help you make her pay for what she did to them."

His gaze burned into hers, and he nodded sharply once before turning his view back out the windshield.

They rode in silence through the night, but they'd shared something in those moments. He'd laid his soul bare, and shared his deepest, darkest secrets. Even the fact he'd touched her intimately earlier, giving her mind-blowing orgasms, hadn't made her feel as close to him as she did now. She trusted him so completely, and she had to believe he felt the same. Right now, she felt like she could take on the world with him. She just hoped it didn't come to that.

* * *

His gaze strayed to Mia again, lingering on her long, silky legs and shapely curves. Sensual and enchanting, she rocked her head back and forth with small motions as she sang low to the music on the radio. In the short time they'd been together, she'd changed into the form of a sex goddess. No doubt, it was part of her transformation and something she could use to attract prey if she chose to. She'd certainly pulled him in and had opportunities to kill him many times as he let himself go completely mindless and vulnerable with her. So unlike him, but she seemed to be able to make him do things he'd never do. Such as tell another soul about the worst moment of his life. He still couldn't believe he'd shared the story with her. Considering even Mac didn't know the whole story, it was surprising he'd spilled every last sordid detail to her, to say the least.

Well, almost every detail. There was still something he'd held back. Yet, for the first time, he'd felt compelled to clear the air. He'd almost told her about his sisters. Maybe next time, he'd tell her the truth about him. Then, she'd know he really was a monster.

He focused on the road again, squeezing the wheel tightly in his fists. More determined than ever to protect her, he raced toward the one place he hoped hadn't been compromised. Of course, he hadn't visited in over twenty years when he'd first set it up as a possible safe haven completely off the grid. With some modifications, the cabin didn't require any outside utilities to function. It was wired with solar-powered electricity, and propane heated the stove and the rooms. Somewhat ironic that a vampire would use the sun to power his home, but it worked. And if all went well, it would continue to work for some time to come.

They'd been driving for around three hours, and he estimated they still had around four hours to go, but the sun would be rising sooner than that. Despite the popular belief vampires burst into flames in the sun, it was more an irritation, one that could weaken a vampire until he or she struggled to fend off attackers, but right now, he was willing to take that risk to get her as far away from Lisada as possible. He didn't need to starve her though.

"There's a place up here where we can feed. Do you want to stop?"

She stopped singing and met his gaze. "Is it safe?"

"For as long as it takes to ingest a little and get back on the road."

Her confusion showed on her face. "Aren't we going to find some place to sleep during the day?"

He shook his head hard. "I think it's best if we just push on."

"Then we'll get there in the early part of the day. We won't even be able to get out of the car."

"I have to get you there. We'll throw a blanket over us or something."

Now she looked suspicious, and he sighed loudly. "That explosion might slow her down, but Lisada will be hot on our trail. We have to keep putting miles between us and staying off the radar as much as possible."

"Well, if we stop for food, won't others see us and rat us out to the big, bad mean-queen?"

He pulled the car onto the exit ramp and drove it down a darkened road. "Let me handle the details."

"Yeah, that's the problem. Something you should know about me. I really don't trust easily. Not without real evidence."

"Haven't I given you reason to trust me?"

Her thoughts might as well be written on her forehead. Clearly a war raged inside her brain, as she decided whether or not to balk or just go with his plan. "I'll be honest, I'm having a hard time knowing who to trust lately."

"What the...? Look, I'm not the kind of man who does things out of the goodness of my heart. Fuck! Don't even think there's goodness left in my heart, but I'm laying everything on the line to keep you safe. What the hell have I done to make you think I'm the type to run around, risking my life, only to throw you under the bus when the opportunity arises?"

She chewed her lip and stared at him in silence a long time. Finally, she sucked in a deep breath and said, "The nightmare I have over and over is about you."

He was speechless. "What are you saying? I'm the one who...hurts you...? That can't be possible."

"All I know is, in my dream, you come at me, fangs bared, and I'm protecting myself from an attack. Makes it hard to build trust when you're chasing me every time I close my eyes."

Her attack at his home suddenly made sense now. "No shit. But, Mia, you've got to believe that I wouldn't really hurt you. I couldn't hurt you."

"Why should I believe that?"

Why should she believe him? Because he cared what happened to her? He had a deep need to keep her safe, but he realized it went beyond that. He wanted to see her thrive, to reach her full potential. Yet, if he were being really honest with himself, it was even more than that. Dammit! He wanted her to look at him as someone worthy of her. *She* was *his.* And he'd do anything to protect her. He'd even sacrifice his own life so she could continue on.

The realization rocked him hard, scared him to his soul, assuming he still had one. His feelings ran deep for her, and truth was, he could lose her in an instant, just like he'd lost his family before. But, he couldn't tell her the truth. It was too much for him to handle. He couldn't imagine how she'd take such intense feelings. He just needed to say what she needed to hear so she'd stay with him, at least until he proved himself.

"Just give me a little trust."

"Okay. I'm willing to follow your lead, Campbell, but it's a short leash."

He chuckled humorously and low. "Now there's an image I'll carry for a long time."

Chapter 14

Mia woke panicked, protecting her neck yet again. She scrambled up and back into a corner of the backseat of the car, a scream caught in her throat. Her gaze traveled around the car's interior, but she was alone. Campbell had parked the car in the shade of a large oak tree, but he was nowhere to be found. The windows were cracked, and the sun was completely gone. Her biological clock must finally be adjusting to her new needs. She'd obviously slept all day with a blanket he must have laid over her before he left, but waking alone was disconcerting. Not a good feeling to be vulnerable while she was unconscious.

Cautiously, she straightened and peered out the window to assess if she was in any kind of danger, but nothing seemed out of the ordinary.

Where was Campbell?

What if he'd had enough of the constant life-threatening situations? Had thrown his hands in the air and walked away from her? She couldn't really blame him. Clearly, she was a danger-magnet, and she had little faith in the hide-away-forever plan they'd settled on. No doubt, something would go horribly wrong. It was the theme of her life lately, and she wasn't unrealistic in the least. They weren't just floating in shit-creek without paddles. They were headed for the falls and had several leaks in the boat.

Anxiety gripped her as the situation sunk in deeper, but she'd never been one to let fate take its course. They had to do something drastic, something that would make the rest of the paranormal world know not to *fuck* with the latest beast off the assembly line. She'd have to prove she was someone to be reckoned with. Of course, she had to figure out where the hell she was first.

Well, she couldn't just sit here all night. She gripped the handle of the door and pulled until it clicked open. With care, she swung the door open and stepped out. Once again, everything seemed ordinary and no odd creatures appeared. The animal sounds continued around her. Birds chirped melodically, bugs buzzed by her head, and everything followed its usual pattern. For the first time in what felt like a long while, Mia felt calm, even if she wasn't sure she'd ever understand what was going on. She felt secure in the fact she wasn't running for her life in this moment.

With surer steps, she pulled free of the car and shut the door behind her. It didn't take long to spot the two-story, wooden cabin up a hill, rising behind more trees. Less than fifty yards to her left, she turned and took several long strides in that direction. She reluctantly admitted to herself she hoped she'd find Campbell waiting for her there. It had been a very long time since she relied on another person, and part of her thought it was probably a dangerous road to travel. But like gravity pulling an object to Earth, she felt the irresistible pull to go in search of him, and she was fairly certain, she'd feel that urge for the rest of her unnatural life.

The minute she breached the cabin door, his hungry eyes lit on her and she felt devoured like the tastiest treat to ever touch anyone's lips. The look slid down her spine and melted into her mid-section, warming her up in her most intimate places. He stopped mid-motion, behind a countertop in a kitchen hardly big enough for one person to turn around, as he was placing something appetizing on a plate in front of him. She had the strangest sensation he could see beneath her layers of clothing and wanted to remove them slowly, intentionally, and skim every part of her exposed skin. At least, it's what she desired deep within her, and she hoped he wanted it, too.

He cleared his throat and shifted his attention back to his preparations, and when he looked up again, his gaze was empty of all the passion he'd hit her with just moments ago. But she knew she hadn't imagined it.

"Glad you found your way. Almost finished up here." Coming around the small island, he carried two plates to a small table and set them down with a gentleness that spoke of care. "I would've come to get you in a few minutes if you hadn't shown up."

She debated asking him about the Pixie, but Mia couldn't be entirely certain the strange creature wasn't trying to warn her about being with Campbell...or being without him. She just wasn't sure. Best to get more information first. "I thought you might have seized the opportunity to find another place you'd rather be without me."

He shook his head, his jaw slackening slightly before, in clipped tones, he said, "I won't abandon you, Mia."

"You probably should. Pretty sure they're never going to stop chasing after me."

"Let 'em come. Too much of the slow-life makes me itch. I could use a good head-on battle, especially now that I'm on my own turf and prepared for anything."

She made her way across the room to the table and sat in the chair opposite of where Campbell stood. The sight of a rare steak on her plate made her stomach rumble, but as hungry as she was, something else was on her mind.

"Why?" She still didn't quite understand the connection between them, and she wasn't really questioning why he made such strong assertions about protecting her. She wondered why they couldn't walk away from each other. What exactly was the strange connection pulling them closer and closer? And when all this was finally over, what would become of it?

He sat across from her and picked up his fork. It was clear he had protection in mind when he said, "It's my job."

Disappointment filled her. What had she expected? An admission that she was special to him in some way? That was ridiculous. Of course she was just a mission to him—a responsibility. Yet, a part of her wished he found her as physically irresistible as she found him. "I should be thankful you were the one they assigned. Someone else might have taken advantage of the opportunity."

He cut into his steak and took a bite. "You didn't ask to be changed. I'd be a royal asshole to take advantage of you right now."

She took a bite and moaned as the flavor hit her tongue. As she met his gaze again, she saw a repeat of the hunger from earlier. Pretty obvious he desired her the same way she did him. Perhaps it all came back to his sense of responsibility. Did he resist the attraction between them because he thought it would be taking advantage of her?

"You're a decent person, Campbell."

He rolled his eyes. "Don't get any ideas. I'm nobody's hero. Just...don't think it's fair for anyone to use you like you don't matter."

"So I matter to you?"

His jaw clenched tightly, and she could see the muscles in his face moving with an unusual tension. "Don't quite understand it, but hell yeah, you mean something to me. I plan to see this through."

The air left her lungs and her heart picked up, pumping double time. She knew he could hear it as well as she could feel it, but his words felt heavy and meaningful. Was he still talking about protecting her? Or did he mean something more?

"What if they just don't stop? How's your stamina?"

A single eyebrow rose on his forehead. "Never had any complaints. You volunteering to test it?" A mischievous smile spread across his face.

She laughed low at his not-so-veiled insinuation, but she chose to ignore it, pushing her mostly full plate toward the center of the table. "You did an excellent job on this, but I can't eat any more."

Concern shined in his eyes. "Can't be full. You haven't eaten all day."

She met his gaze guiltily. "As good as it is, it's not what I want."

"You'd rather drink, wouldn't you?"

Reluctantly, she nodded. "I can wait though. It's not like I'm starving or anything."

"It's more than that. You've completed your transition. That much is obvious now."

The reality of never being human again hit her hard. Tears stung the backs of her eyes. Never again would she be able to feel the sunshine full on her skin, just hang with her friends, or complete her college classes. She'd never have a normal existence again. A painful lump settled in her chest over her heart, and she looked down at her hands in her lap. "No going back now, huh?"

He was suddenly around the table and kneeling before her. "Don't look at it like that. Trust me, it's a dangerous path to go down." He took her hands in his and she met his gaze straight on. "It's the start of a new life. If you've ever wished to try out different ways to live, now's your chance. Look at it as a beginning, not the end."

"Is that how you saw it at first?"

Storm clouds moved into his eyes. "No, but I didn't have someone there in the beginning to protect me. Maybe if I'd had a different experience, it wouldn't have taken so long to understand the opportunity immortality represents. Do-overs are my way of life now."

"How many times have you started over?"

He moved his gaze upward as if the answer might be floating above their heads before meeting hers again. "Too many to count."

She bit her lip, debating whether to ask her next question. Before she could talk herself out of it though, she blurted, "How many women have you rescued...and then walked away?"

"Don't know. You're my first rescue, and so far, I'm still here."

Time slowed as his focus dropped to her mouth, and she felt waves of desire wash through her body, ending in an electric vibration at the very center of her. In that moment, she felt like one touch from him would ignite a fire in her that could never be extinguished. Her attraction to him was too powerful to deny, but more than anything, she wanted to feel close to him, to feel human. She needed to know she wasn't just a heartless monster, that she still held onto a piece of her humanity, a piece that connected with another.

When he lowered his gaze to their hands and made a motion to pull away, she tightened her grip and leaned in to lay a soft, lingering kiss on his lips. He remained motionless as she pulled back, but without further hesitation, pulled her toward him, melding their lips together with swift determination. His gentleness quickly changed into urgency as he swept his tongue into her mouth and landed lightly on one of her fangs. The sweet, delicious taste of him flowed over her tongue, and desire, like adrenalin, pumped through her veins, freeing her to act.

Hot. Wet. Ready to beg. With no more care about what she'd lost, who was after her, or who she could trust, Mia wrapped her arms around Campbell and met his kiss with her own slick tongue, tangling with his skilled one.

He lifted her, allowing her to wrap her legs around his waist as he walked them past the kitchen, through a darkened doorway that led down a hallway and hopefully to a bed. His hardness rubbed provocatively against her as they moved. Regardless of everything else, this is what she needed, and with who she most wanted to be. Tomorrow would bring its own worries, but for tonight, she just wanted to feel the sensations of their bodies joining together until they both collapsed in pure exhaustion.

A thrill of excitement shot through her body as he laid her on the bed and followed to hover temptingly over her, pulling back to give her a sexy grin that said he had her right where he wanted her. He reverently caressed her right side with his hand, sliding it down and up until he cupped the underside of her breast. Her nipples, already tight with need, practically begged for his touch as he grazed a teasing touch around them. A needy moan escaped her mouth and she arched to his hand.

The pounding of his heart picked up, and he pressed the length of his erection to her core, bringing her whole body to life with a jolt of hot desire that he obviously felt just as strongly as she. Every part of her being wanted him with a deep, dark need that she couldn't deny. She arched into him, earning a deep groan from him, all masculine arousal and hungry need.

He ducked his head to touch his lips to hers once again, but his kiss was no longer gentle. It was fierce, wild, and free. He wasn't holding back any longer as he sucked her bottom lip into his mouth. That much was clear, and she didn't want it any other way.

Balanced on his knees, he pulled back a little and used his hands to push the hem of her t-shirt up and over her head. He made quick work of her lacy, red bra too and sucked in a hitched breath when she lay bare beneath him. With a thoughtless throw, they disappeared somewhere behind him. He never took his eyes off her as his own shirt followed, and she finally got a look at his naked chest. Her fingers tingled as she smoothed them over the hard planes of muscle, skin, and masculine beauty hovering above her. When she brushed her thumbs over his nipples, he emitted a low growl and grabbed both of her hands, raising them gently above her head.

Like he'd overused his deep voice, he whispered, "Keep your hands up here. Don't want this to end too quickly."

She couldn't stop the slow grin that slid onto her lips. Not normally vain, she reveled in the idea he was barely hanging onto his control because of her. At some point, she definitely wanted to explore his beautiful body, but right now, she wanted to do this for a while too, so she nodded her head and let her arms relax beside her head, keeping her hands above her. She hoped she looked provocative enough to get him inside her quickly because, with the riot of feeling building inside her abdomen, she wasn't sure how long she could hang on herself.

Desire shining deep in the depths of his eyes, he looked back at her exposed breasts, cupped one and brought the hardened nub in the center up as he lowered his head. Red-hot fire surged through her veins as his tongue swirled and laved at her nipple. All thoughts fled from her brain. Warmth pooled between her legs.

She clenched her hands into fists, barely resisting the urge to sink her fingers into his hair and keep him right where he was.

A slight murmur of protest escaped her lips as he lifted his head, but she didn't have to wait long for him to cover her other nipple and give it the same teasing treatment. She squirmed under him.

"I need more." She could hardly believe the words as they tumbled from her lips. She hadn't meant to speak them aloud, but they had the desired effect. His hand slid down her abdomen and pushed her shorts and underwear down her legs until she could take over and kick them away.

She felt a single finger sliding slowly up her thigh. She shuddered with anticipation. The minute his fingers touched her slick pussy lips, a deep moan of need rose from her chest. If he wasn't inside her soon, she would surely die. In the next moment, he slid a finger inside her, relieving some of the building ache.

Her back arched as she felt the tense stirrings of her need for release.

"That's it. Your reaction pleases me, love. So beautiful!"

She met his glittering gaze and felt her desire ratchet up even higher. His fangs had descended and looked every bit as dangerous as they truly were. She bit her bottom lip, feeling her own fangs descend and throb.

He added another finger, and using his thumb, searched out her clitoris rising above its hood. With circular motions, he continued to dip his fingers inside her as he rubbed her sensitive nubbin. In and out. Around and around. She gripped the sheets above her head and dug her heels into the mattress. So close to the edge. All she wanted was to slip over.

And then, like a launched projectile hitting its highest velocity, she felt the second of free-floating, knowing what came next. The waves of her orgasm hit hard, and she cried out with the intensity of her muscles contracting around his fingers.

As her release faded, she felt his thick erection probing her entrance. Almost involuntarily, she thrust her hips up to meet him. In that moment, she couldn't get him inside her fast enough. Forgetting her agreement, she raised her hands to skim her nails over his back, reveling in the feel of his warm flesh. Mindless in that moment, he didn't seem to notice.

"Don' think I can hold back any longer." His accent thickened, telling her just how far gone he really was.

He pushed inside her with a groan, and she absorbed the delicious feel of being full of him. "Oh, God…" It felt so good as he began to thrust in and out slowly at first, but began to pick up rhythm as they undulated against each other.

For the first time, she felt an almost irresistible urge to sink her throbbing fangs into his skin. It felt as if the joining of their bodies would remain incomplete without that final penetration.

As if he read her mind, he grated, "Bite me, Mia. Now!"

For all of ten seconds, she resisted, but as she watched the pulse at his neck throb, the urge became impossible to tamp down. In less time than it took to draw her next breath, she slid a hand around the back of his head and sank her fangs into his skin. Her eyes rolled back as the first warm rush ran over her tongue. As he shoved deeper, rumbling his obvious approval deep inside his chest, her body felt within an inch of bursting into flames as he stroked her inner walls.

She felt him swell inside her and recognized the signs he was close to release and felt her own orgasm spin upward toward the finale. Their bodies rocked riotously toward that end, purely instinctual, mindlessly, they pumped together in rhythm until her body began to vibrate and she felt the world fall away as she exploded in fiery sensations again. "Campbell..."

As she pulled her fangs free from his neck, he lowered his face to her hair and thrust erratically, spending deep inside her with muffled growls. *Amazing!* She was ruined for anyone else in that single moment. No one but he would ever do again, and she savored the sense of satisfaction and wonder.

With a stroke of his hand over her hair and a shudder, he rolled over to his back, pulling her with him until she was settled on his arm, flush against his body. He pressed a tender kiss to her mouth before throwing an arm over his eyes and muttering, "Damn! That was phenomenal. Deserved a fucking standing ovation. Of course, my legs are jelly, so standing is completely out of the question right now."

"Come on. You've lived a long time. Probably not anything you haven't experienced before."

He lowered his arm and met her gaze, all seriousness. "Never. Not lying, Mia. Never felt like that before. Ever."

She nodded, a slow grin crossing her lips. Feminine pride flowed through her veins, along with the essence of the man beside her. She still couldn't believe how adding fangs changed sex so completely. The intensity of her orgasm lingered still. *Ruined!*

He relaxed again, and she hoped he was basking in the aura of complete satisfaction and overwhelming awe of their connection. She totally was, and had to fight to keep from giving him all of her, including her heart and her absolute trust. Hard to admit just how difficult a battle it was in this moment, and she was pretty certain the war was as good as lost.

A warning voice whispered at the back of her brain. Trusting him felt right, but her grandmother's words came back to her. What if trusting him did lead to her downfall?

She couldn't help thinking back to that voice in her head in the parking lot. It had sounded so much like her grandmother's, and now the doubts about Campbell persisted. *He'll turn on you! Don't trust him!*

But how could he make love to her like that, only to turn on her? Why would he save her time after time? It didn't make sense.

Aaaaahhh! So much to think about.

"I want to lay here and explore your body all night, but there are a few business things I need to take care of before I can totally settle in."

Disappointment hovered in her chest as she watched him dress and something occurred to her that she should have asked before they got started. "We didn't use protection."

He continued to set his clothing to rights as he answered, "Turned vampires don't need to. We can't produce children and our immortality makes sexually transmitted diseases obsolete."

"I hadn't realized...no children ever?"

His focus dropped to the floor as he crossed his arms across his chest. "It's a done deal now, Mia. You've already completed your transformation." He looked up just as she glanced down, unable to look at him just now.

So much taken from me forever. It was a lot to take in. She looked up to meet his gaze, shining with uncertainty. He probably thought she was about to fall apart. Yet, what Campbell didn't realize about her was that she didn't go to pieces easily. And with Campbell on her side, she'd grow stronger and learn to focus on what she'd gained, not what she'd lost. She just had to be careful not to grow more attached to him than he was to her. No doubt, he could probably walk away without the slightest hesitation, but her connection to him was deepening beyond protection and education. She was clearly falling for him.

With a final, smoldering look behind him, Campbell turned and headed out of the door of the bedroom.

It seemed now they were safe, the danger to her heart was just beginning.

Chapter 15

"Shoo, girl, you can sleep like a teenage bear on tranquilizers."

Mia sat up quickly and stared at the small person sitting on the side of the bed, barely making a dent in the mattress. Her crazy, pink hair drew Mia's gaze first, her diminutive size second, and she thought whoever it was might be a child.

"How's life in Fairy Tale Land?"

"Who are you?"

"Who me? Nobody really. Just the person here to save your life. You know, no big."

"Where's Campbell?"

Mia scrambled toward the headboard as the stranger jumbled around until she could throw both legs onto the bed to sit cross-legged adjacent to Mia. The first view of her up front and personal was even more of a shock. She had beautiful mocha skin and neon pink hair cut into a pageboy with two short pigtails. The outfit she wore looked like little girl's dress-up clothes amplified. Her dress was a gauzy, light pink thing that fell to mid-thigh and cinched in at her tiny waist. Her eyes were a light violet and practically glowed as she smacked her gum a few times and looked at Mia again. "He's close. Somewhere in this cabin in the woods. How very Joss Whedon production, but seems to be working for him."

Mia lifted her eyebrows. Not a child, but clearly her mind wasn't quite right. "Here to save me? Could I at least know your name before we get to that?"

She sucked in a sharp breath and covered her mouth with her hands for a few seconds before dropping them to her lap, leaning in, and saying, "How remiss of me. However, truth is, my name isn't important. Like the Terminator, I go by an ominous title instead. It's kind of scary in certain circles when it's mentioned...in a whisper...after checking under all the beds...and in all the closets." She seemed to be trying to give Mia an intimidating stare, but the look was ruined by the huge bubble she blew in that moment. She sucked the chewing gum back into her mouth and said, "They call me the Pixie."

The Pixie? Where was the intimidation-factor in that? "Sounds...like...you know who you are." She held up her hands, flat to the ceiling and shrugged. "I'm Mia, but I think you already know that if you have the means to help me."

"I know you better than you know yourself. As it turns out, you're on a journey to figure out who you are, and I have the information you need."

Mia waited in silence as the Pixie stared at her blankly. "Are you going to share that information?"

"What? Oh, yeah. Sorry. Just went on a mind-vacation there for a minute. The airline lost my luggage, but I always travel with an extra everything in my daydream carry-on bag, so I won't be having repetitive nightmares for weeks or anything. Like some people I know. Like you— hint, hint."

Was she actually trying to make a point? Mia couldn't seem to follow. "I don't get it."

She laughed hysterically, then suddenly grew serious. "Yeah, me neither. Anyway, couple things before I go—Campbell's bite won't kill you, but it will possibly lead to an apocalypse and in the immortal words of my fair Lady Gaga—you were born this way."

Mia's jaw dropped and she felt her forehead wrinkle in tight confusion. "Are you serious right now? None of that makes a lick of sense."

The Pixie pursed her lips and nodded her head slowly. "That's about all I have to say about that—except, you might want to keep this visit between the two of us. Campbell has a listening problem. I told him not to get all punchy on the taste of you, but he did it anyway. Now, he's flat-out addicted to you, honey. He'll tell you whatever you want to hear to keep you close. Best to keep him in the dark that you know me until we see how everything shakes out."

"He's...addicted to me?"

"Um...more like obsessed, bonded, completely connected on a soul level, but close enough. Well, I can't hang around here all day just shooting the breeze with you. Ta-ta for now." A loony smile eased onto her lips and she waved her hand in a large arc before crossing her arms and disappearing with a snap and a loud pop that made Mia scream.

"Wait! Come back."

But she was truly gone. The smell of cotton candy lingered in the air as Mia's brain worked to understand what had just happened. But try as she might, she couldn't put any of the pieces of insanity together. The Pixie possessed rationality rivaled only by a lunatic, and Mia questioned whether she'd imagined the whole thing.

Campbell? Obsessed with her? She doubted it. Maybe he lusted her, but one taste of her blood did not an addiction make. He'd resisted drinking her again. He couldn't possibly be addicted to her. That even sounded ridiculous. Being addicted to a person just wasn't a real thing.

She should probably find Campbell and ask him what he made of the whole situation, but the Pixie insisted he wouldn't be level-headed about the visit. Well, as well as the strange visitor's addled brain could insist. Yet, how could she not go to him? He was the only other person with knowledge about this world, and she needed some answers.

However, as she looked for him, she only found a note stating he'd gone into town and would be back sometime later tonight. Probably for the best. That gave her plenty of time to think about what she should do. She'd just have to make a decision before he returned.

Of course, he'd said it himself. They might be here for 100 years or more. She didn't really have to rush to action. Maybe she should mull over the Pixie's words, try to make sense of them for a while before she talked to Campbell. Yeah, that's what she'd do, at least until she understood whatever the Pixie had been attempting to tell her.

Chapter 16

With the passing of a couple weeks without incident, Campbell began to breathe easier. They weren't completely out of harm's way yet, but they seemed to have found a place to get their feet on solid ground until they could figure out their next move. Of course, the attraction between them grew stronger day-by-day, and he had a hard time concentrating whenever she was around. He wasn't sure if his inattentiveness to...well, anything else...were a byproduct of her transformation, or if she was just his kind of vice. Either way, he couldn't seem to keep his hands off her.

The only time they'd spent apart was whenever he went into town for supplies and information about any nearby strange occurrences. As of now, nothing seemed out of the ordinary. It was quiet, and that worried him almost as much as if there'd been the kind of unexplainable events that surrounded a powerful immortal like Lisada. She wouldn't give up, but she was a clever witch and more than likely had something evil up her sleeve that he wouldn't see coming until it was too late.

It was the reason he needed to stop thinking with the area below his belt when it came to Mia, which was right up there with stopping the primal urge to feed. For a vampire it was a constant battle. He could cage the need, but it never went away. The same could be said of his desire for Mia—he was powerless against it.

Just yesterday, he'd decided to try to put some distance between them because he recognized the signs of his powerful addiction—

seeking her out when he should be working to fortify their safe-haven, thinking of her taste and silky skin long after he should be satisfied, and focusing singly on getting deep inside her again. He was lost, and he knew it. Unfortunately, he'd had no willpower whatsoever and ended up seeking her out in the middle of the night, kissing every part of her body until she'd come over-and-over. Then he sank deep inside her and rocked slowly until he'd found an explosive release he wouldn't soon forget. He just had to accept that she was impossible for him to resist and could be used to weaken him completely if he wasn't careful. As long as he continued to abstain from biting her, he could keep a relatively level-head and avoid the Pixie's dire warning.

The sun had dropped behind the horizon, and right on cue, Mia wandered out of the cabin with a towel over her arm. She glanced his way once with a small smile and a wave before turning toward the forest, walking out of sight.

He wasn't worried. She was headed to the hot springs, and he'd been very good at letting her have that evening time alone. But tonight, without the slightest hesitation, he found his feet moving in her direction. His attraction to her was too strong to resist, and he was tired of trying. He'd been up for an hour, forcing himself not to fantasize about her delectable body and plump lips. He hadn't done a very good job suppressing his desire, and now he planned to take her every which way he could until they both went over the edge, sweaty and satisfied.

As he inched closer, he heard the splash of water, and his cock hardened painfully at the thought of all that hot water sluicing over her naked curves. Her shorts and shirt were slung over a nearby bush. On the other side were her silky red underwear and bra. His heart skipped a beat at the thought of what awaited just beyond the bushes.

Her bare shoulders rested against the edge of the small pool, and he began pulling his own clothes off quickly. "Mind if I join you?"

She didn't turn around, almost as if she'd known he'd been there all along. "Thought you'd never ask."

With precise movements, Campbell tossed the rest of his clothing in the direction of the bushes where hers hung in the breeze. He didn't care if they made it there or not. His only concern right now was getting into the water with Mia and pulling her into his arms for a hot kiss and so much more.

He walked around to the other side where he knew there was a high ledge that could act as a step and stood, mesmerized, for a brief moment at the sight of the water lapping at the tops of her breasts just like he wanted to. At the quick intake of her breath, he figured he was probably an impressive sight himself. He knew what she saw when she looked at him. A male vampire in his prime was nothing to mess with. Once again, the cut muscles and enlarged…everything came with the predatory package when one turned into a vampire. Everything about him was used to catch prey. And though she was his ultimate query tonight, she would never be anyone's prey. It was just kind of an added bonus that his *gifts* finally seemed to work on her too.

With measured movements, he slid into the water and crossed the small expanse slowly, feeling the powerful urge to fuck the immortal beauty before him into complete submission. His cock had never been so hard at the thought of dominating such a strong being, and yet he wanted to be gentle with her. He wanted to take his time and not rush. He wanted to enjoy every kiss, every touch, every thrust until nothing else mattered in the world but the two of them.

He stopped directly in front of her, their gazes locked, and bracing his hands on either side of her, he leaned in for a hungry kiss. The sweet taste of her wild tongue was almost too much for him, and he knew the first time through might end too quickly, but he was all too willing to keep going until they got the timing just right.

He picked her up and twisted so that he was seated on the built-in ledge and she straddled his lap, just barely out of reach of his throbbing cock. Her pert, little nipples, hovering right in front of him, made his mouth water. It was luscious torture to sit still for even a moment without touching her, licking her, tasting her, but he held out long enough to say, "You're the most exquisite creature I've ever seen, Mia."

She stroked a hand through his steam-dampened hair and traced a hand down his chest. "What do you want to do about it?"

He skimmed a hand down her front and began to stroke her sex slowly. With a gentleness he didn't feel, he leaned forward and tongued her nipple, pulling it into his mouth to suck lightly. At her moan, he slipped a finger inside, finding her slick and ready to take him deep. His cock ached at the thought of her sheath squeezing him like a fist. Within a few breaths he could pull his hand free and be seated fully inside her so quickly. *Slow it down!* No doubt about it, he was flat-out addicted.

A glance upward showed her head thrown back in ecstasy, the vein there pulsing in invitation. He felt his fangs slip out of his gums. He closed his eyes and worked hard to resist the urge to sink them into her. After several deep breaths, he opened his eyes and lowered his gaze back to where he could make good use of his mouth. He added another finger inside her and kissed over to the other pebbled peak. He pressed his palm in a circular motion against her little clit and felt her rock her hips, brushing against the tip of his cock, almost painfully. He hissed in a quick breath.

"Campbell...please..."

He might be completely obsessed with Mia, and it was a risk every time he was with her, but he couldn't resist her if he wanted to.

Beneath the water, he felt her searching fingers. She curled her hand around his shaft and stroked his length tightly, giving him the maddening sensation of what it would be like inside her again and again. With determination, she directed the head of his cock into her soft folds, and for one blessed moment, he thought she was going to seat herself over him, gloving him deep inside her, but she only rocked her hips teasingly over the tip, bringing him to the point of madness. Her touch was sensuous and a hungry desire razed through him, pushing him to penetrate her without any more hesitation. *It was over.*

His gaze seized on the pulse at her neck as he shifted until they were lined up, and he felt a little give at her entrance. His fangs lengthened and throbbed with the need to pierce her delicate skin. He ran his tongue over one to try to assuage the ache, but it only made the need greater. He needed to be inside her in every way, and he needed it now.

Inch by inch, he began to thrust upward, feeling her folds grip him and pull him deeper. He wrapped his fingers around her curvaceous hips to steady her as he pushed inside her warmth. *Too much.* Sweat beaded on his forehead, and still he watched the thrumming of her pulse as it sped to fast, rhythmic beats. *Just a taste of her.*

"You want to bite me?"

Damn, he really did. But the Pixie's warning came back to him. The obsession was fueled by her taste. What if he couldn't stop once he'd started?

As if she'd read his mind, she said, "The transition is complete. I'm immortal now."

Fuck! But his addiction would be complete. He would never be able to let her go, would always crave another taste for the rest of his life.

With a growl, he closed his eyes and slammed up into her the rest of the way, pulling her onto his cock forcefully, getting a small sense of satisfaction that for this moment, she was his. Her moan of pleasure heightened his need to send them both over the edge, riding the pleasurable feelings to a final satisfaction. After a long withdrawal, he plunged in again, reckless abandon taking over. Animalistic, he became instinctual, pumping in and out of her, pushing headlong toward a mind-blowing orgasm.

Chapter 17

Mia felt like she was losing him. He was becoming mindless, but she wanted him present with her. With a gentle motion, she stroked up his back and tangled her fingers into his hair. Slowly, she leaned in and touched his lips with hers. With a grunt, he sucked at her mouth, kissing her like he was headed to the firing squad tomorrow, and she felt the tip of his fang brush her lower lip, but then, he seemed to wake up and slowed the pace of his thrusts.

His kiss slowed, became thoughtful again, and though his hunger didn't dissipate completely, he seemed to be in control once more. He slipped his hand between them and searched out her exposed clit, rubbing in circular motions as he lunged upward again and again.

Electricity fired through her bones, igniting the fire building in her mid-section. Time slowed down as she could only make soft cries, feeling his touch to her very soul.

"More!" The word slipped from her lips as they rubbed against his, and he pulled back from their kiss to stare at her neck again. "Bite me, Campbell!"

"Can't!"

"You can't hurt me anymore!"

His gaze snapped to hers, "You doona know what you're sayin'. Different kinds of pain. I doona ever want to hurt you in any way."

"Then just make me feel. I just want to feel you."

"That I can do."

With powerful thrusts, Campbell, held her gaze and pounded into her, but even as crazed as he seemed in his need to find release, and even as his hips pumped hard and long, he continued to circle his fingers over her clit. He clenched his jaw, determination to see her go over first clear in his eyes.

With a small motion, he shifted her body until her back was arched and his penis targeted a bundle of nerves in one particular spot at the top of her sex. The stirrings in her belly quickly ignited into full flame as he swelled inside her, giving her a feeling of fullness and a heightened awareness of every sensation that came with each thrust. Her head fell back on her shoulders, overwhelmed with pleasure, she spread her knees wider and began riding him fully herself.

"Come for me, Mia."

He needn't even ask. She was already there, and with a scream, she went over the edge, feeling her orgasm rip through her body like a powerful ocean wave, pulsing in vibrant bolts of electricity and making her let go time after time.

With groans and grunts, he followed quickly, calling her name and crushing her to him, clearly experiencing the same intensity that even now still quaked in her legs.

In the moments after, when the only sound was their heavy breathing, Mia realized just how deep her feelings for Campbell really were. What they'd just shared was beyond relieving a little sexual frustration. The reality now was that she was approaching the point of never seeing herself being satisfied with an existence that didn't include him.

And yet, she knew what that meant. Immortality together wasn't a light thing to consider, especially for someone who lived as independently as Campbell did. He certainly didn't seem obsessed with her as the Pixie had suggested. It occurred to her again that she could just ask him, but what if by asking, she scared him away. If she wasn't careful, she'd be living with a broken heart for eternity. Maybe she was the addicted one.

She was saved from analyzing the situation any further as Campbell repositioned her on his lap so that her head rested on his shoulder and said, "I was thinking tonight we might go a couple towns over for a little change in scenery."

"You think we can do that safely?"

She felt him nod. "I've been keeping an eye on things, and so far everything seems safe around here. Besides, I need to speak to a few people, but I need different equipment that can't be traced as easily, and I have a reliable contact close to here who could get it for me."

"Okay. Did you plan to go right away? Or do you think we could sit here and bask in the glow for a little bit?"

He chuckled. "I like that." With a shrug he said, "Why don't you finish soaking, and I'll go get everything ready to go. We can leave in an hour or two."

"I can handle that."

With a sigh and one more squeeze, he set her on the ledge beside him and crossed back to the built-in stairs. She watched with rapt attention as he pulled himself from the water easily as his solid muscles rippled under his skin. He was beautiful, and now she chuckled at her first impression of him being too gorgeous to be human. As it turned out, she'd been right.

As he walked away, her humor faded slightly. She just hoped her prediction that loving him being a mistake wasn't nearly as insightful.

Chapter 18

Less than twenty minutes later, Mia dressed quickly and began to walk slowly back toward the cabin. Even with all she'd lost by becoming a supernatural being, she couldn't help but smile at the turn of events. Life was indeed strange in its twists and turns, but at this moment right now, she wouldn't trade a thing. She liked her newly-developing powers, even if she didn't quite know how to use them exactly. She had the time, though, to figure that out. She had freaking forever.

And then there was Campbell. When she thought back to that first day when she'd stormed up to get the moving truck moved from behind her car, and instead, she'd found herself staring speechlessly at a real-life Adonis. All rational thought escaped her brain, but the whole time, he'd known who she was, and he'd been there to protect her.

Now, a scant month later, she was winched-to-the-limit in love with him. She swallowed hard. It was a scary admission, to say the least. Especially since, she didn't have the slightest idea how he felt about her.

As she approached the cabin, she slowed. She heard voices, as in multiple people talking. With the utmost caution, she crouched low and headed for the cover of the bushes at the side of the house. A quick glance around didn't reveal anyone or anything out of the ordinary.

"How thoughtful of you, Campbell, to bring her to this place to wait for me."

The feminine voice was floating out of the window was unforgettable. It was the same as the one Mia had heard in her head in the parking lot. Her heart dropped at the realization that their bubble of safety had just burst. Then, the meaning of the words hit her. Her quick breaths halted for a brief second as they sunk in. *Had he been working with Lisada the whole time?*

Since watching Campbell fight the werewolf in the parking lot, the thought had never occurred to her. It was entirely possible everything he'd done had been a ruse to get her to follow him to an out-of-the-way place where no one else could intervene in whatever the witch's plans for her were. Her stomach heaved at the idea.

Campbell wouldn't betray her like that. He hated Lisada.

But she didn't hear him rushing to deny it. As a matter of fact, he wasn't saying anything.

"Such a good pet, you are. I've missed being away from you, love."

Mia's stomach dropped to her knees. He'd said he'd thought he'd loved the witch, and that she'd loved him. Was it possible he'd never let that idea go? Did he still believe Lisada and he could be together?

The idea felt false almost immediately. With the way he'd called Mia's name less than a half hour ago, there was no way he could be that passionate about two different women. And what of the Pixie's visit? She'd insisted Campbell was obsessed with Mia. Unless she'd been in on it the whole time. Maybe Campbell and Lisada had sent her so that Mia would drop her guard even further. What if everything she'd believed to be true the last few weeks had all been a lie.? The idea made her stomach pitch and roll with nausea.

Suddenly, the low, untamed tone of Lisada's voice made Mia's skin crawl as she said, "And you fucked her, just like you were supposed to. I knew I could count on you for that. Now, if we need one, we'll have a possible back-up to sacrifice to the cup."

Oh my frack! It was true. Though she didn't understand everything Lisada was talking about—back-up, sacrifice, cup—she knew one thing to be certain: she was so naïve. He'd tricked her, and she'd fallen for everything. How had she been so stupid?

Her heart thudded against her chest. Panic was setting in, but before it could get a foothold, she clenched her fists until she felt her new, claw-like sharpened nails begin to pierce the skin of her palm. She set her jaw in determination. It was time to take charge of her own destiny. She had freaking superpowers, or something like that, even if it would take her some time to master them completely—or have the ability to use them just a little bit. Still, she couldn't sit back and become someone's victim.

With careful steps, she inched along the outside of the cabin, under the window. After a few reassuring breaths, she peeked over the sill until she saw Lisada standing in the center of the room, her white hair flowing down her back and an evil grin on her beautiful face. Such a scarily lovely package on the outside, but clearly crazy to the core.

Mia ducked back down quickly. She hadn't spotted Campbell, but she didn't particularly wish to see him right now. The thought that he'd pretended affection for her, pretended he was helping her find safety, made her stomach churn. She didn't want to believe it was true, still had a hard time assimilating the Campbell she knew with one that would be a co-conspirator with this witch. And though deep inside, she couldn't help but think something was wrong about this situation, just once, she wanted to hear Campbell deny it.

Instead, the gruesome image of a blood-soaked, wild-eyed monster standing over her fired into her brain. *Her nightmare!* Maybe it was more than a dream. Maybe it was a vision.

Lisada's voice rang out sharp as she shouted, "You! Go find her! Bring her to me, so we can finally finish what we started."

Mia stiffened. One thing was clear—she needed to act now if she wanted to save herself. With small movements, Mia made her way to the corner of the house and dared a look around. No guards, henchmen, or wild, hairy beasts were anywhere in sight—yet.

She couldn't question her good luck though. She had to go now. With nothing on her mind but pushing herself to run as fast as she had the night she'd escaped her apartment, Mia sprinted toward the wooded area edging the little hidden lane Campbell had used to get them to the cabin. She'd run. Where wasn't important yet. She just needed to get away from Lisada, from this dangerous world...from Campbell.

Mia swiped at the tears falling freely down her face, but she refused to acknowledge she was crying. Betrayal hovered just outside her thoughts, but she didn't have time to analyze every little element of her relationship with Campbell. Certainly didn't need to fall apart when her life was clearly in danger. Right now, she needed to keep it together.

She stepped out of the woods and onto the small driveway. Still no one appeared to be around. It was almost too easy to get away, but she didn't question it for long. She needed to put distance between this drama and herself.

Maybe she had been naïve. Maybe she'd even been stupid, but one thing she wasn't was a person who sat around feeling sorry for herself. She was nobody's fool—at least she assured herself she wouldn't be from this point forward.

As she emerged onto the road, she was still surprised not to see any other beings. Wouldn't Lisada bring reinforcements to squash any resistance or at least call in back-up?

And then it occurred to her, Lisada hadn't expected resistance. If Campbell was on her side, who would fight her?

Well, Mia didn't plan to make it that easy for them, and despite what Campbell had said, she knew she needed to get to Roxy, Hope, and Janna. As her best friends and the only family she had left, together they'd figure out how to keep her safe.

Yet, as she approached the end of the long driveway, something didn't feel right. She felt watched, almost like she should expect red, targeting dots to show up all over her shirt. But as she listened and watched, nothing stirred. The whole forest was quiet, which begged the obvious question. Where were all the forest creatures? Shouldn't they be making a bunch of racket this time of night?

"Miiiiaaaa!"

Campbell's livid bellow split the night. Her absence was clearly noted. Her heart pounded even harder. He sounded like he was ready to kill someone, which meant she was out of time.

Without another thought, she sprinted out past the lane, onto the road that ran perpendicular to it, and all hell broke loose in a single moment.

As if they'd been entirely invisible to her eyes, then suddenly appeared in the instant she stepped onto the road, fifty uniformed figures approached her, guns raised and ready. She wanted to kick herself for not trusting her instincts. Just moments ago, she'd felt them there, but she'd let her doubt get the better of her.

They dropped the pretense and rushed forward, but she held up her hands and in less than a second, they all dropped backwards as if they'd hit an unseen barrier. It brought to mind, the time she'd been able to conjure they same thing to hold Campbell at bay, long enough for her to get away from him.

With that thought guiding her, she ran away from the sprawled figures behind her and away from Campbell. She darted into the woods across the road and picked up speed until the vegetation seemed to come at her in flashes and near-misses. At this pace, one false move would surely knock her head clean off. As if she didn't have enough to worry about.

Behind her, she could hear bodies crashing through the trees, but she knew they'd never catch her as long as she kept up her current speed and made her way to a faster mode of travel, which at her rate of speed, might be a jet plane.

After what seemed like an hour, Mia finally slowed as she approached a clearing with a string of houses, stretching further than she could see. People milled around outside, going about their daily business, and cars zoomed down the road in front of her. If she could just find a willing ride, she could get miles away from here, inconspicuously. But how did one ask a stranger for a ride without arousing suspicions, especially at night?

The answer came to her, but she didn't feel entirely right about it. She had to pull a Campbell. She had to steal a car. It was the only way, but she'd be choosy about which car and from which house she took it.

With her new mission in mind, she jogged to the backyard of the nearest darkened house and edged her way around to the driveway. Unfortunately, no cars sat parked there, so she was forced to move on to the next one.

As she was making her way through the shadows, she shook her head at herself. Who was she kidding? She didn't know the first thing about stealing a car. This was a horrible plan, but it was the best she currently had. Maybe she'd get lucky and find a car with the keys inside. Sure, and maybe there'd be a red carpet leading to the door and snacks and chilled drinks waiting inside too.

Then, she saw something that stopped her in her tracks. As she peered around the next house, she noticed several cars, their lights lighting up the dark night, blocking the end of the street. Clearly, they were waiting for someone...for her. Her heart dropped to her toes. Just when she'd committed to a poorly thought-out plan and everything. Well, putting it lightly, *this sucked duck eggs!*

Suddenly, the sound of a voice on a bullhorn shouted, "Mia Renee Alexander, we know you're here, and we're here to help. We just want to keep you safe."

The voice sounded oddly familiar. One that she'd heard long ago, but the way he pronounced her name is what gave her chills.

Then, it all became clear as the speaker put the bullhorn away and shouted, "Mia, it's me. It's your father. Come to me, so we can get you somewhere safe."

Her father? How was that possible? It wasn't possible. How many times had she wanted to hear the deep sound of his baritone voice one more time? Yet, she'd accepted she never would again. He'd gone down in a plane crash when she'd been a child, and no matter how many times she'd wished it otherwise, he couldn't have survived that. How could he be here? Now? After fifteen years? It had to be a trick, a way to pull her out of hiding. Unfortunately, it worked.

The confusion muddled her brain, and she forgot to hide, instead, stepping in front of the house into the orange-tinted streetlight shining on the sidewalk to get a better view of the one who'd spoken. The downside was it made her more visible too.

"There she is!" A voice called from her left, but she didn't turn her head, couldn't turn her head. Her focus was solely on the one face she recognized. He'd hardly aged, if at all. Again, she had to ask how it was possible for him to be here and look almost exactly the same.

"Dad?"

"It's really me, Mia."

"How?"

"I promise, I'll explain everything, but you have to come with me now. You're in danger."

Danger? Of course she was, but right now, she couldn't think past this surreal moment. Her father, whom she hadn't seen for most of her life, stood before her now as if it had all been a dream...or a horrible nightmare. Her brain was spinning, her breathing heavy, and it was all she could do to not drop in a heap to the ground.

She was confused about so much and felt lost in all her life had become—running here for her life, trusting the wrong person, running there for her life. But, he looked like her father. She sniffed the air, and the scent of wood, campfires, and hard-work sweat. He smelled like her father, and she desperately needed someone she could trust right now. Someone to tell her what the hell was going on.

With a nod of her head, she moved toward him and the waiting crowd of cars and people. Finally, she might get some answers and maybe a chance for a breath or two without having to look over her shoulder every few minutes. They seemed to be exactly what she needed at just the right time.

Now the only question was if she should worry about that little niggle of doubt burning at the back of her brain or totally ignore it, like she'd done for too long.

As she approached the figure that really appeared to be her father, she paused. He opened his arms with a pained expression.

"Mia mine!"

She sucked in a choppy breath. Only her dad had ever called her that. Relief settled over her at the reality of being this close to her living, breathing father. *He was alive!*

She rushed into his arms and felt wetness on her cheeks where they brushed against his shirt. "I can't believe it's really you."

"It's me." He pulled back and stared intently at her. "You're just as I knew you would become."

Confusion washed over Mia briefly. *Did he know what she'd become?* Did he have a hand in it? Questions were racing through her mind, and the time had come to get some answers.

"Dad, we need to talk."

Chapter 19

Campbell woke with a splitting headache and a vague recollection
of what had happened.

He'd been attacked the minute he'd walked inside the cabin. Lisada
had set a thorough trap, and he'd been so muddle-headed from Mia's
sweet body and the security of the last two weeks, he'd walked right
into it without batting a single lash of his eyes.

He'd failed her. Now he had to wonder where Mia was and in what
shape. Had they already drained her? The thought made his vision blur
into a hot-white rage. He'd kill them all.

"Dammit!" He slammed the bottom of his fist into the cold,
concrete floor where he lay facedown. He should have known better,
should've seen it as a possibility. Instead, he'd gone in full-force, head
down, ignoring everything he'd ever been trained to do.

He'd grown complacent in the easy pace of their life together these
past few weeks. It had almost made him forget the danger Lisada posed.
What an idiot he'd been!

Pain shot through his torso as he raised himself up to a sitting
position, and he groaned with the effort it took. They'd done a number
on him if he hadn't healed completely by now. One of the perks of being
paranormal was an ability to heal quickly, but right now, his body didn't
seem to be responding normally.

A glance around showed his surroundings. It wasn't his cabin, and it
certainly wasn't a five-star facility. Stone walls surrounded him on all

sides, except for a thick, wooden door that broke the monotony of one wall. Cobwebs and dust littered every open area where he looked. A flat, wooden slab sat horizontally against the far wall about a foot off the floor. He assumed it was the bed of sorts, in this dungeon-type cell. Other than a bucket in the corner, nothing else stood out noticeably. For now, this was his new home.

Just one question. For how long?

A key rattled in the lock at the door, and with some effort and the help of the nearest vertical surface, he sat propped against the wall, attempting to be ready for whatever they threw at him next.

The door swung open and two hulking trolls stepped through with guns trained on him. *Interesting company you're keeping, Lisada.*

The good news was they obviously expected him to recover at some point if they thought he was dangerous enough. Even in the current shape he was in, he could see they were clearly under Lisada's control.

"Hey, guys. Social visit?" Flippant seemed to fit the moment and had a tendency to make idiots put their guard down. Even when one of them bared his teeth and growled, Campbell only smiled at them. Whatever they were here to dish out, he wasn't about to bend over and take it without some resistance.

"Get up!" They used their guns to demonstrate with a sharp quick lift of the barrels before training them back on him.

"Been working on that. Don't suppose you'd lend a hand, would you?"

They both stepped toward him, and one gave him a hard nudge

with the toe of his boot. "No one's going to help you here. If you think you're helpless now, what about with two *broken* legs?"

Campbell chuckled as he used his hands to push himself up to a standing position. "Now wouldn't that defeat your whole purpose to get me *on* said legs?"

The minute he was between the two of them, shoulder-to-shoulder, they cuffed his hands and shoved him toward the door. By the way his wrists burned like fire, the cuffs were made of pure silver.

With sucked air between his front teeth, Campbell shook his head, "I think I forgot to R.S.V.P. for this party. Hope I don't get accused of being crass." For that smart remark, he got a knock to the head that left his ears ringing.

As they dragged him into a warehouse-sized great room, he was struck by the chaos surrounding them. Weres, witches, warlocks, gremlins, harpies, and all manner of other beasts lined the walls of the room. Briefly he caught the gaze of Andrex, the newly crowned Goblin King and though their connected gaze passed quickly, he felt sure there'd been a message he couldn't quite read there. The Goblin King was a hybrid creature and looked more human than goblin. Campbell had once gotten some intel from Andrex that had panned out in a case that involved a catburgling goblin, but he wasn't completely allied with Sup Co. He was what the youth of today called a *frenemie.* Sometimes friend, sometimes foe. Nevertheless, the contact between them was too short to make sense of anything, and Campbell returned his focus to the craziness of the room. Creatures of all kinds fought each other and watched him with hungry eyes as he was lugged toward the woman of his nightmares, regally seated on a throne that appeared to be made of bleached-white bones. Leave it to Lisada to make such a statement, especially considering she pretty much brought death and destruction wherever she went.

As he got closer, he noticed a large bejeweled golden and crystal goblet on a raised table. She didn't seem to be drinking from it, but it certainly had an ominously prominent place beside this queen of insanity. One thought jumped to mind—the Absolute Glass.

Once they stopped in front of her, the guards pushed him to his knees in front of Lisada, and her lips turned up in a sickening smile he wished he could wipe away with the back of his hand. This witch had brought him so much pain in his long, long life. He just hoped he got the chance to repay her someday soon.

For now, he used the only weapon he had, "Well, this is awkward. Always hate running into an —ex in public."

Her smile slipped slightly before re-pasting itself. "Campbell, I'm so glad you've retained your sense of humor. You're going to need it over the next couple of days."

"How are you even still alive? Last I saw you, you were in pieces."

"Yes, well, I didn't appreciate you leaving me like that, but the thinnest connection remained between my neck and body, and sorry, but I wasn't exactly monogamous. One of my faithful followers, not only saved me, but allowed me to drain him completely. He didn't make it, but it was enough to make me fully immortal."

He'd known she was cruel, but clearly she was insane as well.

"That's loyalty for you."

"Yes, well, loyalty is easily lost. Just ask Mia."

Her words hit him hard, just like she'd planned. God, he hated feeling powerless. "Where's is she? What have you done with her?"

He saw doubt flicker slightly in her eyes before she regained her composure. "Well, that's why you're still alive. Seems after she overheard my little message to her about your betrayal, she slipped through my guards' fingers. Clearly she's more powerful than I realized."

She'd escaped! But as Lisada's words sunk in, his jaw clenched tightly. "What betrayal?"

Lisada laughed lightly, but the amusement was only for herself. "I think she left believing you'd led her straight to me and that you did it because you're madly devoted to our love. How about that show of loyalty?"

Rage shot through Campbell's spine and he struggled to rise and get free of the two trolls who held him tightly. Unfortunately, he got nothing for his efforts except more stinging burns from the silver cuffs around his wrists. *Powerless!* Oh, he'd make her pay. "I detest you! You're a filthy whore, turning everything you touch to ash! I can't wait to get my hands around your neck. I'll cleave it from your shoulders…"

With a flick of her wrist, she sealed his lips, cutting off his tirade. "Oh, your endearments need some work, Campbell. They used to be so much sweeter."

She stood and walked to the goblet, stroking it lovingly. "Do you know what this is? It's our salvation, Campbell. It's my ultimate insurance policy. You see, beginning with you, I've planned this moment for hundreds of years, and though that seems like a long time, it's a drop in the ocean compared to the eternity I'll rule the world and finally be rid of the human scourge."

Campbell fought against his bonds again, but got nowhere once more and stilled as she came closer. As interested as he was in her plan, he knew he wasn't going to like how it played out.

She stroked his face as lovingly as she touched the goblet, a cruel smile on her face. "You will bring Mia to me, so I can drink her hybrid vampire and goddess blood from the Absolute Glass. You've tasted her, and how you resisted draining her is a mystery to me. If you're a good boy, I'll let you have a sip and a taste of what it's like to be a god."

He felt the wrath humming throughout his body, and he shot her a gaze full of the anger pulsing through his veins.

She bent down to meet his gaze on his level. "See, here's how this goes. You bring her to me, and I'll spare her life. Let her live. If you make me chase her, I'll kill you both. It's that simple."

With another flick of her hand, his lips loosened. He pulled long breaths into his lungs. Though he didn't technically have to breathe any longer, he liked the feeling a lungful of air gave him. It made him feel in touch with his humanity, unlike the creature in front of him, whose human qualities were long gone. "I don't trust you, bitch. You've proven over and over just how little your word means."

The room broke into laughter behind him, and she straightened her spine to stare them down until they all fell silent. For all her show, it was clear she was hanging onto this motley crew by a thread.

Her heat-filled gaze returned to him. "Oh, you'll do it. Or I'll bring back every single one of your three sisters as my own personal Revenants. They'll be mine to use and abuse for all eternity."

"You couldn't do that. Only ashes remain of them."

She tsked loudly. "You know me better than that. I like insurance. After I killed them, I removed their hearts in a way that you'd never even notice. I have all I need to bring them back, and there's nothing you can do about that."

"Why can't you let them rest in peace?"

Her facial expression changed to exaggerated surprise. "That's on you, Campbell. I will leave them in peace if you bring me what's mine."

"She doesn't belong to you!"

"Oh, but she does. I made her what she is. Not in that lab as all you idiots assumed, but many, many years ago, combining the genetics of her vampire father and goddess mother. She is my creation, and I intend to use her for what I made her. To turn me into the most powerful being to ever live."

The room erupted again, this time in loud support of her outrageous claims. Poor bastards had no idea the level her cruelty would climb. As the room grew quiet again, Campbell shouted, "I don't care what she promised you...the bitch won't keep her word."

"I promised them the same thing I promised you...life on the winning team. Now, are you going to be a good boy and bring me the final ingredient? Think of your sisters."

He hated how trapped he felt. He hated that she had him by the short and curlies. "I'll go to her."

"And bring her back to me?"

"Sure." He sighed and spoke to himself under his breath, "No way she'd go anywhere with me now anyway."

"Trust me. You're all she can think about, and she'd crawl over glass to get to you right now."

Yeah, thanks to what Lisada made her believe, she probably couldn't wait to see him again. "To kick me in the nuts, no doubt."

She laughed that humorless laugh again, and chills broke out on the back of his neck. He had a feeling she knew something he didn't.

"Quite the contrary. She's literally starving to see you. You see, her kind can only drink from one source—you—until the soul-bond is broken through death."

"So, she's starving right now?"

A nonchalant shrug from her renewed his rage. "You better get going if you don't want her to die forever."

Chapter 20

"How are you alive?" Mia stared into the oddly familiar green eyes of her father, Riley Spencer, across the table from her. She winced at the cramps squeezing her abdomen. Her hunger was beginning to get out of control, but so far nothing offered her had stayed down. She was starting to worry but hadn't brought it to anyone else's attention. She hoped it was just a passing phase of her transformation or some kind of paranormal bug she'd caught somewhere along the way.

He sighed heavily. "I should have known better than to trust Lisada, but your mother and I didn't see the danger until it was too late."

"My mother? Is she here too?"

His lips thinned into a grim frown as he shook his head back and forth slowly. "I haven't seen her since sometime after the crash."

"You mean, there really was a crash? But you both survived? I...I don't know what to say."

Uncomfortable silence sat heavily in the room for a few long seconds before he finally said, "I'm sorry you had to deal with that loss. Need to tell you how it all began."

Mia leaned forward and nodded vigorously.

"I am an original vampire, naturally-born from two mortals thousands of years ago, and through some sort of mutation, was given life. My parents cared for me and raised me with strong values of right and wrong, but nothing they did prepared me for the likes of that witch." He paused, dropping his head, and when he looked at her again, she saw the guilt in his eyes. "Like so many, I was under Lisada's spell. I would have done anything for her. So, when she asked me to give my vampire genetic material to combine with your goddess mother's to create a hybrid being, I didn't question her. I did what she asked, and as your mother carried the implanted embryo, we grew closer until I began to wake up to Lisada's ultimate plan to use you to make herself stronger. By the time you were born, Desside and I were deeply in love. We'd decided we needed to take you and run, but Lisada was so strong and would have halted any escape plans before they even got off the ground. You see, she always knew where we were at all times. She had a supernatural connection with us that we couldn't break.

"That's when her sister Hepseba agreed to help us. She had the ability to mask our presence from Lisada, and with her help, we were able to get away. We changed our names and laid low. Unfortunately, as you grew older and your own supernatural abilities began manifesting, it became harder to hide all of us, and when you were five, Lisada found us. We escaped, barely. And that's when we decided the only way we'd be safe from her was separated. We left you where you'd be safest—with Hepseba, the woman you knew as your grandmother, and your mother and I staged the crash and ran, hoping the concoctions Hepseba gave us would allow us to confuse Lisada's connection, forcing her to break it, as only she could."

"Lisada's sister was my grandmother?" She shook her head back and forth in disbelief. "I had no idea. She protected me until she couldn't anymore. She passed away last year."

"I'm afraid it was Lisada's doing."

"She killed her own sister?"

He nodded grimly. "Trust me, it's the least of her crimes. But Hepseba would have gladly given her life to protect you. She loved you, much like your mother and I do."

Mia felt tears stinging the backs of her eyes. The loss of someone so special to her had been devastating because Hepseba had been more than a wonderful grandmother. She'd been her only parental figure through most of her youth, she'd given Mia more love than a child could ever expect, and knowing now how she'd used her supernatural abilities to keep Mia safe, brought her sacrifice into perspective. She hoped it hadn't been in vain. "How did Lisada find me?"

"Hepseba had placed great magic spells around you before she passed. They followed you wherever you went, kind of like a force field surrounding you always, and they suppressed your abilities in order to keep you undetectable, but whatever substance they gave you during the research study in which you participated recently negated the protection of her magic. Essentially, it was an antidote to her medicine."

"Well, that explains a lot."

"I'm sure it does. I joined the Supernatural Council's Special Forces to help in fighting Lisada's plans, but she went way underground and couldn't be located for these many years." A crooked smile slid across his face. "I was always close to you though. Hepseba kept your mother and me updated about every one of your accomplishments, but we knew we had to stay away...until the research study changed everything and brought Lisada out of hiding. The minute I found out what was going on, I sent my best man to protect you. I knew Campbell would do everything in his power to keep you safe."

"That's where you were wrong. He was working with Lisada the whole time."

"What? No that's not possible. He hates Lisada to the core. She's the reason his family is dead."

Mia stared, confused. Though what her father told her matched up to Campbell's account of events, she knew what she'd witnessed had actually happened. "But I overheard them together. She was thanking him for bringing me to her. She spoke like they were long-time lovers."

"Believe me. Campbell would never work with her, not after what she did. Something about the situation isn't quite right."

A sudden shot of intense pain struck through Mia's abdomen, doubling her over with a moan.

He was around the table in a second, crouching at her knees, his hands planted on the armrests of her chair.

"Are you alright? What's wrong?" The concern in her father's voice was clear and if she weren't in heavy agony, she might appreciate having someone else to care about her again. As it were, she just didn't want him to worry and fuss over her, not when all she could think about was feeding—from Campbell. How could she still want to have anything to do with him? Of course, now she had to consider that what she had assumed she'd overheard may have not been the situation at all.

But, she wasn't an idiot. She knew what she'd heard, and even if her instincts still screamed for Campbell, she couldn't afford to be stupid anymore, not when so many were willing to kill to possess her.

Her father's hand rested on her shoulder comfortingly, and the cramps began to dissipate enough so she could sit up. She met his worried gaze and slid him a tremulous smile. "I'm hungry, but I can't keep anything down."

"Dammit! Why didn't you tell me?"

"I figured you had enough to worry about what with psycho-witches trying to take over the world and all."

He stood tall over her with a wide stance and crossed his arms. His eyes glowed neon green. Anger was scary on him.

"You bonded with Campbell."

"What? Of course not. I don't want anything else to do with him."

A raised eyebrow demonstrated just how badly convinced he was. "Well, he's definitely bonded, but more than likely both of you are, if you can only feed from him. Did he feed from you?"

She chewed her bottom lip and felt like she'd just got caught making out on the living room couch. She had to remind herself that she was a grown woman now, and though he hadn't been there through much of her developmental years, she had nothing to be ashamed of.

"Once, but he always refused to after that, said he didn't think he'd be able to stop."

He actually growled...out loud...and she almost laughed at his display of fatherly concern. "That's because he knows what's good for him. Feeding isn't just an ordinary process for vampires. If there's affection involved, it can create a bond. If the bond gets strong enough, then, well, you get your situation where nothing else will satisfy your hunger."

She looked at her hands, folded in her lap. "Well, I think it's obvious who's still bonded then." *How freaking embarrassing!*

"That's not how it works with vampires. You can only feed from him because his bond to you has grown near unbreakable. I know you believe what you heard was real, but clearly he's not working with Lisada because..."

A screeching alarm sounded, drowning out any more conversation, and her father sprang into action. As he headed toward the door, he turned back and pointed in her direction. "Come on! I'm sending you to a room upstairs. You'll be safe there."

Her heart pounded loudly in her ears as she realized something that scared her more than anything else ever had. The bonding thing with Campbell went beyond just physical hunger. He was here, he was desperate, and she could sense he wanted her.

* * *

He felt her hunger, and it made him crazed to get to her. *She needed him! Now!* And he would go through anyone to find her and keep her unharmed, despite his deal with Lisada. He'd swore to bring Mia back to her to prevent an unimaginable fate for his sisters, but he hadn't sworn not to kill Lisada once he'd completed his task. Then, he'd make sure Mia was safe always—away from those who would use her— and even from him.

As he crossed the wide, grassy area in front of the looming, three-story block building, he stuck to the shadows and slipped up behind two guards.

Despite being a blood-sucking vampire, his first instinct was not necessarily to kill them. They weren't hurting anyone, just doing their job. In his long life, he'd done his fair share of killing and chose a different path whenever possible. With as little movement as possible, he smashed the butt of his gun on the back of one's head and threw a right hook at the other guard just as he turned in reaction. If they'd been ordinary men, the strikes would have been enough to put both on their asses. As it were, one was a shifter, and from the smell of the other, he was a dragon. The shifter guard he'd hit with his gun went down stunned but not out, and the dragon came back at him swinging, his eyes an eerie glowing green.

Campbell ducked and came back with a left uppercut and a hard right jab, feeling like he was hitting concrete blocks. The guard stumbled back far enough that with one hard kick to the side of the head, Campbell was able to knock him unconscious just as the other guard rose from the ground. Campbell hung back and waited for the guard to make the first move, but as the shifter lunged forward with a growl, he suddenly jerked back, bowing his back as if he'd been hit from behind. As he fell to the ground face-first, Campbell saw a thin projectile jutting from his left shoulder. Someone had shot the guard with a tranquilizer dart.

With almost perfect night-vision, Campbell scanned the area but saw no one. Had someone helped him? Or had the guard leaped in front of the dart's actual target—in front of Campbell?

When a piercing alarm sounded and light flooded the area, Campbell sunk low and misted, floating just above the ground to the few shadows against the outer wall of the main building where he knew she was. He returned to human form and clung to the wall. Well, he clearly wasn't sneaking in the back door now. Who would have triggered the alarm?

Truth be told though, he didn't have time to figure that out. He needed to get to Mia immediately.

He misted again and rose up the side of the building until he hovered over the rooftop. As he formed into a human once more, what he was looking for caught his attention. Slightly out of breath from his exertion, he misted again and drifted toward an open ventilation unit and slipped silently inside.

Once inside, he flowed through a long air shaft, twisting and turning as he sensed her growing nearer. Finally, he found the room where he felt the intensity of her suffering. Like a black waterfall, he surged into the room and materialized into his human form. The minute her heady scent reached his nose, his fangs elongated. *How long had it been since he'd eaten?* Now that he thought about it, he hadn't eaten since she healed him at the safehouse. To be honest, he hadn't wanted to feed from anyone else. Only Mia. *Shit!*

The sight before him nearly pulled him apart and made him forget his own needs for the moment. She was doubled over at the waist, moaning in agony. *This was all his fault.* The strength of his affection for her had grown so passionate that she could only get her nourishment from him. In his opinion, it was a cruel side effect that often resulted in vampire pairs dying together because they refused to break the bond. There were artificial means for breaking the connection, and as soon as she was well again, he had every intention of pursuing them. He never wanted to be responsible for her suffering again.

He rushed to kneel in front of her and lifted his arm to her mouth. "Drink, Mia."

Her head whipped up and the sight of the anguish in her eyes nearly undid him.

"Campbell? What are you doing here?"

"Your hunger drew me. You have to drink."

Determination steeled her facial features as she turned away from his offer. The sheer willpower it must have taken to refuse his blood showed just how betrayed she felt.

"I know you think the worst of me. I don't know exactly what Lisada said because I was unconscious at the time, but I can assure you I wouldn't do anything to hurt you." *God, he hoped he could keep his word on that.*

She met his gaze again, and he could see how much she wanted to drink. It was torture for her to resist.

"Dammit, Mia! No matter how you feel about me, you have to feed or you'll die."

When she shook her head, her eyes blazing with defiance, he marveled at her strength. But he couldn't let her die. He used his own fang to slice a gash near his wrist, much like he'd done the first time she'd drank from him. He hoped she'd find it irresistible again.

Yet, she still held out, and he marveled at her strength. "Here's the deal. We have to escape because Lisada will stop at nothing to possess you." *Not a lie.* "I know a way to break our connection, but you'll have to drink to strengthen yourself first."

Hope shined in the depths of her gaze, and with only another short moment's hesitation, she fell on his arm, drinking deeply. Her pale cheeks pinkened, her hair became fuller, and he could see the power begin to flow throughout her body again.

As before, he found himself hard as rock and grabbed the wooden rails of the bed on which she sat to keep from laying himself over her and grinding her hot body into the mattress. He squeezed the wood tightly in his fists and felt it splinter into dust in his hands. The bed collapsed and she rolled off it and onto him. She didn't come unattached even once, instead straddling his hips and rolling her sex over his straining erection. Damn, he wished he could get rid of the clothing separating them.

He threw his head back as the pleasure overtook him and he uttered mindlessly, "Ah, there's a good lass." Only she lifted his hard-fought suppression of his Scottish brogue. He'd worked with great difficulty to make his accent more American, especially as it changed over the years and as he traveled from place to place. Now, in one passionate moment, she wiped all his work away.

His fangs ached with the need to sink them into her neck and his hand was inches from undoing his jeans and ripping her own flimsy shorts from her body when she pulled free from his arm and crab-crawled away from him. Her breathing was heavy and he could sense her sexual need, but she held up a hand and created an invisible barrier between them. He rubbed a frustrated hand over his aching groin.

"You need to go, Campbell. My father will be back in a moment."

"Your father? How is that possible? I thought he was dead?"

She dropped her gaze to her lap. "It's complicated, and Lisada's plotting is at the heart of it all."

At his growl, she looked up at him as he stood. "Then help me defeat her once and for all." He began to pace, never breaking her gaze. "She expects me to bring you back to her or she'll make my sisters zombie slaves."

"Then it's true. You're working with her. You'd hand me over to her?"

He slammed his fist on the floor, causing a long, jagged crack to snake its way across the concrete. "Over my eternally dead body."

Mia stood slowly. "But what can we possibly do? She's so powerful."

"She fears you."

Surprise widened her eyes. "Me? Why would she be afraid of me?"

He nodded to the invisible barrier in front of him. "I'm not sure any of us know everything you're capable of, and it was clear she was surprised by your escape, maybe even a little fearful she wouldn't be able to control you...or me. I think that's why she sent me and then set off the alarms."

"I'm still not going anywhere. My father told me to stay here, and that's what I plan to do."

Grim acceptance thinned his lips. "Fine. Then, I'll stay here with you. I'm not leaving your side until I know you're safe."

"I'm safe. Okay? If you want to make me safer, go and do whatever it was you could do to break our bond."

"Is that what you want?"

She turned her head and looked to the left. "Yes. It's what I want you to do." Determination shined in her eyes as she met his gaze again. "I don't want to be dependent on you anymore. I don't want to be dependent on anyone ever again."

He had to admit her words hit him harder than he'd expected. Despite the unrealistic feasibility of being her only source of nourishment, he didn't mind the feel of her bite. For the first time in a long time, he felt like so much more than a monster because he could do something good for another person. But she made it clear that the feeling wasn't mutual, and he couldn't blame her. Trust was a major issue in her life, and right now, she couldn't, maybe shouldn't, trust him.

They both stood up straight as the alarm suddenly stopped. Something didn't feel right.

He tensed and turned to stand in front of Mia as the door swung wide. To his surprise, his commander, Riley Spencer, stood in the frame of the door.

"Reid." His first hint that Spencer wasn't happy with him was the way he growled Campbell's last name. The second came as Campbell was shoved up against the concrete wall. "What did you do to my daughter?"

Fortunately for Campbell, he didn't need to breathe, but it was clear Spencer would happily crush Campbell's windpipe to prove how displeased he really was.

"Father, let him go. Please!" Mia was at his arm, pulling and pleading. With little effort, she pulled Spencer off of Campbell and shoved him into the opposite wall, where he crashed to the floor. Her strength was like nothing Campbell had ever seen. No way was Campbell letting her get anywhere near Lisada's Absolute Glass.

Campbell rested his hand at his neck and stared between his commander and Mia. "He's your father? But, how is that possible?" For some reason, this question kept coming back.

"He...he left to protect me from Lisada, but when I participated in the research study at the lab on campus, the spell protections dissipated, leaving me vulnerable."

Spencer stared at Campbell. "I trusted *you* to keep her safe. Instead, you put her in more danger, leading her right to Lisada."

Campbell clenched his jaw. "That was never my intention, no matter what she led Mia to believe. And why the hell didn't you protect her yourself?"

"Lisada tracked me no matter where I went. I couldn't shake her."

"You could've at least told me she was your daughter."

Riley ran a rough hand through his hair. "Trust me, I wanted to, but I wasn't sure who I could trust with that information. Lisada seemed to be aware of everything the Supernatural Council discussed. I assumed she had people on the inside. It was best to give you as little compromising information as possible. But I sure as hell didn't think you'd run right to Lisada. Thought your hatred for her was solid enough to make you want to crush her into oblivion."

"You thought right then. Don't hate anyone more than that witch."

"Why, for the love of all that's supernatural, did you lead her back to Mia then?"

"Again, not my intention. Lisada made it clear Mia was starving and could only feed from me. I couldn't let her die."

Spencer stood and started across the room. "Well, you don't have to worry about that now because I'll work tirelessly until I find a way to break the connection."

Campbell met him in the middle until they stood nose-to-nose. "No need to worry. I know what to do, and I'm on it already. But I'm not doing it for you. It's for Mia."

"Don't get any more ideas, loverboy. You're coming with me. I've got a special place for you on the other side of the compound." He pointed at Mia. "Whatever set off the alarms is gone, but you need to stay here. I'll have guards posted at the door. If you need anything, just ask one of them, and they'll get the message to me."

"I can't stay in this little room forever."

Spencer steered Campbell toward the door. "It won't be forever. Just give me a little more time to set up your transportation to a Supernatural Council safe facility. Lisada wouldn't dare come after you there."

"Ugh! Why can't I just go back to my old life?"

Campbell looked over his shoulder and felt his gut clench at her forsaken look. "Your life will never be like it was, but you can always create a new purpose for your existence—something that makes a difference in the world." He held her gaze until he exited the room in front of Spencer.

Not known for his optimism, Campbell's words resulted in a raised eyebrow by his commander as he closed the door behind them. "Since when are you the vampire guru?"

Two guards Campbell recognized stood outside the door, one on either side. They nodded as Spencer and Campbell passed between them. Chris Devlin and Simon Lopez were men who'd been with the Supernatural Council's Elite Force almost as long as Campbell's one hundred years. But right now he didn't like the idea of leaving them to guard Mia...not when it should be him.

He ignored his insistent need to stay rooted by her side and walked on, answering Spencer's question, "Since I met Mia and felt connected to another being for the first time since the loss of my family."

"Yeah, about that. You have to walk away from her. It's not healthy for her to rely on you to live."

Campbell nodded. "I'll walk away as long as you recognize you have a traitor in your guard."

Spencer sighed heavily. "I know I do, but I don't know who it is. The only one I trusted was you, and now I even have to question my judgment on that."

"You know you have my loyalty always."

They turned a corner and continued down a long hallway where

Spencer's entourage with Kerenth at point waited by the elevator for them. The commander lowered his voice and said, "That's why I have a job only you can do."

Campbell stopped, standing still in the hallway, and Spencer turned to look at him. He lowered his voice and explained, "I still need you to watch over Mia, but I need the traitor to believe you're nowhere near her."

Something about the plan didn't feel right to Campbell. "You're going to use her as bait?"

"I don't like it either, but Lisada's not going to stop, and until I know who among my guard is working with her, she'll never be safe. I need to draw him out."

"So, what do you need me for?"

"I'm going to lock you into your room just as everyone expects, but we both know that won't hold you. Get back to her side and hang back enough to give the traitor room to think he can grab her. Be close enough to stop him." In a low growl he added, "But keep your damn hands off of her."

Campbell clenched his jaw and started walking again. He wasn't going to make promises he knew he couldn't keep. Avoiding the command altogether, he said, "Let's go then. I don't want to leave her vulnerable for long."

Spencer gave a humorless chuckle as he rubbed at his lower back, reminding Campbell of the way she flung him across the room like she was swatting a fly. "She's a lot of things. Vulnerable isn't one of them."

Chapter 21

Mia woke, hands protecting her neck. Nightmare, again. A frightening visage of Campbell, again. A look at the clock showed the time as 2:34 again. It was becoming a routine way for her to wake. The only difference now was that her body had adjusted to sleeping during the day, and she didn't have to look out the window to realize the sun was high in the sky.

The minute he cleared his throat, she knew it was Campbell. "How'd you get in here?"

"It really wasn't that difficult. Kind of lax security, if you ask me."

Mia sat up and swung her legs over the side of the bed just as Campbell sat down beside her. "You shouldn't be here."

He moved a stray piece of hair out of her eyes, and she couldn't help leaning into his hand.

"Probably not, but I couldn't stay away. Seems I'm as hooked on you as you are on me."

"That's not funny. Turns out, I can't sink my fangs into anyone else but you."

Campbell stared at her mouth with shining, green eyes. She ran her tongue over her lips self-consciously, and his gaze narrowed. "What if I told you, no other source but your blood satisfies my cravings?" He leaned in and nuzzled the pulse at her neck, causing a tingling sensation to run down her spine and warm up all the right places.

She tipped her head ever so slightly to give him better access. "I'd say you're lying."

The feel of his lips and tongue sliding over the small heartbeat growing quicker with every whispered touch. His hand slid up her back and pulled her closer. She knew she was getting into dangerous territory with him but couldn't seem to make herself pull away. *Why couldn't she resist him?* There was still a chance he'd betrayed her. Shouldn't her body be on board with what her mind questioned?

Ha! Like her heart was? Maybe she was ten times the fool, but she knew what the connection between them really meant. Her bond with him went way beyond mere attraction or even affection. It was so clear to her as she relished the feel of his hands on her, of being encircled in his arms, of being cherished by his kisses. *She was in love with him.* And it hurt because, it was obvious, in no way did he feel the same. She knew he felt something for her, but she'd bet her new set of fangs his feelings hovered closer to lust than love. Such a horrible realization that she might be in love with her own downfall, but even that wasn't enough to dampen the intense feelings raging like a violent fire deep inside, completely out of her control.

Against the skin of her collarbone, he rumbled, "Won't drink from you because no artificial spell or talisman would ever be able to break my bond to you once I do. Would stay bonded to you until the day I starved to death." He cupped the back of her head and met her gaze with his oh, so serious one. "One taste of your blood was enough to make that clear. We would be perfect mates."

An electrical current bounced between them and the air around them thickened, but Mia was the first to blink. "I...I don't think that's possible for us."

A momentary sadness coated his features, but he nodded in resignation. "I'll respect that." His focus was back on her mouth. "But for tonight, I need to feel that connection one last time."

Her whisper was soft, but the sentiment was strong. "Me too. Make me feel good once more, Campbell."

Mia stroked her hands slowly over his chest, felt the hardened nubs under his t-shirt and explored the chiseled planes, so much more meaning in her touch than ever before. Love was new to her, but it was clear it changed everything.

Campbell made quick work of her nightshirt. Once again, she'd chosen to go braless, and once again she was thankful. His hungry gaze landed on her puckered nipples and a groan slipped free from his lips.

"Beautiful." His voice ground out reverently as he ducked his head and slipped a nipple into his mouth.

Her head dropped back on her shoulders as the sensation of his tongue swirling over her sensitive nerves overwhelmed her. He pulled free and moved to the other side, giving equal greedy attention.

His hands lowered and he broke long enough to remove his own shirt before continuing to worship her body with his kisses, moving to her collarbone and up the column of her neck. With the way he seemed to cherish each touch of his lips to her skin, she could almost imagine he loved her, and it nearly broke her heart in two. She didn't want to think about that though. If the connection really could be broken, this could be the last time they were together, and Mia needed to feel the strength of that connection one last time.

Her hands clutched his head, tugging him up to her lips as he laid them down onto the bed. They made quick work of the clothing they still wore and tangled their limbs together in a wild, possessive embrace. Pulling her hips toward him, he thrust deep and she saw his struggle in the clench of his jaw. He was on edge, and she was right there with him, feeling desperate for release with each stroke.

"More!" Mindless, her nails curled into his ass, urging him on the only way she knew how.

His fangs descended in response and deep inside, Mia's stimulus-response took over. She wanted his mouth on her. She laid her neck open to his bite and felt a desperate desire to feel him pierce her skin. "Come and get it, Campbell."

"Canna do it."

She knew he was losing control, even as she felt the stirrings of her own climax rolling closer with each push of his hips. His speech pattern regressing back to the Scottish brogue of his youth was a sure sign he was close too.

Her desperation was building. "I need to feel your bite."

"Aaahh!" He raised up on his arms and threw his head back. "The bond talking."

"So close."

He lowered his head until their gazes locked and reached between them, pressing his thumb to the sensitive nub that would push her over the precipice. He brushed his thumb back and forth. "Come on, lass. Let go."

Every nerve fused at her core until the tension broke and she cried out with the most intense orgasm she'd ever experienced. With her pelvic muscles squeezing tightly, she gyrated her hips and rode the wave even higher, feeling him swell inside her. With erratic thrusts and a strained, "Mia," Campbell followed her with his own release, and they finished together, breathless and spent. Their heavy breathing filled the silence, and Mia thought about the guards posted just outside her door.

"Do you think anyone heard us?"

"Possible. Can't quite care right now."

She punched him in the shoulder. "It's my reputation on the line."

"True. Good point, but technically you're alone. So, probably will just result in a few perverted looks next time you catch a guard's eye."

"Ugh! Not helping, Campbell."

He chuckled and rolled to his back, pulling her tightly to his side. "You're so easy to tease. Truth be told, if they'd heard your moans and screams of pleasure, they'd probably be in here right now thinking you might be in trouble."

"Of pleasure, huh? Think pretty highly of yourself, don't you?"

He lay in silence a few extra heartbeats before answering, "Not for a long time, but I certainly feel different...better...when I'm with you."

She knew his thoughts had turned to his family, and her heart squeezed at the sadness she felt rolling off him. "You've suffered so much."

A glance at him and she watched his jaw muscles work as he remembered the past. "No, I caused my suffering, over and over. Don't make me out to be the martyr."

"Lisada took everything from you."

He slid his gaze sideways until he met hers in the dark. "Make no mistake. I am as much to blame for the loss of my family as she is. I've learned to push the guilt way, way down, just to function, but I'll never forget finding my parent's beaten and bloodied bodies, where she'd set her other vampires on them."

"That must have been horrible."

"Worse still? The smell of their blood, made my fucking fangs descend, as if I could feed from those I cared the most about." His gaze was devastating in that moment. The past seemed agonizing for him to remember, and she had to wonder what he was holding back from her. What wasn't he revealing?

She didn't dare break his stare in that moment. "Instinct of a vampire. I understand that now."

"I swore I'd never feed from someone I cared about...ever." His message was clear. He cared about her, and she reveled in the tentative tingles running around inside her mid-section. He glanced away for just a second before looking at her again with a glint of steel in his ice-green eyes. "That night, I buried their broken bodies and thought things would never be right again."

"I can only imagine."

A sad smile lifted one corner of his mouth. "Then I met you."

"Yeah, I changed everything for you. Not buying it, Campbell." The sarcasm in her voice expressed her continued struggle with doubt and even hurt. He'd lost what little trust he'd managed to gain with her, but a small part of her wanted to believe him, wanted his words to be more than a way to get her back to Lisada with him. She wanted him to love her the way she loved him.

"But it's true. Don't expect you to believe me now, and I'll make sure our bond is broken, as you wish, but I can't let you think otherwise for the rest of your life. I haven't felt anything for another being for hundreds of years. Until you."

She turned away as her heart ached with a need to believe his words. Yet, so much of her life she'd been told one thing and now she was finding out things were so different in actuality. She had to harden herself against the vulnerability she was feeling, especially when it came to her feelings about Campbell. He was her ultimate weakness. He could break her heart completely if she let him in. "You're right. I don't believe you." *She couldn't believe him.* She faced him again. "I think you should go."

"Can't. Been asked to look after you."

"By whom?"

"Your father."

She laughed and crossed her arms. "Doubt it."

"It's true. Someone in his guard is a traitor and working with Lisada. He knows it's true, but he doesn't know who it is." She cocked her head and opened her mouth to say something, but he held up a hand and stopped her, "Not me, before you even suggest it."

"Well, what are you going to do? Hang around here all day and night until someone makes a move? They won't if they know you're here."

He acknowledged her words with a nod. "Which is why your father made such a big deal out of locking me away." With his hand, he rubbed his stubbled cheek and shrugged. "At sundown, I have to meet a being about a talisman to sever this thing between us. Other than that, I plan to be right here day and night until the threat to your existence passes."

Her chest felt like it was caving-in with the thought of no longer being linked to him, but it was what she wanted. No, she couldn't lie to herself. It wasn't what she wanted, but it was clearly what was best for both of them. Didn't lessen the ache of her heart, and she nicked her tongue with her own fang to keep from begging him to wait just a little longer. It wouldn't help either of them to drag their relationship out.

"Do you need to feed?"

She did, but she refused to do that to herself again. The moment her fangs sank inside him, she thought of nothing else but their hot, sweaty bodies connecting and writhing toward an explosive release. Her heart couldn't take much more of that.

She shook her head. "Not hungry."

"Let me know if you change your mind. I'll be close."

"I won't change my mind." She didn't know exactly who she was trying to convince, but she knew one thing to be true. If anyone was likely to crack, it wasn't going to be Campbell.

* * *

Campbell gripped the crystal amulet, fingering the gold inlay framework and small ruby jewel in the center. He drove up the long driveway to the compound. He figured he was back on Spencer's good side since there'd been no guards to give him any trouble, which gave him a slight twinge of concern. *Where was everyone?* Maybe they were in the middle of a shift change.

Yet, as he approached the main building where Mia waited to be set free of their bond, he felt good about accomplishing what he'd set out to do. Though witches weren't top of his list lately, one sorceress in particular could always be trusted, and just as he'd thought, she'd had a solution. He'd thanked her with ten bags of sour gummy worms, which he knew just happened to be her favorite, and a plane ticket to Wales to help her in her quest to find her mother.

The talisman in his hand contained a drop of his blood, and once Mia's was added, he'd pour the contents of the small vile in his pocket into the hollow vessel inside the amulet. As the final step, they'd each take a sip of the mixture. This process would make him forget the taste of her blood and should do the same for her. Once all was done, he'd wear the talisman around his neck for all eternity, and she'd be free to drink from any source she desired.

Nevermind the fact that just the thought of her drinking from anyone else made him want to slam the amulet into the dirt and ground it under his boot until it was useless. *Dammit!* But he was doing this for her. At this point, he just wanted to free her and let Spencer take her to a secure place where Lisada couldn't hurt her...and neither could he.

Didn't help that his thirst was starting to affect his mental state. If he didn't drink soon, he'd be crazed with bloodlust and would probably attack her despite his good intentions. He'd sooner dive into a pool of liquid silver than hurt her in any way, but his instinct to feed was becoming near to impossible to ignore.

A wave of anxiety rolled over him again, and he worked hard to suppress it. A quick glance at the dashboard clock showed the time was two in the morning. He hadn't meant to leave her alone for hours, but at least he'd let his commander know his mission before he'd gone. He'd made sure she was protected. Then why the hell did he suddenly feel he needed to get to her right the fuck now?

He pushed the accelerator down harder and felt the tires spin on the gravel a touch as they pulled him closer to the looming building in front of him. With a sense of urgency riding him, he stopped in the gravel drive and flung the car door wide, not bothering to close it as he ran toward the front door. *What the…?* The guards posted at the front door were on the ground, unconscious but alive. His heart thudded, picking up speed as he took in the scene in front of him. Clearly, something wasn't right.

An electrical current sparked in the air. Whatever had knocked them out had happened recently, which meant Mia could still be secure in her room, and Campbell needed to get to her now.

He rushed through the front door and felt the prickle of power all around him. A thick mist hung in the air, and he could feel it seeping into his skin and lungs. Lisada was here, and she was pissed and ready for a fight. Everywhere he turned, the entire legion of soldiers lay on the ground, out for the count. If he'd been here, would he be flat on his ass right now too? Leaving Mia vulnerable to attack?

Even now, he felt an urgency to get her out of here and to the one place a witch couldn't go, at least according to the source of the talisman. Linnetha was a long-standing member of the Elite Guard for the Supernatural Council and one of the smartest people he knew. If she said he could keep Mia safe in a local cemetery, that's where he'd take her. Then for fuck's sake, he'd blow Lisada off the face of this dimension and all others within paranormal-gate-jumping distance.

The further he walked, the more he felt the effects of the fog around him. *Shit!* The vapor began to float inside his brain, and he could feel himself slipping into delusion as he began to see shadows all around him. His thirst grew, and he could sense Mia's closeness. The temptation to sink his fangs into her skin was growing unbearable, but he fought to resist. Time seemed to slow down as he worked hard to clear his brain. Lisada's ability to get her claws inside a person's mind was her greatest weapon, and she used it well. She'd used her skill to manipulate and control Campbell once, he refused to let her do it again.

With the goal of getting to Mia as quickly as possible, he misted and felt the effects of Lisada's magic lessen immediately. He slipped through the halls and observed the unconscious bodies of the guards. They were strewn in awkward positions, like they'd dropped where they stood, almost immediately. Nobody had seen Lisada coming, except her co-conspirator. Campbell needed to learn who the hell the traitor was sooner rather than later in order to protect Mia long-term.

As Campbell slid closer to Mia's room, he noted a complete lack of guards. Clearly he was walking into a trap, but he didn't have any other choice if he wanted to get to Mia. He'd have to anticipate Lisada's next move. Easier said than done.

He eased into the ventilation system and worked his way to her room. With restraint he didn't know he had, he observed the room before rushing in to Mia. She lay unconscious on her bed. No one else appeared to be in the room, but he knew all too well that the scene below was a fucking set-up. Something didn't feel right.

A quick glance at the clock showed he'd taken almost a half an hour to get to her room. He must have been under Lisada's spell longer than he realized. Why did he feel like he was following a well-plotted plan? Probably because he was.

With as little commotion as he could make, he slipped into her room and took on his human form again. He approached the bed, glancing at the glowing numbers of the clock—2:33. He had enough time to get her to the cemetery and into the tomb where Linnetha assured him Mia would be safe. He bent to scoop her body from the bed but stopped at the sound of the low laugh behind him. *Lisada!*

"I knew you couldn't resist coming to her rescue."

Campbell swiveled, fangs descending, ready for the coming fight. "And I knew you had to be the cause of this chaos."

"Chaos? Or revolution?" She stepped toward him, her eyes glowing. His muscles tensed to defend. "Think about it, Campbell. The Supernatural Council would be powerless to stop us from reaching our destiny. Humans would be the ones running and hiding instead of the most powerful creatures on the planet. We...would be gods!"

"At what cost? The Supernatural Council was put in place for a reason. Without them, not only human existence is threatened. All life would be endangered without the order the Council brings. If you go around killing indiscriminately, you better be ready for the shit-storm coming back at you."

Her smile spoke of things he apparently didn't know, and he could tell she was ready to enlighten him. "None of the things I've done have been indiscriminant. From you, from Riley and Desside, to getting that fool college professor Tipton to find her and keep Mia coming back to the research facility until the effects of my sister's spells wore off completely. Everything has been part of the plan. They've all been upon orders from my Master. He's thought out every possibility, and he can't be defeated." Her strides were long and smooth as she approached him. He growled when she dared reach a hand toward him. "I had such high hopes for you. I told him you'd come to our side eventually. I so hate being wrong." *Who the hell was she even talking about? Her Master? As in, head-boss in charge?*

He was about to demand she explain who was orchestrating everything when she turned and looked at the opposite side of the room. On cue, the outer door opened, and Campbell felt his heart drop at the sight before him. "No."

Three creatures with the palest of skin and long, stringy black hair stared at him from familiar faces. Two damning puncture wounds, the cause of their demise, remained on each of their necks. Lisada had brought his sisters back from the dead, but as revenant slaves.

Campbell went to his knees and cried out in frustration and anger. "Why couldn't you let them be?" All the guilt and sadness rushed back over him at the sight of the worst thing he'd ever done.

"I thought you'd be happy to see them alive again. After all, you are the reason they were dead in the first place."

His head snapped up. "Because of you, you heartless bitch. You made me believe they were enemies and a threat to you. I didn't see them for what they were until it was too late."

"Such is life. We never know what we've got until we've completely drained every last drop of blood from it." With the ease of hopping over a puddle in the rain, Lisada leaped into the air and landed on the bed behind him. Campbell stood and lunged for her, but she only laughed and rose out of his reach. "You'll have to try harder than that. Or are you too weak? You haven't had a drink in a while, have you? Doesn't she look delicious, Campbell?"

Damn him! She did look beautiful laying on the bed, vulnerable, her head turned so her neck was bared to his aching fangs. He could just take a sip. That way he'd gain enough strength to face and defeat Lisada. It wouldn't take much. He inched toward the bed, lowering himself to her side.

He paused. Something about this didn't feel right. There was a reason he hadn't drunk from her again after she'd healed him. Something about her blood was off-limits, but he struggled to remember what the exact problem was.

"Here. Let me help you decide." She reached down with her nail and ran the sharp point across Mia's neck where a thin, red line appeared. The sweet, sugary aroma hit his nose, and he felt the lapse in logic that took hold of him. He switched to pure instinct as he leaned closer to that tempting nectar at her neck. Just a little would give him the strength to take on Lisada.

Just as he felt his fangs elongate, and he inched closer, Mia's eyes opened and she scrambled backward, away from him. "Campbell? What are you doing?"

Lisada sprang into action, knocking Campbell across the room with a backhand. "Get away from her!"

Campbell shook his pounding head to clear it. What was going on? He didn't feel in control of his own body and mind. Only one other time in his life, he'd been this disoriented and when he woke, he'd drained his own sisters to death. Lisada had been in control of his mind, but he'd let her in then. He never would again.

"Oh, my dear, you were nearly attacked. But don't worry. I won't let him hurt you," Lisada practically purred.

Mia turned her gaze and focused on Lisada. Confusion shined in her eyes. "Campbell wouldn't hurt me."

Lisada swung her hand out and pointed across the room. "No? Look what he did to his own sisters."

With a slow perusal, Mia swiveled her head to stare at the three, strange creatures creepily standing in a loose triangle across the room. Lisada hadn't planned to create slaves of his sisters. She wanted to use them to scare Mia.

Campbell pushed to his knees. "Mia, you can't believe a word she says."

Lisada stretched closer to Mia. "Think about it. Who was ready to sink his fangs into you when you woke? Look at those poor girls' necks. They trusted him to keep them safe, and he killed them instead." She lowered her voice. "Did he ask you to trust him?"

Mia leaped from the bed, and Campbell sighed in relief that she was away from Lisada, but then she did the exact opposite of what he needed her to do. She edged around his sisters and made her way toward the door.

"Mia! Wait!" But she was gone before he could rise to his feet. He was so very weak, and he was sure Lisada made him weaker somehow.

"Campbell, go after her."

He took a threatening step toward Lisada. She gathered energy in her hands, reminding him he wasn't strong enough to take her on in a fight. His pride demanded he do it anyway, but he was more concerned about keeping Mia safe. Everything inside him resisted following Lisada's command, but he couldn't let Mia go out there without him. She'd be vulnerable, and Lisada would have guards ready to snatch her the minute she stepped outside.

He moved in the direction of the door and paused just a moment to look at his sisters in such a dire existence. He needed to find a way to give them peace, but it would have to wait until Mia was safe and Lisada was no longer a threat to the whole fucking world.

Chapter 22

He was coming for her. This wasn't a nightmare. This was actually happening. Campbell was coming after her to sink his fangs deep into her neck, and it would be the end of her. He'd said it himself. He would drink her until she was drained. She had to run. She had to escape from him, from this place.

She sprinted down the hall and to the stairwell. After two flights, she didn't even bother running down them anymore, instead leaping over the ledge and falling to the bottom. She landed in a crouch, completely unharmed, and looked up stunned. She really needed to remember she was a freaking supernatural being now and could do things she'd never done before. Could she turn around and take Campbell on? Too risky. As much as she knew what she was capable of, she didn't know how to control those powers. She just needed to get out of here and away from him.

At the sound of a stairwell door opening high above her, she booked it in the direction of the exit. She still had to pass the lobby area, and surely Lisada would have guards there ready to take her prisoner. She'd been working on creating the shield at will and had had some luck with it, but she still wasn't completely confident she could produce the protective barrier on cue. No time like the present to give it a sloppy-wet, dry run.

Mia eased the stairwell door open and edged into the darkened hallway that led to the lobby. Bodies of guards lay littered throughout the scene, but it was clear they were still alive. The creepy feeling that they would all open their eyes and come after her sent chills up and down her spine. Yet, she had to move past them to get out the door.

She hugged the wall as she stepped quietly forward. An unusual silence engulfed the facility, and it made her more cautious to be ready for an attack. But the sound of something loud crashing down the stairwell pushed all her good intentions way out of sight. She rushed the front door, looking right and left, expecting someone to come at her from the dark, but no one moved an inch. It was downright freaky, and she paused for just a moment with her hand on the handle of the door to the outside. What if she was following the exact path Lisada wanted her to? It did seem a little too easy of an escape.

The door to the stairwell crashed open and Campbell stood in the doorway, breathing heavily. "Mia!" His tone sounded furious and pleading all in one, and she couldn't decide if he posed a great enough threat to push her to run outside the door into the unknown. He hadn't exactly hurt her yet. Instead, he'd done the opposite all the time she'd known him. He'd made her feel amazing and accomplished. The combustion of the two of them together was impossible to forget. It made more sense to trust him than Lisada.

At the moment she'd decided to turn around and throw herself into his arms, sure he'd never hurt her, he stepped into the scant red glow of the emergency lights, and she caught a glimpse of the monster from her nightmares. He seemed to have tripled in size, his eyes glowed icy-green—their usual color on steroids—and his fangs looked longer and more menacing than ever.

As he continued slowly toward her, she gave a small squeak and pushed at the door, but it wouldn't budge. She couldn't take her eyes off of him as he stalked forward, getting closer.

"Doona dare go out that door, Mia."

His accent was slipping. He was losing control.

He sped up his steps, and she knew he'd be on her any moment. She slammed her hands over-and-over into the door, banging on it harder as she felt it give some. For just a moment, she dared take her gaze off Campbell and saw through the glass that the unconscious body of one of the guards blocked the door from opening.

A quick glance behind her showed Campbell almost upon her. She cried out defiantly in frustration and held her hands up in front of her. The glass shattered around her, but she didn't waste time mulling over this newest of powers. She jumped through the makeshift opening, over the unconscious guard, and flung herself into the night.

The smell of blood surrounded her, but she ran on, trying to put distance between Campbell and herself. Her speed was incredible, and the world was a blur as she dashed across the expanse of grass between the building and the outer gate. No way would Campbell be able to catch up to her now.

But just as she sucked in the air for a sigh of relief, she felt her feet fall out from under her, and she hit the ground, face-first. As she lay stunned, she felt a clawed hand grip her ankle, and she felt warm blood flowing from her nose and mouth.

"Never doubt. You are mine." She didn't recognize his voice, and as she looked back at him, she didn't recognize the look in his cold, green eyes. Now. Now would be the time to use her powers, but no energy built and she couldn't seem to get a grip on the pinging alarm going off inside her head.

His grip accommodated as she flipped over and swiped the mud and hair out of her face. "Please, Campbell. You said it yourself. It's best if we aren't tied to each other. Let me go."

"Never!"

"No other choice—kill me now. I'd rather die than be a slave to your blood for the rest of my life."

He pulled her toward him, hand-over-hand, until she sat at his feet and stared up at him defiance in every fiber of her being. He met her gaze, confusion slowing his movements.

"Doona want to kill you. Want to save you."

She leaned closer to him, pleading in every word as she said, "Then you have to let me go. That's the only way to save me."

"Canna! Willna! Will make you mine forever." He shifted over her, fangs descending, his focus on the racing pulse she felt in her neck.

With a strangled cry, she threw her hands up in front of her neck to protect herself, just like her nightmare, but she wasn't covering her neck to keep him from biting her. She was trying to generate an invisible shield to push him back. And likely scenario, nothing...abso-freaking nothing...happened.

Except, Campbell stopped. The look of confusion overtook him again, and Mia realized he was fighting inside his own mind. When he cried out and shook his head back and forth, she understood, it wasn't confusion in his eyes. It was pain.

For a heartbeat, their gazes met, and she dropped her defenses, reaching a hand toward him instead and stroking his cheek. His eyes slid shut, and he leaned into her touch. *He didn't want to hurt her.* He was holding back. She read it in the edgy way his muscles ticked under his skin.

His eyes flew open as he reached out a finger and swiped the blood from her face. Then he jerked backward, leaping into the air, feet away from her. He pulled a couple objects from his pockets, and she watched, baffled.

With deft movements, he added her blood to a small container, along with the contents of a tiny vile. He thrust the container toward her, and she recognized it as a round, metal flask on a long, leather string. "Drink this! Now! Before I change my mind."

"What is it?"

A muscle in his jaw worked visually as he ground his teeth together. "What you asked for. This will end your need for my blood. Drink it!"

She sucked in a breath. From the moment she'd known she was essentially addicted to Campbell, this is what she'd wanted, but suddenly the idea of no longer having a need for him made her chest feel hollow and her heart sink. But she really didn't want to be tied to Campbell for the rest of her days, did she? She couldn't live like that for all of eternity. He would inevitably resent her, and she refused to be a burden to anyone.

Without another thought, she reached out her hand to take the small container, but before she could even get a finger on it, it flew from his hand, landing a few feet away from them. They both turned to see Lisada closing in on them, magic sparking red from her fingertips, her shock-white hair snaking out in blowing tendrils.

"Now, why do you want to go and ruin my fun? No breaking the bond just yet. Not until my plan is complete."

"If you're plan was to be a total bitch, mission accomplished." Campbell's words earned him a scathing look from the powerful witch.

Yet, as legions of guards surrounded them, she smiled, triumph in her eyes. "How droll, Campbell. Always the smartass to the end, eh?" She turned toward one guard in particular and commanded, "Kill all inside. No survivors."

"No!" Mia thought of her father. She'd just found him. She couldn't lose him all over again.

"Don't worry, my dear. In just a little while, you will join them."

Mia felt her strange, new powers beginning to build inside her. Like a pot churning to a boil, she could feel energy rising from deep inside. If she had to, she'd blow them all to tiny pieces to save her father, Campbell, and herself. She raised her hands, ready to shove a shockwave in the direction of Lisada, and the energy began to flow. Yet, before the tingle in her hands fully manifested into the deadly power she could generate, she was hit from behind. She heard Campbell curse Lisada, and she dropped to the ground as her world went black.

Chapter 23

Campbell woke thirstier than he'd ever been. He tried to run his tongue over his dry lips, but he was having trouble making the effort because he was so weak. Certain he must lie abandoned in the middle of a sun-soaked desert, he was sure he was on his way to a true death. His only regret was not protecting Mia better. He should have anticipated Lisada's manipulation all along. From the beginning, she'd been working the game board to get the pieces in just the right positions for the win. *Damn!* He hated being someone else's pawn, and he especially hated being used in the same way twice.

He pried his eyes open with great effort, but shut them almost immediately. The brightness of the room made pain shoot hard behind his eyes. He was in bad shape and struggling to find motivation to even try at this point. Lisada was going to be damn hard to defeat, and though he wouldn't ever give in completely, he was having a hard time moving any part of his body.

And then the sweet, sugary smell hit his nostrils, and his eyes popped open with recognition. His fangs descended and throbbed with the need to sink deep inside her and drain every last drop from her body.

With effort, he rolled to his side and braced himself with his hands, trying to ready himself to balance on his hands and knees. After accomplishing that much, he used his strength of will to push up to a kneeling position and turned his head until she came into focus. Her body lay at an awkward angle against the wall to his right. Clearly, she was still knocked-out. Seeing they were in a room as small as a supply closet, he was only a couple feet away from her. He could be over there, incisors sunk deep in her neck, eyes rolling back in his head as the spicy warmth of her blood slid down his throat before she could take another shaky breath.

"Dammit, Lisada! Get out of my fucking head!"

A loud click sounded above him, and a thin, but familiar, voice came through a speaker in the ceiling, "Campbell, we both know you don't have the willpower to resist taking what you want for very long."

"Fuck you!"

"Oh, you did, but that's old news. Hundreds of years ago and not even worth thinking about. And yet, you were talented with a woman's body, as I recall. It's too bad, really that you're not important to my Master's ultimate plan. I might like keeping you around as a pet."

"I'd eat my own hands before I touched you ever again." He took a deep, rattling breath. As weak as he was, he needed to keep her talking. She had a tendency to have too much pride in her own actions to keep her intentions to herself. She liked to brag, and that's what he needed her to do. "Who the hell is this fucking-idiot you keep calling Master? I don't give a damn about that son of a bitch's ultimate plan. Do what's good for you and let us go before I have to dig a deep pit to Hell to drop both your ugly asses into for eternity."

She laughed like he'd just relayed a well-executed punchline. "Really, Campbell. My Master would find that quite humorous seeing as he finds Hell a rather pleasant place to be. Now, stop messing around and drink her to the marrow." Her voice dropped to an ominous octave, "You know you want to."

Damn, he really did! His heart pounded heavily, and he clenched his fists to keep from reaching for her. His muscles twitched uncontrollably, but somehow he fought the urge to give in to Lisada's manipulation. He glared at the ceiling, sure she had a camera somewhere up there, watching her game unfold. "You lose, witch."

"Oh, Campbell, I can't lose. I hold all the pieces." He heard some rustling before she continued, "Give him another hour. He'll cave once his stomach twists and turns with a hunger so hard he'll think he's swallowed volcanic ash."

He heard the click of the speaker turning off and felt the immediate danger of being alone with his greatest temptation. He didn't want Lisada to be right, but he really couldn't guarantee that in an hour, he'd still be holding out and doing the right thing by Mia. With the sight of her long, beautiful legs, smooth pale skin, and the smell of her delicious vanilla and lavender scent, odds were, he wouldn't even last ten more minutes.

* * *

Mia woke, the sound of a low growl was too close. Every muscle and sinew ached, and she felt the oppression of fear. Her head pounded. It took three attempts to open her eyes fully and raise her head to see where the animal noise was coming from. The sight that greeted her was the stuff of nightmares...literally...her nightmares. Campbell sat crouched, ready to spring, eyes glowing that eerie ice-green, fangs bared. She got the feeling he didn't really see *her* in that moment. She felt like the weakest prey to his high-level predator.

"Campbell? It's me. You know, Mia." She scrambled into the corner, away from him, but it didn't put more than three feet distance between them. He definitely wasn't himself.

He didn't seem to be aware, like he'd dissociated, and in this moment, he was more monster than human. With slow, measured movements, he began to close the distance between them, reminding her of a sleek, jungle cat in hunting mode. She cringed into herself, pushing back against the wall as far as she could, still keeping her gaze locked with his. If he decided to attack, she wasn't sure she could do anything, considering how little control she had over her powers. What good was having supernatural abilities, if you couldn't manifest them when you desperately needed to? The earlier fiasco in the courtyard in front of the building came crashing back and her heart dropped to the pit of her stomach. *Her father.* He could already be dead. She didn't think she'd survive the grief if she had to mourn him a second time.

Surprising her slightly, Campbell paused and watched her, head cocked to the side. He seemed to be assessing her, but for what? Did he sense her desperation? Maybe he no longer saw her as easy prey. It gave her a boost of confidence. She wasn't the type to lay down, bare her throat to make it easier for her attacker, and die without a fight. Even if it was Campbell, even if she didn't want to hurt him, even if she believed she...loved him, in a short minute, she'd lay him out flat, render him defenseless and harmless.

He raised his hands to either side of his head and shook it as if to clear it. She felt the magic pour into her hands, and she sighed in relief. But she didn't attack, instead she held her power in check, waiting to see his next move.

His eyes narrowed and his gaze dropped to her parted lips. *Was he thinking of kissing her?* Why did the thought of licking every inch of his body sound so good at a time like this? Her stomach quivered at the thought, and she suddenly became aware of a charge in the room. Her powers were beginning to envelop the two of them, but she had no idea how she was doing it. With a thought, she pulled them together, until she felt the cool skin of his leg against her own naked thighs. *And that's how it's done.* Her pulse jumped at the contact, and she barely resisted stroking her hand over his chest...and—a devilish grin stretched her mouth—lower.

As she looked him over, concern overtook her and completely quashed her feelings of desire. Sweat dotted his brow and though his eyes had seemed bright just a few minutes before, she realized they'd lost most of their glow, like a battery running out of juice. When he raised a shaking hand to cup her cheek, she recognized the signs of illness in him.

"What's wrong with you, Campbell?"

"Nothing now. So beautiful. So perfect." His eyelids drooped even further, and for a moment, she thought he'd drifted off to sleep. Yet, his thumb continued to stroke the side of her face lovingly.

"When's the last time you ate?"

"Don't know. Doesn't matter."

She gently pried his hand away from her face and cupped his with both of her hands. "It does matter. You need to drink...from me."

He shook his head back and forth slowly. "No. It will weaken you further. I...I won't be able to stop."

"But it will strengthen you. You'll die otherwise."

A lopsided grin lifted a corner of his mouth. "Already dead."

"You know what I mean." She pursed her lips and dropped her hands to her lap. "Feed. Now. No argument."

With quick actions, she lowered her own fangs to her wrist and bit down until blood began to flow. She raised it to hover in front of his mouth, recognition caused his eyes to pop wide as he scrambled backward, hitting the wall of her protective barrier.

"No, Mia. You don't know what you're doing. I won't be able to stop. It's happened before...to those I cared about."

"But you did stop with me last time—when I healed you."

His face crumbled, as if in terrible pain. "I...I still don't know how I managed that. I don't think I could do it again."

She let out a frustrated groan. "And I can't watch you die." Her mind made up, she rose to her knees and pushed her arm against his lips. "Feed now, while you still have some control. Otherwise, you will kill me."

With a loud cry, he turned his mouth away. "You don't understand." He locked his gaze with hers, and she could feel the tension building like dirt being piled on top of them in a hole. "Mia, I killed them."

For just a moment, she was sure he was becoming delusional. His admission didn't seem to have anything to do with the two of them at that time. Yet, she could sense his immense guilt, and so she asked, "Who? Who'd you kill, Campbell?"

The silence in the room was oppressive as he struggled with the words. She saw the moment when he made his decision, and part of her wanted to stop him, just in case what he was about to admit would change the way she looked at him forever. Finally, he spoke, his voice quavering with each word. "My sisters. Lisada was my parents' killer, but she isn't solely to blame. I killed them. Lisada starved me for weeks and dropped me into a locked room with them. She got into my brain. Made them seem like enemies, and I was so weak. She didn't kill them, Mia. I drained every last drop of blood from them. It's my fault. All my fault."

His pain was palpable in the small space. With effort, he held in his emotions, but his clenched jaw told her just how much guilt he was holding onto. Guilt he'd held onto for hundreds of years. No way should he shoulder that level of blame when it was so clear Lisada had been in control of Campbell from the minute she'd brought about his transformation. But Mia knew Lisada wasn't in control of him any longer, and Campbell needed to know that too. She needed him to know she saw the situation differently. She saw *him* differently because he had changed. He was not the same naïve person who'd fallen for Lisada's lies before. Somehow she believed it would matter for him to know this.

"No, Campbell. She wants you to believe that, but she manipulated the situation from the start. Your sisters ultimately died because of Lisada's actions. You were just a playing piece in her game—like me. She literally manipulated my genes to create a being she could then use to become some ultimate paranormal don't-mess-with-me witch-bitch. But you're not her creation anymore, and neither am I. Now, you have to work with me, so we can stop her." She shifted her wrist to his mouth again. "Drink! It's the only way."

He hesitated still, and as hungry as he was, she didn't know how he held out so long. Finally, she felt the tentative touch of his tongue, and the sensation made her moan as the nerve-endings all over her body lit up in pulses that ended at her core. He sunk his fangs into her skin, and she threw her head back as tendrils of desire shot up her spine, pulling the breath from her lungs. With little effort, he pulled her closer until she straddled his lap, and with a lick of his tongue he pulled free from her arm and as she tilted her head to the side, penetrated her neck with a growl. The effects hit immediately as she felt liquid flood her sex and the hardening thickness in his pants.

He sunk his big hands into her hair and held on tightly. Nothing could have stopped her from undulating her hips and riding him hard as he gripped her waist and continued to suck from her neck. He was taking long pulls, and she grew light-headed with sexual need. She rubbed her hands through his hair and over his shoulders, growing desperate as she lowered her exploration and sunk her claws into his back. So turned on, she was right on the brink of coming, but something didn't feel right.

A sudden weakness pervaded her body, and she began to panic. Her arms dropped to her sides, unable to support themselves any longer. No matter how hard she tried, she couldn't even pull even the slightest bit of her powers to the surface. She couldn't believe how quickly things had changed.

"Campbell...stop." She swiped at his body, but had no strength to get his attention. He was locked in, and after a few weak attempts to pull away from him, she realized she was in real danger. He was mindless and would drain her completely in the next few minutes.

She mustered as much energy as she could to raise one arm and yank at his hair, but he only growled and held her tighter. Switching tactics, she began to slap at his face, hating the feeling of helplessness. Yet, she might as well be stroking his cheek for as much attention he paid to her strikes.

Finally, as she felt herself fading, she changed tactics. With no more vitality left, she used her words, which came out slurred and whispered. "Campbell, I love you. Don't blame you. You...are good and decent. Lucky you found me. Love you."

Unexpectedly, he paused, and as if coming back to himself, pulled free of her neck, throwing himself backwards away from her. But as she began to flop to the concrete floor, he scooped her into his arms and cradled her to his chest.

"Ah, Mia, what've I done?"

She reached up a shaky hand and stroked the hair away from his face. "You stopped." Then, everything faded to black.

Chapter 24

He rested his chin on the top of her head and worked to calm his racing heart. He'd nearly drained her, and though that alone wouldn't have killed her outright, it would have weakened her for months, assuming Lisada wouldn't swoop in and use what remained for her world-domination plan.

Actually, she surprised him. She was strangely absent from the scene and hadn't burst into the room, along with her guards, to pry Mia from his arms. Yet, the way he felt in this moment, he'd like to see them try.

Gone, was his weakness. He felt the strength of a thousand suns pumping through his veins. Right now, he wanted them to come at him. Right now, nothing could hold him back.

He glanced at the door on the wall opposite from where he sat. Surely it wouldn't take more than a single slam of his fist to make the steel crumple like aluminum. Time to test this new-found intensity flowing like a rushing river throughout his body.

As gently as he could, he set her to the side and laid her carefully onto the floor. He stood and crossed the short distance to the door. With several, deep breaths, he drew back his fist, but just as he readied to crush the barrier between them and their freedom, he was knocked off his feet by an earth-shattering blast somewhere close by. Dust and debris fell from the ceiling, but nothing more than a smattering of foamy pieces.

"What the…" Once everything calmed down, Campbell glanced over to make sure Mia was still secure. She still lay where he placed her earlier, her breathing shallow but even.

However, he suddenly didn't feel so good. He was sweating and nauseous. His vision blurred then re-focused. Something wasn't right. Something felt very, very wrong.

His lungs began to restrict, and he struggled for each breath. Poisoned. He'd been poisoned. He glanced at Mia again. Had Lisada somehow used Mia's blood to poison him? Now her insistence that he drink from Mia made sense. Once again, she'd manipulated everyone to do exactly as she wanted.

Dammit! He really needed to anticipate Lisada's moves. If he made it through this alive, he vowed he'd never be used by that witch again.

Right on cue, he heard the metal clang of the lock being pulled and the door slowly pulled open. He expected Lisada to step through, a smug smile planted firmly on her ageless face. Yet, he never had to suffer her look because she wasn't the one to come through the door.

Instead, a familiar visage stood before him, one of the last people he ever expected to see—The Goblin King.

Other than his high cheekbones, long straight nose, and two small horns mostly hidden by his dark hair, he looked like no goblin Campbell had ever seen. But the rumors were he was a hybrid. The question was what beautiful species would mate with a goblin to produce such attractive offspring?

Campbell rasped, "What the hell are you doing here?"

The Goblin King stepped into the small space and crouched just out of arm's length from Campbell. "Is that anyway to greet the person here to save you?"

With a shaky hand, Campbell reached a shaky hand up to swipe the sweat from his brow. He stared at the liquid pouring off him. "I think you're too late for me."

"Nah, I'm not that lucky." He reached into his pocket and pulled out a syringe full of liquid.

Campbell balled his fists. "Don't even think about sticking that into me."

"Oh, that's classic. A vampire afraid of needles." He raised the syringe and removed the protective cap. "This is the antidote for that screaming rager going on inside you right now."

"I knew that bitch Lisada poisoned me."

The Goblin King shrugged his shoulders and pursed his lips. "More like forgot to give you all the details. Turns out, a little of Mia's blood would give you god-like powers. All of it, would turn you into an atomic-bomb. You overdosed on the drugging effects of her hybrid vampire and goddess blood. Now, the good news is you didn't drain her completely. I can tell by the fact she's starting to rouse."

Sure enough, Campbell focused his wavering gaze on her, and relief flooded him as he saw her eyes flutter and her limbs begin to move.

"So, you managed to hold back just enough that there's only mostly a chance we'll all explode before I get the contents of this needle into your bloodstream. Now, what do you say you morph into the perfect patient and let me take care of business before Lisada and her henchman arrive to drain you of that liquid fire inside of you?"

Campbell growled as The Goblin King inched closer. "I still don't trust you. Let me do it myself."

"Yeah, that's going to go well. You can't even steady your hand enough to hold the syringe, matter alone inject the contents."

"How do I know Lisada didn't send you here to finish me off? Last I saw, you were hanging out with her cronies."

The Goblin King sighed heavily. "Believe what you want, but I was waiting here for Mia's arrival, and not for the reason that's getting you all worked up right now. Dude, calm down before you have a stroke. That vein in your forehead looks like a roadmap to the last fiery blast we'll ever experience." He lifted the syringe again. "Let's just say, her mother sent me with this because she knew where all this was going to end."

"Her mother?"

"Yes, the Goddess of Fire and Light. She's been watching over Mia all this time but is unable to cross back over to this dimension right now. She told me to tell you that if you kill Lisada, your sisters will live, not just as revenants, but as living humans. They'll get a chance to experience a human lifespan, and though she can't give them immortality, she believes it would relieve you greatly if they could just be given the chance at a life they never had before."

Stunned. He wanted to believe every word. It was everything Campbell needed to hear. Maybe it was all part of an elaborate trap, but at this moment, as his insides seemed to be turning to fire, he was willing to put his sisters' lives first. If what The Goblin King said was true, it was all he'd ever wanted.

He thrust his arm out and rested it on the ground beside him. "Do it."

As The Goblin King inched even closer, readying the syringe, Campbell held up his other hand and stopped him briefly as something about this situation niggled at the back of his brain. "One thing first. Your word that you'll get Mia to safety, no matter what happens to me."

He paused in his actions before saying, "I give you my oath. As Andrex, son of Tothen, the now deceased Goblin King, you have my word I will protect Mia at all costs."

"I know of your father. But...your mother?"

"I've already mentioned her. Desside, the Goddess of Fire and Light."

"Then, you're Mia's..."

Andrex nodded. "Her brother. Well, technically, half-brother. Different fathers, of course."

The reality of Andrex's motivation sunk in. He was here to save Mia. All objections faded away, and Campbell presented his arm once again.

As Andrex moved in, Campbell noted the neon-yellow glow of the liquid. Clearly the contents were anything but ordinary. The needle slid into his arm, and the antidote stung as Andrex pushed it in slowly. Yet, he felt the relief immediately. A cooling sensation started in his arm and flowed throughout his body until every ill effect he'd felt just moments before faded back to normal.

Campbell sat up slowly and rested his arm on an upraised knee. "How long do we have before Lisada shows up?"

"I'd say we're down to less than a minute. The earlier explosion created a diversion, but she's not going to be duped for long."

Sure enough, Campbell could feel Lisada's mental fingers creeping into his mind. She was close. Both men stood, and Campbell lifted Mia into his arms effortlessly. He appeared to have recovered completely. "Let's go then. Right now. She's going to be royally pissed you ruined her plans, so I don't want to be here when she returns."

"Do you need some help with her? Hate for you to drop my sister before I get the chance to meet her."

"I got this. Now, move."

Andrex nodded and moved toward the door. "Follow me. I'll show you the way out and then I'm going after the Absolute Glass."

"Sounds like a shitload of wasted time. Let's get the Glass then we'll all get the hell out."

A pained look crossed Andrex's face before he said, "I don't think it's a good idea to have you two near the Glass, but damn if you aren't right about the time issue."

"Lead the way."

* * *

Mia blinked her eyes and worked to comprehend the situation she suddenly found herself in. Her head was pounding, but her heart was beating, which meant she'd survived. The last thing she remembered was being tangled up with Campbell well on her way to an incredible orgasm when everything went completely black. Now, she was in someone's arms, in quick motion, going who knew where. But, she was thankful to be alive.

Cautiously, she turned her head to see who carried her. Relief washed over her as she saw Campbell's chiseled jaw above her. She started to say his name, to let him know she was conscious, but stopped when she sensed someone else moving in front of him.

Campbell asked a question, his voice sounded gravelly and little-used. "So, if Lisada created Mia to put her blood in the Absolute Glass and become some all-powerful freak-of-nature, why didn't she just put her blood into the damn cup and drink it herself?"

An unfamiliar voice answered, "Uh...hello. Weren't you paying attention a few minutes ago when you almost made an explosive trip into little pieces? She couldn't inject as much of Mia's blood without something to act as a catalyst, to make it tolerable for her to consume—you. Once you'd drained Mia, she'd be two steps from dead, but the real prize would be all that churning lava-blood changing into a drinkable concoction inside you."

"Why me? Why not any one of the current freaks following after her, hanging on every word she says, and willing to become her eager sacrifice?"

Mia turned her head to try to get an idea of who Campbell was talking to. But from this angle, all she could see was a wide back and dark hair that fell to the collar of his dark shirt. His voice was rich and deep, with an appealing quality to it, especially as he explained, "The best way I can explain it, though it feels like some outrageously implausible rom-com plot, you are Mia's parallel soul, also known as a kindred soul. You were the only one who could blend her blood into a form that would turn Lisada to the bad-ass world-dominator she thinks she will be."

"Parallel soul? Mia and I are parallel souls? Like two-halves of the same whole."

"Yes. Born hundreds of years apart, but thanks to Lisada's handy ties to magic and to Hell's most powerful demons, you were brought together. Beautiful, ain't it."

Campbell stopped briefly. "Lisada's working with demons?"

"One really. The one she calls her Master—Rendyon. He's the one who made you into the vampire you are, Campbell."

They started moving again, making a few more turns before stopping right outside two large, curved doors. She guessed they led to a prominent part of the building, and it was where they were ultimately headed.

"Wait, you said the bad-ass world-dominator she *thinks* she will be. What's that supposed to mean?"

"Let's just say, the pawn has been deluded to believe she is the player. Her Master has no intention of letting her drink the contents of the Absolute Glass. He'll kill her and take it for himself. It's the only way he could roam the earth dimension permanently."

"Surely she's not that stupid. You'd think she'd at least suspect a freaking demon would pull a double-cross."

For the first time, Mia got a thorough look at the new addition to their party as he turned in Campbell's direction. He was handsome, in a very exotic way. His hair was longish, but didn't quite cover the two, short horns protruding from the top of his head, and his sharp cheekbones, longish nose, and deep amber eyes drew her gaze. He was staring back at her as well, and a small smile lit his lips as she studied his oddly familiar face. Had she seen him before?

"Don't forget, he's strung her along for hundreds of years, making her believe he's with her because he loves her, just waiting for this time and this place. She'll never see it coming until it's too late."

With this new, unknown guy's gaze locked onto Mia, Campbell finally glanced down to her face. "Hey. You can put me down now, Campbell. I feel fine."

He set her gently to the ground and gazed at her like the most fragile china cup he'd just shattered into a million pieces. "Mia...I'm so sorry. I shouldn't have fed from you in the first place."

She reached up and cupped his cheek again, staring hard into his eyes. "You should have. You were weakening by the second. I'm still amazed you stopped when you did."

"It wasn't easy. Your blood is like the most delectable of desserts. The only thing that stopped me was..."

"What? How did you stop?"

He shook his head. "I can't imagine a world without you in it, even for a second."

A snort came from behind Campbell, and Mia remembered they weren't alone as the third wheel spoke derisively, "Look, can we continue this feeling-fest another time. We kind of need to get this over with as soon possible. You know, to save the world and all."

Mia peered around Campbell to the man standing behind him. Whoever he was, he had a flair for sarcasm, and she kind of liked that. With a heavy sigh, Campbell turned with a smirk. "Mia, this is The Goblin King, Andrex. Believe it or not, he's here to help."

Something passed between the men when they exchanged a look. Some message Mia wasn't meant to intercept, but she figured, as usual, there was more to this story than either was willing to reveal right now. Either way, she wasn't waiting around for the made-for-TV-movie. She wanted out of here. She needed to check on the status of her father, and she wanted as far away from Lisada as she could get. "Nice to meet you, Andrex, but if you two don't mind, I'd rather save the introductions until after we've blown this pop stand and made it out the exits. Now, what do we need to do and can we please get doing it?"

Campbell nodded. "Do we just go through the front door? Seems a little obvious."

Andrex shrugged. "Not the stupidest thing I've ever done." And with that said, he reached for the handle and swung the door closest to him open. They all pulled back to the sides, just in case someone had been waiting for them.

Yet, as they peered around the open portal, the room appeared to be completely empty. Mia inched closer and noticed it looked like an auditorium of some sort, with rows and rows of padded chairs and a low stage at the front of the room. The entire room was bathed in dim light that disappeared at the edges of the large space. It had an old-time creep-fest-movie house feel to it. On the stage, a podium-sized column stood in a spotlight shining down from above, and a single, crystal goblet, with gleaming gold trim stood on top.

"The Absolute Glass." It had to be.

Chapter 25

Campbell led the group into the room and down an aisle way between the rows of seats. They moved at a jog, attempting to stay ahead of Lisada and the motley crew doing her bidding, but as they jumped up onto the stage, light flooded the room, and Mia couldn't voice it any better as Andrex groaned at the sight in front of them. All manner of creatures lined the walls of the auditorium and hundreds more glared at them from the balcony above. They shouted and jeered, a cacophony of evil noise surrounded them. Yet, the one that worried Mia most was the white-haired witch sauntering down the same aisle they'd just exited, an impudent grin planted on her lips and three zombie-like females following in her wake. Campbell tensed at the sight, and Mia could only imagine the guilt he felt in that moment.

Lisada held up her hand, and the room fell silent. "Nice try, Andrex, but I knew you weren't here to join my cause. It was clear your mother sent you the moment you showed up at the foot of my throne. Now, the surprise was your boldness knowing my Master's arrival was surely imminent. How did you ever believe he or I would let you leave here with The Absolute Glass?"

She felt Campbell at her back as Andrex stepped forward in front of Mia, blocking her view of Lisada and clearly attempting to protect her from the witch. "Do you really believe he intends to share the Glass's powers with you? You're a fool to trust him. Rendyon is a fucking demon."

Her eyes blazed, and her hair stood on end. Spit flew from her mouth as she screeched, "Never speak his name in such a manner. He deserves your worship, and soon you will bow down to the new King and Queen of this realm. You will regret choosing the wrong side."

"You still didn't answer my question. Lisada, there is no way he'll ever let you sip from that damn cup. You'd be better off to side with us against him. Send him back to the depths of Hell where he belongs."

"Fools! You can't stop him. You can't stop us. All you can do is join us." She continued toward the low stage. "Well, you can, Andrex. The other two have a different fate ahead of them."

Mia was surprised to see Andrex tense his muscles and tighten his hands to fists. Whatever the reason, he didn't like the idea of Lisada using Campbell and her for her ultimate-evil plot.

"Do you really think I'd let my sister be sacrificed to your insanity? You're an even bigger idiot than I first believed."

His sister? What did he mean by that? Like maybe he meant sister as in a consolidated front against *the man who was keeping them down*, but she really didn't think that's what he was getting at. And seeing as she was supposed to be said sacrifice, it could only mean one thing. *Andrex was her brother?* She had a brother. How was that possible?

Of course, how was any of this possible? From the moment she'd met Campbell, nothing was off the table of possibility.

"Believe what you want, Andrex, but everything will become clear to you now because...he's here."

A shadow fell over the entire auditorium, and a sinister vibe edged into every fiber of Mia's being. Whoever Lisada's master was, he wasn't on a low rung of the ladder of Hell. Mia felt certain they were dealing with a high-level demon, and though she was new to the paranormal world, even she understood the unfavorable position they were now in.

The dark presence moved over the room, and Mia could feel it slip in behind them, at the back of the platform. Suddenly, Andrex lifted off the ground and flew through the air like a piece of paper on the wind. He landed about twenty rows back from the stage, leaving Campbell and Mia as a united front. Mia swiveled and latched herself to him as Campbell pulled her in tight to his side.

They turned toward the newest threat, and Mia sucked in a breath at the sight in front of them. Instead of the horrible, disfigured creature she'd expected, the demon in front of her looked like he could star as lead in the latest Hollywood blockbuster. His hair was dark brown with caramel highlights that glistened in the spotlight still shining down on them like actors in a production. His eyes were a brighter blue than any sky Mia had ever seen, and his features were perfectly symmetrical and proportional in every way. His body oozed sex appeal as he filled out his red t-shirt and low-slung jeans. He looked like the fallen angel that demons were purported to be.

"Lisada, why do I see these two still alive? We agreed on a plan. By the time I arrived, the process should have been taken care of. Yet, I see them before me, very much...animated."

Mia didn't dare look behind her. Not when the substantial danger was standing right in front of her, but she heard the quiver in Lisada's voice as she slipped closer to them.

"My most-exalted Master Rendyon, everything went according to plan, but the process was interrupted by Andrex's untimely explosion and hypodermic of angel's blood, which he injected into Campbell."

His voice was calm, but an edge of danger swirled in the blue depths of his eyes. "Angel's blood? You allowed him to inject the catalyst with angel's blood?"

Her voice shook as she explained, "He…he planted the bomb in the chamber where I slept. I spent a good portion of the evening regenerating the body parts that were blown off." She held up her hands. "I still don't have all my fingers back." Sure enough, her hands looked disfigured and gross as she twisted them in the air for all to see.

"And what good are these useless creatures that surround you? Why weren't they given orders of what to do in just such a case?"

Mia sensed Andrex's return to consciousness just as Campbell spoke up, "Look, if you two need some privacy to settle this dispute, we can leave."

Yet, in that moment, Mia felt paralyzed and like a puppet on a string, like she was controlled by someone else's power. Magic was at work because she couldn't move even if she wanted to. Like the rafters above her head were now pressing down on her shoulders, she knelt on the ground, completely under someone else's control. Her arms stiffened against her sides, and her neck cocked, exposing the fast-beating pulse there. As she watched, Campbell went through the same set of motions, and a sense of hopelessness came over Mia. There was nothing they could do to stop this.

The demon's features changed. Became sharper, more defined,

menacing. His beautiful, blue eyes changed to a raging red. "Useless. They're useless now, Lisada! I can't drink a mixture tainted with Angel blood."

She walked past Mia, toward the demon. "I will drink the mixture. I'll purify it. You can drink from me."

He stared at her, his mind at work. "Yes! You could do that for me. I know you would do that for me." He strolled around Lisada and approached Mia first, running the backs of his fingers over her shoulder. Campbell growled in reaction, yet he was frozen in place too. "But…instead, I say we go back to the original plan. I possess your body and I consume every last drop of her blood."

"Though I'm willing to do almost anything for you, my Master, if I allow you to take over my body to exist on this plane, you'll never be allowed to leave me." I didn't have to see Lisada to know she was treading carefully through a metaphorical minefield. Saying no wasn't going to go over well, and even paranormal-newbie Mia knew a demon could surely do some serious damage with the flick of a finger.

The sound of his voice was next to her ear, as the demon said, "You owe me, Lisada. If I hadn't intervened, your pet Campbell would have finished you off permanently."

"Of course I'm grateful. My soul is already yours for eternity. Sacrificing my body just seems…extreme."

The demon hovered over Mia for several silent seconds before turning to the crowd of supernatural beings watching with rapt attention. "Do you hear her? After all I've done for her, she can be so selfish. What has she promised you? I'm not so sure you'll be dealt with fairly by Lisada the Vampire-Witch. I think if she will double-cross me, the one who brought her back from the brink of Hell, she will certainly trod roughshod over each and every one of you bastards."

Lisada rushed to the front of the stage, out of Mia's sight, brushing by the two captives where they still knelt, motionless except for their eyes. "No! That's not true. Those who have been faithful to me will be rewarded." The air grew heavy as Lisada cleared her throat. "Do it. Take my body as yours, my Master. I would be honored to serve you in this capacity."

Mia couldn't believe it. Lisada, the white-haired witch, had seemed so bad-ass, but she had one major fault. It appeared her one weakness was loyalty to the wrong being. It didn't fit with her brand of evil, but as Mia met Campbell's gaze, she picked up on a message shining there. He kept looking behind her, where the demon and Lisada performed their macabre act of reluctance, guilt, and capitulation. Yet, it wasn't concern, but triumph, Mia saw swimming in the depths of his stare. Hope bloomed deep in her chest, and she felt her powers surge through her veins, centering in the palms of her hands.

"Lisada, you have been my most faithful servant. Your reward is soon to come."

She let out an ear-splitting scream, and Mia wanted to turn to see what was happening. With great effort, she tensed her muscles and felt intense magic rush through her body until whatever gripped her lost its paralyzing hold and she could once again move her body. Yet, as she turned, she froze at the sight in front of her. Lisada was stretched with her hands above her, her feet pointed toward the ground as she floated in mid-air. As the demon laid a hand on the witch's hip, Mia tried to stand, but throwing out his other hand in her direction, he pushed Mia back into a kneeling position. She couldn't even release the frustrated groan that built in her chest.

"Don't get excited. I'll be with you in a moment." He focused his attention back onto Lisada, and Mia watched, realizing she would have had wide eyes and dropped jaw if she wasn't paralyzed in this moment. The demon transformed into a thick cloud of black smoke and seeped into Lisada's skin within a matter of seconds.

Chills broke out on Mia's skin as she watched Lisada's body slowly lower to the ground. Her arms floated to her sides, and she eased around to stare with reddened eyes at Mia and Campbell.

As she spoke, her voice came out deep and hoarse, like she spoke through a harsh, Lord Vader-type mask. "Now, let's take care of the real reason we're here."

Lisada's skin seemed to roll, like something living was settling into her muscles as she approached Mia. It was clear, though, she was no longer the one in charge as she stepped toward them, reaching for the Absolute Glass and an intimidating knife with a gleaming edge from the column still in the spotlight.

The male voice grated from Lisada's throat. "Better safe than sorry. I think we'll be using the knife instead of the teeth."

Without wasting another minute, he slipped the blade across Mia's throat and caught the blood that gushed out. The demon repeated his actions with Campbell but missed the cup on purpose. "Probably best if you're incapacitated too, even if I can't have what's flowing through your veins any longer. No need for you to get any heroic ideas."

They both dropped to the floor and watched helplessly as the demon lifted the cup to his lips and took the first sip.

The red eyes rolled back into Lisada's head, and the demon looked down at their prone bodies as blood continued to pour out onto the ground around them. "Behold! Witness the power your blood manifests. Soon I will become unstoppable. A creature that inspires fear and awe. I will be your worst nightmare and completely indestructible on this plane." He smiled icily at Mia. "Don't worry. The loss of blood won't kill you, and if you're nice to me, I might even let you live. Unfortunately, I can't offer the same to Campbell."

He laughed in celebration, like things had worked out better than he'd ever expected, but just as he lifted the goblet to swallow another gulp of the liquid inside, Mia sensed Andrex's presence moving closer. The crowd of supernatural beings around them went ballistic, and chaos erupted, but the demon only laughed louder, and Mia could only assume he thought it was in support of his triumph.

Andrex leaped from behind a row of seats and charged the stage. The demon turned and threw up his hand as if to stop her brother's progress, but Andrex continued advancing. Creatures from all over the room began running toward the front of the auditorium, and Mia cringed as she realized they weren't coming to her rescue.

Yet, the demon yelled, "Stop! Don't come any closer. I don't need your help, and frankly, I don't trust you bastards. I'll kill anyone who dares step on this stage." Mia could only guess he was guarding the Absolute Glass and its contents.

Whether they believed him or not, they all stopped as one and crept back, away from the stage. All except Andrex, who ran faster in the demon's direction.

The demonic-Lisada set the goblet back onto the column, raised the knife again, and readied himself for Andrex's attack. As her brother neared the stage, he pulled his own knife that seemed to already be dripping blood from the blade.

"Andrex, you need to learn when enough is enough. You can't kill me with a knife, silver or otherwise."

As Mia's brother grew nearer, he slowed and crouched just out of reach of the demon. "No. The knife alone would only irritate you, but this knife has been soaked in something that will do so much more to you. It even has an injectable cartridge full of angel's blood inside that will pretty much obliterate you from this dimension and all others forever."

The demon took a step backward, showing vulnerability for the first time. "You lie. Not like angel's blood is easily accessed on every street corner."

"No lie. Not even from a goblin such as me. But once I told my supplier what an ugly asshole I had to kill with it, she was all too eager to help me out."

The demon shifted his gaze toward the restless crowd surrounding them, grinning evilly as he shouted, "Friends, I'll share my cup with the being who takes Andrex down."

Cheers sounded and Mia watched, horrified, as werewolves, vampires, and other creatures she didn't yet recognize bounded over the seats toward the stage. She didn't think—just reacted. She held one of her hands to her healing neck and raised the other hand as adrenalin surged through her battered body. She threw up a large shield in front of the stage, laughing in disbelief that she'd actually accomplished it. One-handed, no less. The creatures hit the barrier she'd created and bounced back. Coming at it again and again. Yet, no matter how much force they exerted, she held it easily.

Andrex nodded in her direction and stepped closer to the demon, but the demon stepped in front of the cup, and Andrex swiped through the air with the knife, but just missed Rendyon's arm. The demon came at Andrex with a growl, bowing his body to keep out of reach of the deadly weapon. He brought his fist around and caught Andrex on the side of the face. Even in Lisada's body, his strength pushed her brother to the ground. In a second he was back up, slicing for skin.

The demon seemed to tire of the slow dance, and leaped into the air, feet first, straight into Andrex's chest. Her brother flew backwards and dropped the knife to the floor. It clattered out of Mia's reach. Once he hit the barrier, he didn't waste time licking his wounds. He charged back at the demon, but with a swipe of his hand, he sent Andrex flying to the right until his body smacked into the side of the stage. He slumped to the ground, dazed but still conscious.

Mia began to feel the pressure against her shield as the adrenalin coursing through her body began to wear off. *What now?* She looked around for Campbell, but he wasn't on the floor any longer. His neck was almost completely healed. So quick. *Lingering effects from drinking her earlier?* Now, he was standing next to the column, with the goblet in his hand, staring hard at the contents and realization hit her.

"Campbell, no! You'll die."

But in one of those as-quick-as an eye-blink moments, Campbell downed the contents of the cup, gripping his chest as the glass fell from his hands to the ground with a clatter.

The demonic-Lisada stared in awe as Campbell writhed and dropped to the floor, bowing low to the ground and groaning as the mixture entered his system. The demon began to laugh, full and derisively as Campbell struggled. "What did you expect, fool? That you would be as powerful as I? All this will do for you is destroy you from the inside out."

Rendyon dared a few steps forward, and Mia felt her powers fading. It was only a matter of seconds before the clawing creatures broke through from the other side.

Campbell began to glow with orange light, harsh to the eyes, and clearly leading to an explosion of immense proportions. If only she could get to Campbell, she could hold him one last time before they were both obliterated by the imminent blast.

"This! This is what I created all those hundreds of years ago?" Demonic-Lisada kicked Campbell in his side, just below his shoulder. "Pitiful. I expected so much more from you, Campbell. Don't get me wrong, I always planned to sacrifice you to become immensely powerful, but I just can't believe that power will be generated from a creature as weak as you."

With a sudden raise of his hand, Campbell brandished the injectable knife, lifting it high to slam down quickly into Lisada's foot, pinning her to the ground. "I'm not the one with an intolerance for angel's blood."

The demon cried out and attempted to pull back, but Campbell grabbed both legs and yanked them out from under Lisada. He jerked the knife out, holding it ready to do some ultimate damage as he scrambled to straddle Lisada's body. "What do you say, you fucking die, Rendyon!"

He gripped the hilt of the knife in both hands and lifted it above Lisada's heart, but before he could plunge it in, Lisada spoke, "Wait! Campbell, wait! It's me. The girl you fell in love with. Rendyon warped my mind all those years ago. I need you. Save me, please."

Mia didn't know why Campbell paused so long. He seemed to be contemplating her words as she continued, "I can save your sisters. I'll put them back into the grave, peacefully and with care. You help me and I'll help you."

The nod he gave her shocked Mia. Had he really fallen for Lisada's lies? She was clearly trying to manipulate him once again, and the thought weakened Mia even more.

Unable to block the creatures any longer, Mia dropped her arms and the creatures stampeded toward the stage. This was it. Mia was out of ideas and clearly out of luck. She focused on Campbell as he breathed heavily over Lisada. He glanced at Mia and her heart skipped as he winked and gave her a cocky grin.

He lowered his gaze back to Lisada. "I'll help you go to Hell!" Then he swung his arms high and plunged the knife into the witch's heart.

Her scream echoed throughout the auditorium, stopping the progress of the beings, as they threw their hands over their ears and dropped to the floor in disbelief. A few leaped onto the stage and stood over Lisada in utter shock. Others shook their head, as if to clear it from a dream and looked around as if they didn't quite know where they were. Apparently some had been under her spell, literally.

Andrex limped over to stand over the body, just as Campbell fell to the side, his back on the floor. "The witch is dead, but the demon got away."

Campbell focused on the lifeless body next to him. "Are you sure?"

"Yeah. Saw him ease from her body into the floorboards. He's long gone now."

"Dammit!" Campbell sat up slowly, resting his arm on an upraised knee. "Well, at least we got the cup."

But as Mia searched the area where it had rested just moments before, it was gone. "Where is it?"

She looked at Andrex and Campbell, but both just shook their heads in disbelief.

Andrex cursed a few times and spoke up, "The question is, does the demon have it, or did one of the others take it?"

"How can we tell?"

Campbell stood up and reached for Mia to do the same. "Doubt we'll be in suspense very long. That's just the kind of thing that keeps rearing its ugliness on a regular basis."

He pulled Mia into his embrace and pushed a wayward wisp of hair off her face. Her neck was almost completely healed. "What I'm more interested in at the moment is kissing my parallel soul and celebrating the fact she's finally safe from that damn witch."

His lips met hers soft at first, then the kiss deepened quickly as she felt the full extent of his relief and satisfaction at the final outcome.

Chapter 26

Mia couldn't shake the smile from her face as her father approached. He was alive, and the relief that overcame her was shocking. She hardly knew the man, but she couldn't help but feel something for him.

The burly, military vampire marched up to her and enveloped her in his embrace, urging a squeak of surprise to bubble out of her throat.

"You're okay. Thank goodness." He pulled back and stared behind her, over her shoulder. "Andrex, I knew your mother would find a way to get you through. Thank you for watching over your sister."

Andrex stayed behind Mia and Campbell, but explained, "She had exactly one dimensional travel amulet, and she used it to send me here. There are no other ways into or out of the dimension, and it's not even visible to most beings, including me. I don't even know how I'll return, but she was desperate. My mission was to help Mia and get the cup back. I'm glad I was there when my sister needed me. Wish it would have turned out differently though. We lost the cup and the demon."

With a stern look around, Mia's father shouted, "Search the perimeter for any sign of either of them."

Andrex's words stopped their movement though. "You won't find them. I've already searched. Whether the demon and the cup are together or another creature nabbed the Glass, they're both long gone."

"That's a worry for another day." Her father assured him. "I'll send a few of my men to still complete a search, if you don't mind?"

"Have at it. Won't offend me, sir."

Her father gave a curt nod and whispered some orders to a couple soldiers close by. Then, he turned back toward her, but stared at Campbell instead. "Can't thank you enough. You were there for her when I couldn't be."

"You've got it wrong. We're alive because she held off an attack until we could take down Lisada and Rendyon. She's a born warrior."

Her father's gaze dropped back to Mia. "Just like her mother. A beautiful warrior."

A longing rushed through Mia. "Wish I could meet her."

"That can be arranged. At least, you can communicate with her via inter-dimensional video. Other than Andrex," he stared deeply at the Goblin King as if trying to discover something in his eyes. He shook his head and continued, "no one's passed through that gate in many years. Like he said, there's no way to physically connect the dimension in which she currently is and the human world. He was right that we can't even find where it is physically because it changes constantly, but we can arrange an inter-dimensional call of sorts."

As the possibility sunk in, Mia grew excited and nervous all at once. Yet, no doubt about it, if there was an opportunity to see her mother alive again, she'd take it. "Hells yeah! Toss me the magical cell-phone. I'm on board with that."

"There's only one place to access it. We'll have to go to the Supernatural Council Headquarters."

Campbell stepped forward. "Will she be safe there?"

Her father nodded gravely. "You have my word. No way will I allow anyone to do her harm now or ever. She'll be accepted as a hybrid creature, and I'll defend her to the end."

His voice held no room for dissension as Campbell growled, "Where she goes, I go. And my sisters too. According to Andrex, there's a way to bring them back as mortals instead of revenants."

"Of course." Her father turned to the other figure standing in the background. "And you Andrex? Will you go with us as well? You're always welcome."

"No sir. Still have a mission to complete. Until I get the Absolute Glass back to the Dimension of the Fae, I won't be sitting still in one place for long."

"Indeed. We can send a contingency of soldiers with you, if you'd like."

Andrex shook his head. "This is my mission alone. Mother decreed it so."

With a slow nod, she caught a glimpse of her father's profile as he turned. Sadness rested there for just a moment, and Mia had to wonder whether it was at the mention of Andrex's and her mother. Something to explore at a different time though. For now, she just wanted to get to a place where she could see her mother's face once more.

Her father shouted, "Let's move out."

Everyone shifted toward the vehicles, and Campbell slid his fingers into her hand, gripping it tightly as they walked together. It was such a sweet gesture, and she'd been craving contact with him, but she'd been imagining a little more of the "clothing optional" kind.

What would become of them now? If she was being honest with

herself, she wanted him for her own. She wanted to be together now and forever, but she never wanted to be a burden on him. Never wanted him to be with her just because they're souls matched in a way she never would with anyone else. She'd accepted the truth. She loved him. It basically came down to one concern—did he love her too or did instinct make him want to be by her side?

Definitely a conversation worth having after she'd rested and wasn't feeling so vulnerable. Then she'd lay her feelings out for him, and hope he felt the same.

Insecurity sucked normally, but when the heart was involved, it was enough to make a person want to crawl into another dimension and never come out. A part of her wondered if that's what happened with her parents, but she knew their separation was based more on the safety of Mia and themselves.

As they climbed into the all-terrain vehicles lining the small field outside the church behind them, she took one last look back. She loved Campbell, but she refused to be in Lisada's situation. She'd never love someone more than they loved her in return.

Campbell would love her as completely as she loved him, or she'd walk away, heart crushed to a pulp.

"You okay? Seems to be some pretty deep thoughts going on over there."

She met Campbell's gaze and smiled. "Just looking ahead now that I'm not constantly running for my life."

He reached for her hand again and brought it to his lips, brushing over her knuckles briefly before lowering it back to the seat between them.

Yep, her heart was in serious trouble.

* * *

Relief hadn't sunk in completely. Campbell still felt an itch of concern he couldn't quite scratch. After all, they still didn't know who had fed Lisada and the demon inside information along the way. And that alone was enough to keep Campbell on high alert.

Even as they pulled up to the familiar building of the Supernatural Council Headquarters, he struggled not to tell the driver to keep on driving, far away from here.

Mia seemed on edge though, and he assumed it was because she was about to talk to her mother for the first time in a little over twenty years. "Ready for this?"

She gave him a crooked smile that caused a tightening in his chest. "Strange how nervous I am. Will she like me? I mean, though I have goddess tendencies, I have fangs and drink blood for nourishment now."

"You're her daughter. She'll love you."

A shrug lifted her shoulders. "I suppose you're right, but nothing says she has to love me."

An unanswered question hung in the air. *Did he love her?* It had been so long since he'd allowed himself to feel anything for another that he wasn't sure he was capable of it any more. Yet, as he stroked her arm, he realized he hadn't been able to stop touching her, his thoughts had been on her since he met her, his instinct to protect her bordered on obsessive, and he admired everything about her. Was it love? He wasn't sure, but he was willing to stick around a while to see just how intense this mating of the soul became.

He began to tell her that when the car came to a stop and their doors were pulled open.

"Right this way, Ms. Alexander."

Campbell stepped out also and watched her walk toward the front entrance.

A soldier he didn't recognize stepped in front of him, drawing his attention. "Mr. Reid, if you'd like to clean up, I'll show you to a place you can do that."

"Yeah. Okay, let's go."

Next time he saw her, he'd tell her the truth. Pretty damn clear as she slipped out of his sight. He didn't have to think on it any more. He loved her.

Chapter 27

"Mia, you're more beautiful than I could have ever imagined."

With tears in her eyes, Mia stared at the familiar face of her mother. She hadn't changed at all, which was normal for immortals such as herself. Though she was thousands of years old, she appeared to be in her mid-twenties, her hair fell in long, golden waves, and her eyes glowed an electric blue Mia had never seen in nature before. She was gorgeous.

"And your father explained your recent battle in which you held off a mass of creatures with your newly acquired powers. Amazing! I don't think I could have done anything near that level just after my supernatural skills set in."

Mia opened her mouth to speak but struggled to form words as she cradled the handheld mirror with the image of her mother staring back at her. A sob escaped.

"My dear daughter. I've missed you terribly. Thought about you every day and fretted that I couldn't be by your side without leading Lisada right to you."

"I missed you too." The words spilled out through her tears, and Mia knew it was going to turn into an ugly-cry. Yet, the emotions welled-up, and she had no way to suppress them. Wouldn't have wanted to anyway. "Thought I'd lost you forever."

Her mother reached toward the glass but couldn't actually touch Mia like she obviously wanted to do. Tears ran down her face unchecked at the limited contact. "It was necessary at the time. Hate that you weren't told the truth. For the best."

Mia nodded. "I know that. I don't blame you or dad. It was for my protection."

"Yes. Didn't make it any easier on anyone though."

"Let's just let the past be in the past. Start over, in a sense."

"I would like that tremendously."

They continued to talk and catch up until the conversation rolled around to Campbell.

With a grin she couldn't wipe from her face, Mia sighed, "I think I love him more than he loves me."

"You would be surprised how little feeling a man shows outwardly, especially an immortal man. They've had a longer time to perfect their poker-face."

"What should I do? Wait him out? Even with all the time in the world now, I'm not that patient."

A look of sympathy covered Desside's face. "Let me give you some advice that will guarantee he'll be unable to resist expressing his love."

But in that moment, something like static began to affect the connection. Her mother said something that Mia couldn't understand.

"What? I can't hear you clearly."

Yet, after a few more tries, Mia realized the connection was completely broken. With a frustration born of being so close yet so far away…literally…Mia slid the contraption closed and walked slowly out of her room. Her father waited for her there with a smile.

"Was she well?"

"Seemed to be. Our connection was broken before we could finish our conversation."

He embraced her tightly. "I'm sorry, dear. She's very far away, and it's hard to maintain communication."

"Is there any chance she could return to us?"

"We're working on that. But to be realistic, we've been trying for twenty years. When she left, it was a slim chance we'd send her to a dimension from which she could never return. Where she is isn't one of those planes, but it's harder than others." He pulled back and met her gaze. "We'll keep trying."

Mia nodded solemnly. To be able to touch her mother again would be amazing, but at least she'd gotten to speak to her. The idea her parents were alive was still surreal, but she was beginning to accept it. "I want to help too."

He stepped back. "Of course. I'll keep you in the loop."

"Thank you." She stepped back too, pursing her lips with a new concern. "I need to find Campbell. We still have unfinished business."

"He's downstairs, in the debriefing room. I'll take you to him."

Yet, in the next minute, everything happened quickly and took on the consistency of a storm of shit. Her father dropped to his knees, and Mia's mouth and nose were covered from behind. She felt a momentary surge of her powers as the warmth rose from her chest and rolled down her arms to her hands, but before she could so much as flex her pinky, she felt her eyes roll back in her head and everything went black.

* * *

Campbell sat in the debriefing room, head in hands as he explained...yet again...what had happened to The Absolute Glass and how it could have disappeared so close by without him noticing just who happened to get their grubby hands on it.

"Telling you...my focus was on Lisada. You know, plunging my knife into her cold, evil heart, saving us all from her evil plan to rule the world and all that."

No one laughed. Campbell knew his interrogator well. They'd gone through early training together about a hundred years ago. Lieutenant Mace Ward was a tough, sonofabitch and a douchebag extraordinaire. Not one of Campbell's favorite people, he was the front-runner for Campbell's fist-to-the-face award, soon to be announced. A tall vampire with eyes the color of muddy grass, leaned down to Campbell's ear. "While you make your jokes, someone has one of the most powerful weapons ever loosed on this or any world, and you better believe, they're going to use it. Now how about you shut the fuck up with the sarcastic bullshit and tell me what I want to know, soldier."

"I've told you everything I know—step-by-step—multiple times. What else can I say?"

"Why don't you start again, and this time leave nothing out—including *why* you thought it was a good idea to drink the contents of the cup?"

Enough! Campbell ground his teeth together and gritted through tight lips, "Why don't you take your questions and your ugly-ass head and stick them right up…" He stopped himself, his head snapping up, gaze wide with realization. He hadn't stopped because he was afraid to put Mace in his place, but he stopped because he could feel Mia's power surging like she was in danger then extinguishing suddenly. Something was wrong, and he had to get to her…right…fucking…now!

He didn't ask to be excused, just shoved the chair back, letting it fly into the wall behind him and took two strides to the door.

"Reid! Where do you think you're going? We're not finished here!"

Campbell didn't pause. He rushed through the door and broke into a dead sprint for the stairs. Last he knew, she'd been in one of the satellite rooms. Those rooms were wired to pick up inter-dimensional communications, and she'd been contacting her mother. What the fuck could have possibly gone wrong?

The thought of the demon somehow breaking past the multiple wards and spells of The Supernatural Council Headquarters seemed impossible, but Campbell could think of no other feasible explanation.

He didn't bother with the elevator. Instead, he took the stairs three at a time, feeling energy soar through him with each leap upward. Whoever had dared to touch Mia would regret ever even stepping in her direction when he was finished with them. He felt his muscles swell at the very occurrence of the thought. His fangs elongated, and he began to emanate a blue, electric heat from his hands.

What…the…fuck?

Since when did he glow?

He gripped the metal handrail and felt it crumble to mere, flaky shavings in his fist. Heaven help him, he paused and stared for a moment before recovering and continuing to bound up the stairway toward Mia.

Could the power of that damn cup have affected him in some way? Was he becoming some mutant monster? As if being a vampire wasn't enough of a freak show?

He reached the level where Mia should be and crashed through the door to the hallway, not even pausing to try the handle. She wasn't anywhere in sight, but he spotted a crumpled figure, lying on the floor halfway down the hallway. He was crouched by his captain's side before he could suck in a lung-relieving breath.

Yet, as he reached a hand out, he realized he wasn't even a little out of breath. Something was definitely different about him, and he used a little more caution when he rested a finger on Spencer's shoulder.

Spencer groaned as he moved stiffly and turned over. His eyes fluttered open. "Mia?"

"Hoping you knew where she was. It feels like she's in trouble."

He reached a hand up to touch the back of his head gingerly, pulling away fingers laced with blood. "Last I remember, I was with Karenth. Son of a bitch must be the inside mole. You've got to get her back."

Campbell ground his molars together. Like an itch in the middle of his back that he couldn't quite reach, he felt like this nightmare would never end. When he got his hands on Kerenth, there'd be nothing left of him because anyone who hurt Mia was Campbell's number one target.

One thing was sure, once all this was over, no one would come between Mia and him again. She was his, and he was hers.

"You have my word."

Campbell lifted his nose in the air. He scented Mia's distinctive smell. She was close, not even off the grounds yet.

He took off down the hallway and burst into one of the front rooms. It was an unoccupied conference room filled with a long, banquet-style table and multiple, plush chairs surrounding it. He leaped over the whole set-up and without a moment's hesitation, broke through the tall window fronting the room and the building.

Five stories up, the ground rushed at him as he waved his arms in slow circles and watched the darkened grass getting closer. Maybe he'd been a bit rash, but movement far to his left had him zeroing-in his gaze on a figure moving through the shadows. Somehow he sensed it was Kerenth.

Just before his feet hit the ground, he loosely tucked them up to his abdomen and braced himself for impact. He landed in a low crouch, completely unharmed, but sending a shockwave of energy rippling over the area around him. He looked over his skin, not even marred by a single cut, and marveled at this new set of capabilities.

He didn't take long to ponder over his god-like talent to...well, live...through death-defying stunts like jumping out of five-story windows. Instead, he took off at a stunner sprint toward the shadowy creature moving through the trees to his left.

Sad really. Kerenth didn't even have a chance to get away now that he was in Campbell's sights, but he had to be cautious in order to keep

Mia safe.

He slowed as he got within striking distance and climbed high in a large oak, balancing on a rather thick limb until he was hanging right over Kerenth. From this vantage point, he could see Mia unconscious in Kerenth's arms. He watched as her chest lifted and depressed with heavy breaths. The bastard had probably drugged her. He'd pay for that, among other things.

"Dammit! Where the hell is he?"

He was expecting company. The demon maybe? That would be a happy ending if Campbell got to take both out with one shot. Then again, he didn't want to drag this out any longer than necessary for Mia's sake.

Another option might be he was waiting for Campbell. Well, he certainly didn't like to disappoint.

With a whisper through the leaves, Campbell dropped to the ground behind Kerenth. Kerenth swiveled to face him. His eyes widened as Campbell stood to his full height. *Definitely taller.*

"You drank from the cup." The awe in Kerenth's voice was chilling. He had, but what's the difference. He'd also drank directly from Mia, and the effects had been mind-blowing...almost literally. Yet, what difference could some supernatural chalice make?

"Yeah. The changes have been surprising."

Kerenth stared for what felt like a long time before finally shaking himself from his stupor. "Doesn't matter. I still have to complete what I came to do."

"And that is?"

He hefted Mia higher in his arms, and Campbell tightened his fists in reaction. He really didn't like seeing Mia unconscious in Kerenth's hands. He needed to change that and soon.

"You're going to see what's it's like to lose the only thing you live for."

Campbell felt confused for just a moment before he realized none of Kerenth's nonsense mattered. "Just hand her over, and maybe I'll let you walk to your dimensional prison with only a permanent limp."

But Kerenth didn't react at all like expected. An evil grin slid onto his face, and his eyes lit up in delight.

For a moment, Campbell was confused, but he took a step forward with a growl and felt a sense of satisfaction as Kerenth took a step backward, losing his smile as his feet hit a tree root behind him. Clearly, his confidence was shaken. No doubt things weren't going exactly as he'd planned, but he didn't seem ready to back down yet.

Somehow he managed a smugness as he said, "You'll pay for what you've done."

"And what is that?"

"You took her from me...twice. And this time, she's gone forever."

Campbell felt his confusion grow. "Mia? She was never yours."

He set Mia on the ground beside him, with her back against the tree. She didn't even stir. "Not Mia! Never Mia. She was just a means to an end. Lisada was mine, and I hers. I saved her the first time you took her from me, but I had to make a deal with that devil. Now, there's no way to bring her back, and you'll pay for that."

So many pieces fell into place in Campbell's mind. Yet, one thing still puzzled him. "But you're not a vampire. Not even an immortal."

"True. I'm no blood-sucking vampire leech." His lopsided grin grew fevered. "I am immortal though. A side-effect of selling your soul to bring back your one true parallel soul. To make matters better, thanks to my curse to die and resurrect over-and-over, my immortality is undetectable. A side-effect that seemed horrific at first has protected Lisada and me over many years."

"What the hell are you then, Kerenth?"

Kerenth stepped away from Mia, into the moonlight and rolled his shoulders. "Talking-time is over. Time to show you exactly what I am. And then I'm going to kill you both, but I'll start with her and make you watch."

A low growl rose from Campbell's throat as he stepped forward again, but he stopped as Kerenth threw his head back with a howl and began to shake and convulse, as his body changed. A pained scream escaped him as his legs elongated and his shoulders broadened. His mouth and nose pushed outward and his skin stretched agonizingly thin across his face. His eyes glowed red and ominous as he lowered his gaze to meet Campbell's.

Impossible! This was the werewolf that had attacked him in the store parking lot. Something about him had seemed different—wrong somehow—now Campbell knew why. His change was unnatural like Campbell's, and the side effects were a bitch with that kind. Natural-born werewolves didn't take on the wolf-like features so literally. They still looked humanoid, but everything about them slid into a more feral, beastly look.

Once he was fully changed, he stood over seven-feet tall and snapped his four-inch fangs at Campbell. "Yeah. Definitely one of those things one has to see to believe."

Far from mindless, his red-eyed gaze bore into Campbell as if giving him one last sneer before he acted. At last, he turned his feral look on Mia and Campbell felt his own transformation coming on. His fangs elongated once more, and the electric-blue energy began to build in his hands again. Under his skin, his muscles tensed in quick succession, as if his body was readying for the battle of a lifetime. If Kerenth even took a step toward Mia, that's exactly what he'd get.

Just as he made a motion in Mia's direction, Campbell slammed his body into Kerenth with his full force. They flew backward, crashing into the trunk of a tall oak, taking a huge chunk out of the side of it. Kerenth's claws dug into Campbell's flesh, but the invasion only served to push Campbell even closer to losing complete control of his transformation. Would he explode like a mega-ton bomb if he did? Damn, he hoped not, but the way he felt right now, he was certain pressure was building inside him.

Campbell pulled his fist back and slammed it into the side of Kerenth's snout. With a snarl, Kerenth lunged to bite at Campbell's shoulder, but he twisted at a backwards angle and cleared the space just as Kerenth's teeth snapped shut on thin air. Campbell threw a few more punches into Kerenth's torso and flung him to the ground.

A loud growl rising from his throat, Kerenth sprang from the ground, leaping above Campbell's head and came at him with claws wide. Unable to move quickly enough, Campbell took the blow and fell into the mangled tree behind him. His head hit the unforgiving wood, but again, he marveled at how little his body was harmed. He came back at Kerenth with his legs kicking out and fists flying until they connected and Kerenth dropped to the ground. Campbell leaped onto him, punching his fists into his face wildly. With his new level of strength and ability, this fight would be over in the next few minutes. Kerenth couldn't defend against Campbell's superior power.

"Time to give it up and go to prison with the other assholes like you, Kerenth."

Campbell recognized the look of humor, even on the canine-type features. Again a sense that Campbell didn't have all the information hit him, made him cringe inside. If he couldn't save her…

Kerenth shifted under him as Campbell continued to pound and tear at him. With a sudden motion, Kerenth shoved his fist into Campbell's ribs and threw his head back with a triumphant howl. Campbell frowned. *What the hell was he so happy about?* Kerenth's blood and bits of flesh were flying into the air and all over Campbell's fist.

But the pain hit him suddenly, and he rolled onto his back, feeling the cool, wet ground soak into his shirt. No, something else was pooling around him. He glanced down to the spot where Kerenth had struck him. His own blood bloomed and was wetting the front of his shirt as he watched. The silver handle of a weapon glimmered in the moonlight.

Damn silver! He should've seen it coming. Should've expected the werewolf to play dirtier than dirty.

The silver edged through his system like fire in his veins and locked him in unbearable pain. As he felt his lifeblood seeping from his body, regret washed over him. Though he'd been certain he had, he should've killed Lisada completely. Should've suspected something wasn't quite right with The Supernatural Council. Should've protected Mia better. She'd trusted him, and he'd failed her.

Kerenth lifted himself from the ground slowly and turned toward Mia. A growl started low in his throat and hoarse words sounded as he stepped forward, "Now...she...dies."

"M...Mia..." Campbell called to her weakly.

She stirred and opened her eyes briefly, but she remained sprawled at the base of the tree, very little sign of consciousness. Her fingers fluttered, and she issued a low moan.

Campbell tried again, "Mia...wake up, honey."

If she could just get up and run into the open field. Maybe one of the guards might see her and take Kerenth out before he could get his monstrous claws on her.

With the last of his energy, Campbell rolled to his side, facing her and called her name again in a strained voice. "Get up and run!"

Her eyes popped wide and as if the whole situation became clear to her in an instant, she erupted from the ground and began to emit a vibrant electric white energy, almost like a visible aura all around her. She bared her fangs as they grew longer and her hair blew back from her face, revealing the fierce, supernatural warrior she was made to be.

She was the most beautiful thing he'd ever seen.

To give Kerenth credit, he actually paused, as if considering the foolishness of taking her on in her powerful glory, before shrugging off any logic he might have had and stupidly rushing at her headlong. She threw him backwards into a tree across the small clearing with the flick of her wrist.

With an effort he really didn't have the energy for, Campbell rolled to his hands and knees, inching up to a standing position. He leaned back against the closest tree, feeling the rough bark abrade his over-sensitive skin. His heart was slowing, and for all the years he'd cursed his existence, he didn't want it to end. Not now that he'd found Mia…his soulkind. Somehow it seemed like a grim irony that he'd hated himself and all that he'd become until he'd used his abilities to protect Mia. For the first time, he saw a purpose to his existence, just as it was ending.

At least he'd die with the awe-inspiring sight of Mia coming fully into her powers, and as she annihilated the idiot foolish enough to take her on.

Mia's voice boomed as if she spoke into a megaphone, "Cannot defeat me now. Only a fool would continue to try."

As if proving her point, Kerenth charged at her once again, and it occurred to Campbell that maybe he was trying to die. A suicide mission to join Lisada in Hell.

She allowed him to get dangerously close while white energy built in her hands to a blinding degree. As he leaped in the air, claws raised to split her in two, Campbell felt his breaths growing shallower. He needed to hang on just long enough to see the outcome.

In a flash, she raised her hands, straightening them in front of her in Kerenth's direction. As the beams hit him, he stopped in mid-air and threw his head back with a painful howl. Her energy continued to pour into him, lighting him up like a Christmas tree. As if he were made of nothing more than silky dust, he exploded into a million glowing particles and filled the air for several seconds before fading into nothingness.

Regenerate from that, mother fucker.

Campbell grinned and slid back down to the ground, feeling the silver dagger dig into his internal organs. He could die happy now, knowing she'd survived, and he'd done his part to make it so.

Chapter 28

Her feet touched the ground gracefully and the energy surrounding her faded as she rushed to Campbell's side. "Campbell! Campbell, tell me what to do."

"Too late. Silver's in my system."

Mia's eyes dropped to the dagger handle protruding from his ribs. She reached for it, but he jerked backwards, away from her.

"Don't touch it. Can't let it hurt you."

"Dammit, Campbell! I don't freaking care!" She grasped the handle and the air left her lungs on a small scream as a sizzling sound emanated from where her hands met the metal and excruciating pain oozed up her arms and flowed into her body to her toes. With intense focus and determination, she gritted her teeth and pulled the knife free, tossing it to the ground behind her. Blood poured from his side, but a sigh of relief escaped his pale lips to have the offending weapon gone from his body.

"There has to be something I can do." Tears slid down her cheeks as her heart clenched in her chest. She couldn't let him die. Not now, not ever. He was her soulkind, and she knew it was true. She felt to her bone that she'd die without him...or at least no longer have a will to live. What was the use of being immortal if you couldn't be with the one you loved the most in the world?

"Let me go. No way to save me."

"Bullshit! I'm a freaking vampoddess or goddampire or something like that. There has to be something I can do."

He laughed lightly then wrinkled his forehead like it caused him great pain. "I like goddampire. Sounds badass, like you." He suddenly broke into a fit of coughing, and she could hear a rattle in his chest. She was going to lose him forever if she didn't figure this out quick.

"I need you, Campbell. I'm not badass enough to make it without you."

His face relaxed unnaturally, pulling her heart even harder into panic-mode. He was fading right before her eyes. "You don't need me. Never did."

"Dammit, Campbell. I don't just need you." She paused and sucked in a deep breath, trying to steady her quickly deteriorating mental state. "I...I love you." She hung her head and let the tears fall unimpeded.

He reached up a shaking hand and caressed her wet cheek. "Love you more." He sagged, unconscious but still barely breathing.

She ugly-cried over his chest with hard, wracking sobs, gaping mouth, and unchecked fluids. Her only concern was that she was about to say goodbye to all hope, all chance for immortal happiness, to the best thing that had ever happened to her. Campbell had become irreplaceable to her, and her heart squeezed painfully in her chest.

"What's with all the waterworks, noob?"

Mia lifted her head and turned it slowly, surprised to see the blue-haired Pixie she'd met at Campbell's home. It felt like years and years ago, and seeing her here felt surreal. She had on a pair of Hello Kitty pajama pants and a shirt to match. She held a dripping ice-cream cone in her hand and looked genuinely perplexed.

"He's...he's dying."

She licked the ice cream without breaking her confused stare and took a few dainty steps forward. "Why?"

"Silver. Kerenth stabbed him with a silver dagger, and there's no way to stop the spread through his system now."

"Ba-loooon-ey!"

"But it's true. See for yourself." Mia backed away slightly to give the Pixie a better view.

The Pixie waved her hand dismissively. "No, I meant the flavor of the ice cream. It's fried bologna, but I couldn't place it until now. They had pickle-flavored. In your current condition, you might enjoy that."

Mia was confused by the turn of the conversation. What did she mean by her *current condition*? Freaked the hell out? Ready to curl into a ball and die as someone she loved faded to nothing forever. "Isn't there anything you can do? To save him?"

"Hmmm. I'm pretty awesome, but that's beyond even my abilities. Fortunately, I have some swanky connections. I know someone who can save him."

Mia released a hopeful puff of air. "Who? Can he get here like...two seconds ago?"

"Nope."

With a heart-wrenching squeak, Mia hung her head in defeat.

"Well, sort of."

Mia was getting tired of having her emotions played with, and she was ready to do some damage when the Pixie got the strangest look, like she'd just delivered the biggest duh-moment in history.

"Because *she's* already here." She took another lick of the dripping dessert in her hand and wrinkled her nose like it tasted gross. "It's you, Mia. You can heal him."

Her head flew up in an instant. "What? Me? But how?"

"You're a vampiroddess or goddesire or one of those weird hybrid things that have powers from both factions. Just do your glow-y thing over him and feed him some of your superpower blood. He'll be full-strength in a snap."

Mia felt her chest rise and fall several times as the information sunk in. Like Dorothy, she'd had the freaking power all the time. That had always made Mia want to bitch-slap Glenda. Couldn't she have revealed that little tid-bit sooner? "So, I can do this. Okay. I can do this."

She closed her eyes and felt the warmth begin to flow into her hands. It was becoming easier to pull her powers to the surface. She laid her hands onto his chest and pressed into him. His body jerked as if electricity shot through him, but she held her palms to him and continued to pump waves of energy into him. His eyes shot wide, and his fangs elongated as she met his gaze. She felt his body stiffen…everywhere…as life flooded through him.

From behind her, Mia heard the Pixie say, "Well, this is getting awkward."

Mia glanced at the Pixie long enough to say, "Thank you."

"Yeah, well, maybe you can pay me back sometime. You know, if you have any way to get a hold of that yummy Hemsworth fellow—either one will do." She shrugged and gave a little wave. "Oh, and just so you know, you can get knocked up by the vamp—totally preggers. If Lisada couldn't use the two of you, she'd wanted a back-up plan, like a baby you two made. Just thought you'd like to be aware."

A vapid look covered her face in an instant as she stepped into the shadows of the trees behind her. "Well, I'd love to stick around, but you'll just have to let Campbell know he's welcome for the tranquilizer dart at just the right moment. I don't have time to hang around and rub it in his face. I've got other places to be just now. Got to see an ice cream vendor about a refund. Pretty sure I asked for grilled hot dog flavor. Like the other kind of belly-button—I'm outie." With a loud pop, like a hundred balloons bursting at once, the Pixie disappeared as quickly as she'd come.

With a bewildered shake of her head, Mia turned back to one, very alive, very at-attention Campbell Reid. Had he heard the Pixie's last revelation? Mia still wasn't sure she believed it, but she placed an absent-hand on her abdomen and stared into his green eyes.

"Thought I'd lost you there."

He nodded, a passionate fire blazing in his gaze. "Thought I was going to lose you, but you were magnificent."

"I know, right?"

Campbell shifted until he was sitting up completely. He still seemed weak, and Mia remembered she needed to feed him her *super* blood. She bit her wrist and moved it toward his mouth. With a tighter grip than she would have expected from someone who'd been moments from death, he wrapped his hand around her arm and stopped her.

"You need this."

"No argument about that. You should know I meant what I said. I love you, Mia."

"I love you too, Campbell."

"Honestly, I think the first moment I saw you suffering in the sunlight in front of my apartment, I knew I could fall fucking hard for you. I didn't realize you'd become everything I ever cared about. You are *my everything*, Mia. And though I wish my sisters hadn't suffered at my hands and would change that part in a runner's heartbeat, I no longer regret Lisada turning me...because I would never have known you otherwise. And yes, someday, I'd like to have children with you. Little vampodesses and goddampires all over the place."

He lowered her wrist to his mouth and took greedy pulls, causing all her nerve-endings to fire deliciously throughout her body. "You know I love you too. Yours for eternity." She threw her head back in abandonment as she straddled his lap and reveled in the first stirrings of a mind-blowing orgasm.

She lowered her gaze to meet his, wanting to watch him as he gained his strength and power. With a lusty smile, he licked her wrist and leaned back against the trunk of the tree.

"Thank you, Campbell."

His whole body came alive beneath her, and he raised her up just enough to undo his pants and free himself for access. He slipped her flimsy thong to the side and entered her in one star-seeing thrust. A low moan rolled out of her mouth as she rolled her hips.

"For what?

She met his lips in a searing kiss, riding his cock as he plunged into her from below. "For making my wildest fantasies, my reality."

His smug grin said it all. "Baby, I'm just getting started."

He gripped her ass in both hands and watched intently as she dived over the edge, feeling her sex clench around him in a shattering climax. She shouted his name over and over, loving every minute of it, loving every minute with him. She couldn't believe her luck. Immortality was hers, and with Campbell by her side, it would be amazing.

# # #

Did you enjoy The Vampire Next Door? Keep up with new releases in The Love Next Door Series and other stories by Cherie Marks by signing up for my New Release Newsletter here: Happily Ever After the Write Way Newsletter

Please consider leaving a review of this book at your favorite e-tailer. E-mail me the link, and I'll send you a free copy of another of my e-books of your choice.

About Cherie Marks

Twitter: http://twitter.com/cheriemarks

Facebook: Author Page

My blog: http://www.authorcheriemarks.com/

It all started with an old fashioned typewriter. When my family brought it home, for the first time, I knew what I wanted to do. All those stories rolling around in my head could finally get out. The press and click of the keys were satisfying in their own right, but when I pulled out a finished page, I knew this was for me. Since then, I've graduated to a laptop, but the stories still find a way out.

I'm a breast cancer survivor, a teacher, a wife, a mother, and a writer. I continue to strive for less procrastination and more tact. The battle wages on.

More Books by Cherie Marks

The Fae Next Door

Janna Thompson believes she's going downright mental. In the past few weeks, she's seeing things no one else can see and can't shake an ominous presence. Yet, when a hot cop with a protective instinct moves into her apartment building, things might be looking up.

Cade Lanter is no ordinary being. The son of a human policeman and a Queen of the Fae, he lives in the human world for now. When an enemy of old threatens the balance of both the human world and Eiru, Land of the Fae, he must fight the would-be usurper in the human realm. Of course, that might require more focus than he can muster lately since a certain, sexy neighbor keeps him distracted.

Their two, unlikely worlds collide when he becomes The Fae Next

Door.

Excerpt:

Someone...or something...was following her.

Janna Thompson moved quickly down the sidewalk toward her apartment building, throwing furtive glances over her shoulder. An acrid smell of smoke and decay floated in the air, yet no one else around her reacted to it. Couldn't they smell it? Couldn't they feel the impending doom that hovered like a cloud, smothering the light and any sense of goodness? No one behind her stood out as a creepy creeper, but she could feel darkness, like a chasing fog, inching toward her to engulf her. This wasn't the first time in the last week she'd felt it, and even more nerve-wracking, it was growing stronger and, to be perfectly honest, scarier.

A hot, bubble bath had been calling her name after a few grueling tests today. Her classes were getting harder at South-central Community and Technical College, and so far, she'd risen to the challenge. She'd loved every minute of her anatomy class--until today. Studying for exams was obviously going to require more than an overnight cram session. But, somehow she'd survived it, and pulled a slightly above-average grade. A little celebration had been on her mind. But not now. Now, that was completely wiped away. She clearly had a blip on her radar—one that felt particularly threatening.

God, what was she thinking? A darkness chasing her? Could she just be imagining the whole thing? Not quite sure how to integrate this incident, the latest in a series of inexplicable episodes, she hurried on, hoping to make it to her apartment before whatever it was caught up to her.

What was wrong with her? Was she just shoulder-deep in a paranoid delusion? When she had no history of them? It was beyond strange and frankly made her concerned for her sanity.

Janna picked up her pace as her building came into view. She was close now, but as she drew nearer, it became obvious, like a flashing storm cloud, the dark presence had shifted to the front of her. *What the...* Without thinking, she veered toward the park across from her building, preferring complete avoidance to a possible confrontation with some unknown evil manifestation. Since when had she become the ghost-freaking-whisperer?

Her attention was still focused on the energy behind her as she turned past the hedges and iron fencing that fronted the park. She didn't see the body in front of her until she'd collided full on with a tall figure clothed all in blue. She let her gaze start on the heavy, dark utility belt and rise up the shirtfront, past the buttons and the strong chin, past the straight nose into the impossibly blue eyes under his adorably wrinkled brow. He was the most beautiful thing she'd ever seen. And though she clearly had never met him, something about him felt familiar, like she did know him somehow. But without a doubt she'd never forget someone like him if they'd ever met before.

"Whoah! Everything okay?" His voice ran over her like warm, soapy water and heated her up from the inside out. Relief bloomed in her chest as she recognized the blue uniform of a police officer. And a gorgeous one at that. The burning in her lungs began to ease as her pounding heart thudded still. She suddenly became aware of his hands wrapped around her upper arms and his concerned gaze scanning her face and body. He'd asked her a question, and she needed to give him a believable answer.

But what could she say? *There's something evil blocking the entrance to my apartment building.* Her breathing sawed in and out heavily at the very real possibility. Yeah, that would go over like a pile of smelly garbage in the middle of a pristine white showroom. More than likely, he'd rush her off to the nearest in-patient treatment center. But he was staring at her, and she needed to say something.

She's back, she's hotter, and he's in trouble.

Lost in New Falls

Lost in Love

Cherie Marks

Lost in New Falls

Blurb:

Twenty-eight-year-old, former fat-girl, Kate Delaney left New Falls, Tennessee, heartbroken and determined to be a screenwriter. She's spent ten years in Los Angeles, but is back, fifty pounds lighter, California hotter, and she's written *The End* on a screenplay, which a Hollywood mega-producer believes is movie magic. Just one problem— a nerve-nuking thief absconds with her laptop, attached USB back-up, and the contents of her underwear drawer, and just in case that wasn't enough, the heart-breaker from ten years ago just walked through the door wearing a sheriff's badge and looking more hormone-carbonating than ever.

Quentin Taylor likes the new and improved Kate, but to be perfectly honest, his feelings aren't new. Unfortunately, when a teen-aged Kate bloomed, her older brother Reese established a no-look, no-touch, no-anything else rule. Quentin figured it was the *anything else* that worried him most. She'd been attractive then. Now she was near irresistible, and he wanted to know one thing. Did Reese's dictate still stand? Of course, he has more pressing problems—a meddling, matchmaking mother, a gossiping dispatcher/receptionist with an obsession for the color orange, and a small-town burglar who steals thimble collections, garden tools, and underwear, along with the usual electronics and jewelry. Nevertheless, he agrees to help Kate find her missing script, and the time together sparks undeniable chemistry.

Yet, once Kate's screenplay is back in her hands, will she return to L.A, leaving Quentin behind forever, or is their romance destined to be a blockbuster?

Excerpt:

"I don't think you've been hanging out with the right people."

"Oh, and who would be a good person to hang out with?"

He crested a hill and the lake came into view. "Someone with a good heart and a huge..." he paused for effect, "...fascination with you."

He felt her gaze like a heated wind until she turned away. What was she thinking? She stared quietly out the car window. "Did you have anyone in particular in mind?" She chuckled and his abdomen tightened.

"I might know someone."

She seemed to hesitate, but spoke quietly, "I realize I'm kind of a little-sister figure for you, but I don't appreciate you teasing me about this."

Don't tease her? Hell, if he had his way, he'd tease her all the rest of this weekend and beyond. Time to lay his cards out and make his play. "What if I'm being totally serious? What if I'm attracted to you, Kate? Always have been?"

Her mouth dropped open as she shifted to face him. "I call bull, Quentin. You can't pretend I didn't come onto you ten years ago, and you can't deny you pushed me away. I was there. That did happen."

And there it was. The biggest mistake of his life thrown back at him, and for the first time, he saw it from her perspective. She'd thought he didn't want her. In her mind, he hadn't found her appealing. How did he convince her the opposite had been true? He'd wanted her so badly, he'd been ready to sacrifice a friendship with the one guy who'd been like a brother to him, with the one guy who'd stood by him when everyone else had run.

The minute he saw a gravel drive on the right side of the road, he pulled off and parked the car. He turned to stare at her for a moment. Her hair was down and fell in large, loose curls he wanted to twist around his fist, and her fiery blue eyes were wide and expectant, even as her lush lips pursed and her cheeks flushed in annoyance. Like this, she was his fantasy come to life, and she didn't even know it.

"Truth—and this might be a little vulgar, but I'm just going to say it—I wanted you that night and would have gladly taken what you were offering. Kate, you've always turned me on. But I couldn't do it because Reese would have gone ballistic. He'd already told us all to keep our hands off his little sister."

"What are you talking about?"

"That night at the lake, I wanted you. I thought I'd won the ultimate lottery when you pulled me in for a kiss, but then at the last moment, I remembered a promise made to a friend, and I knew I couldn't do it. No matter how irresistible you were to me, I couldn't do that to Reese."

"So, Reese told you not to kiss me?"

He chuckled. "Yeah, or anything else. I think he was more worried about the *anything else.*"

Her face twisted as she contemplated his words, and he was sure it was news to her that all the boys had lusted over her. He wasn't going to enlighten her about the others, but he wanted to make his own attraction clear.

"No doubt about it, Katie. You turned heads ten years ago. And the minute I saw you in your cabin yesterday, even before I recognized you, instant attraction hit me like a log roll on the loose. I still want to know."

"Know what?"

"Well, seeing as I screwed it up the first time, I want to know what it's like to actually kiss you."

Her gaze met his. Electricity sizzled between them. His heart raced.

What would she say? Would she kiss him or had he blown all chances ten years ago?

"What about Reese?"

What about Reese? They were all adults now, and Kate was fully capable of making her own decisions without Reese. And, hell, Reese would surely understand.

He smiled. "I don't want to kiss him."

She laughed lightly, but her eyes closed half-way, and the heat between them intensified. "I mean, what do you think he'd say now?"

"I don't know, but I'm at the point, I'd rather ask for forgiveness than permission."

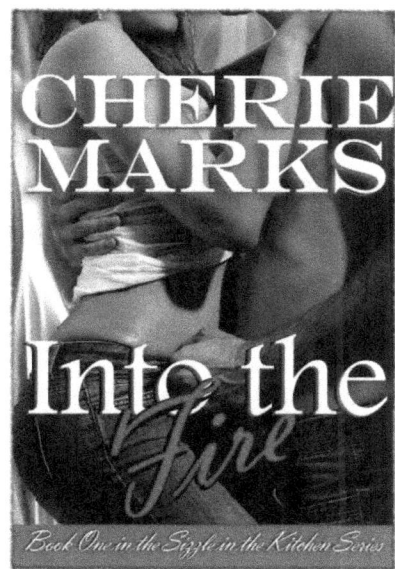

Into the Fire

Months after he stole her affections—then her executive chef position—Shyann and Luke meet again under sizzling circumstances, competing head-to-head on a televised cooking show called Kitchen Twist. Each arrives with a motive: Luke intends to win back Shyann's heart, even as she wants closure on the not-so-tasty heartbreak he once served up.

Luke knows culinary masterpieces require a delicate touch, but that knowledge is tossed out with the leftovers as he works to show Shyann he's not such a bad guy. Now he pushes his skills to the limit to win the competition and satisfy a bet.

Can two top chefs resist each other as they move out of the pan and into the fire?

Excerpt

Silence reigned for half a minute before he reached out a hand and touched hers like a breezy whisper. Her head went a little fuzzy at the warm contact. He shouldn't still be able to affect her so strongly.

"I regret it went down the way it did, but why did you show me the exit before giving me a chance to explain, not to mention—dress? Enlighten me, sugar cheeks?"

With a jerk, she pulled her hand free. He was really asking for it. Sugar cheeks? Seriously? Now she knew he was only messing with her. She could give as well as she got.

"Tell you what. You win tonight, and I'll give you your chance. You lose, we go our separate ways, and you walk out all by yourself, big boy."

A crooked grin formed on his face as he reached a hand toward her hair. He fingered an escaping curl before she pulled away, leaving his hand hanging in mid-air.

"You can call me big boy all you want, but I'll do you one better. How about if I win, I take you to dinner, and you let me explain the whole situation?"

She felt her eyebrow rise and knew he'd read it as interest, but she didn't care at the moment. "I honestly don't want to hear any explanation from you now or ever, but if I win? Which I will, of course."

"Then I'll leave it up to you. If you want me to walk away, I will." He took a step closer, placed his hand on her shoulder, and leaned down, his mouth right next to her ear. "But if you want me to call you darling, sweetheart, and sugar cheeks all night long, I'll do that too."

www.ingramcontent.com/pod-product-compliance
Lightning Source LLC
Chambersburg PA
CBHW060523180626
46817CB00002B/473